AGNES HOPPER
TACKLES MAYHEM
AT THE MANOR

THE ADVENTURES OF AGNES HOPPER SERIES

AGNES HOPPER SHAKES UP SWEETBRIAR

AGNES HOPPER BETS ON MURDER

AGNES HOPPER TACKLES MAYHEM AT THE MANOR

AGNES HOPPER
TACKLES MAYHEM
AT THE MANOR

THE ADVENTURES OF AGNES HOPPER SERIES
BOOK THREE

CAROL GUTHRIE HEILMAN

AGNES HOPPER TACKLES MAYHEM AT THE MANOR
ISBN 978-1-62268-169-3

First Printed: June 2022

Also available as e-book: ISBN 978-1-62268-170-9

Poem "Blue" by Betsy Thorne - Poet & Artist, used by permission.

Cover illustration by Craig Faris – www.craigfaris.com
Author photograph by Mary Eaddy.

Book design by Bella Rosa Books.

BellaRosaBooks and logo are trademarks of Bella Rosa Books.

10 9 8 7 6 5 4 3 2 1

Dedication

For three strong women who lived with
courage and grace:
Evelyn, my mother-in-law,
Ethel, my grandmother,
And Edith, my mother, the inspiration for Agnes.

A lie gets halfway around the world
before the truth has a chance to get its pants on.
~ Winston Churchill

However, Sir Winston, truth eventually rises to the top
like cream in a milk bucket.
~ Agnes Hopper

CHAPTER ONE

It was as plain as our newest resident's chin mole sporting two long, wiry hairs. The administrator of Sweetbriar Manor was a thief.

Yesterday afternoon, Mr. Lively drove his beloved red convertible across the street to Mike's Motor Service. "Routine maintenance," he said with a wave as I glanced up from sweeping the front porch. Two hours later he hadn't returned, but our yardman had finished his mowing, blowing, and trimming, and expected his payment promptly. That's when I unlocked Mr. Lively's office to get some cash.

Well, sir, if I had been wearing false teeth, they would've fallen clean out of my mouth. The gray metal box sat on top of his desk with the lid thrown open. Thank the good Lord enough money remained to pay the young man so he could be on his way.

I didn't confront Mr. Lively immediately upon his return to the Manor, which was not like me at all. But the shock of such a discovery had me bumfuzzled. If he were innocent, wouldn't he have reported the missing money?

The next morning, after hardly sleeping a wink, I threw on my chenille robe, padded barefoot to his upstairs living quarters, and knocked on the door. When he didn't offer to explain how nearly two hundred dollars disappeared from our retirement home's cash box, I told him he could no longer remain in charge of the money. Without any explanation or denial of his misdeeds, he huffed his way down to the office with me behind him, hard pressed to keep up.

Once he handed over the box, I carried it to our cook, Shirley Monroe, someone I could trust not only with the money but with my life. A former shampoo girl at the Kut N' Loose, she had been a godsend to our home. I considered her efficient and practical, not to mention an excellent Southern cook. Maybe even better than Paula Dean.

After patiently listening to my tirade, she shook her head of blonde pouf and said, "Lord-a-mercy. That man's gonna be our ruination. Whatcha plan on doing?" Interrupted by a smoking skillet full of thick-sliced bacon, she rushed to the stove.

I shrugged and returned to my room to dress for the day. Yes indeed. I needed to come up with a plan.

At lunch, even though I hadn't eaten one bite of breakfast, Shirley's chicken salad loaded with grapes and walnuts tasted as bland as saltless grits, and the chatter around our table might as well have been from the Tower of Babel.

Mr. Lively's stunned expression was all I could think about. He had offered no denial, no retort, no thumbing of suspenders, or even rocking back on his rundown loafers—as he was known to do before he expounded on most any subject. His silence had hummed like a beehive. Or maybe it was my new hearing aid acting up again. I immediately touched my ear and wiggled an adjustment.

Had I made a hasty decision? Wasn't our administrator the only one, except myself, who had access to this money? My argument went back and forth. With myself. Especially since my husband, Charlie, was as quiet as . . . well, as quiet as most dead people.

That afternoon I welcomed the usual routine with my friends. After lunch and before naptime we gathered on the porch of our retirement home as I awaited a visit from my pet pig, Miss Margaret. Wisteria, dripping from a nearby trellis, sweetened the air. But even that didn't help my worrisome thoughts one iota. As the new owner of Sweetbriar Manor, I chose not to make the residents of this retirement home aware of my dilemma. Pride would not let me.

Weeks before the money went missing, I had convinced Mr. Lively—a cantankerous sort yet seemingly efficient—to stay. After all, our home needed someone to run the place. We had always been at odds with each other, right from the first day when he bent down, looked me square in the eye, and called me a troublemaker. But I had determined we could put our differences aside and begin anew. As fresh as the jonquils in our front yard kissed by morning dew.

Who was I kidding? Now my mind whirled. Should I show him the door or wait until I could actually prove his thievery?

In this day and time, every employee infraction had to be documented or we risked being sued. Gee whiskers!

My dearly departed husband often said, "footprints don't change." So why was he not talking to me now when I needed his advice the most?

I humphed as I took up my knitting and repaired another dropped stitch. Before I got any further, Miss Margaret's hooves clickety-clacked up the wheelchair ramp. My son-in-law Henry turned with a wave and left to open his hardware store. After I hugged my little pig, she climbed onto her pillow, turned around three times, and settled down with a sigh. I reached down and rubbed her behind her ears. "I would bet my last nickel Mr. Lively has been a no-count swindler his whole life, and now it's finally caught up to him," I whispered to her. With another sigh she closed her eyes and started snoring while my dilemma swirled in my head.

Someone clomped up the side-porch steps, yanking me out of my thoughts. Perhaps it was Nellie, the one with the wiry chin hairs. The one who wore old-fashioned lace-up shoes. Probably returning from no telling where with no telling what in her pockets, one of her many quirky habits. Not only was she our latest resident, she was a bona fide kleptomaniac who also claimed to be Minnie Pearl's cousin, twice removed.

Instead of black, schoolmarm shoes, bright-pink, wedge-heeled sandals worn by a skinny young woman sashayed over to my rocker. She wore a sleeveless, flowered dress, revealing arms overrun with tattoos of stars and planets. A diamond stud sparkled on her right nostril, and a tiny gold ring hung below her left eyebrow. Her indigo eyes peered from underneath a mass of electric-blue hair. My knitting dropped into my lap—and my heart into my stomach.

She thrust out her hand. "I'm Zelda Dee, though most folks call me Dee. Hear you're in need of a manicurist? Been one nearly all my life. You must be Miss Agnes? They told me to look for the little old woman with curly red hair." Her voice was as husky as a smoker's.

Did she say *old*?

Her handshake, strong as a farmer's, released a puff of lavender. "Bless my soul," she said as she peered down by my feet. "Ain't that little pig a beaut?" She squatted and leaned forward as her hair swept the porch. Miss Margaret, asleep with her stuffed monkey underneath her chin, awoke when Dee stroked her head. My precious gazed up at this girl who gave her a final pat before she stood.

I finally found my voice. "Well . . . uh . . . we could use a nail person for sure. But I haven't placed an ad for one." Hadn't mentioned needing one, not even to Shirley. Well, except for running it past my Charlie. Since he had crossed over Jordan, he didn't talk to anyone. Except me. If he took a notion.

Dee moved closer, brushing her skirt against my slick jogging pants, my latest garage sale bargain. I glanced around, but not one of my friends met my eyes. What if I needed some help here?

"It would only be part-time," I managed to squeak out. "Where did you acquire your experience? Have you had any training? And what about references?" I squirmed in my seat as Dee pulled an empty rocker over to face mine, plopped down, and studied me as I sized her up. Surely, a young woman would not want to work a mere few hours a week for whatever the residents offered in tips. That rule had been set by Shirley, who did our nails whenever she could fit us in between her various kitchen duties.

"Who suggested you come here to ask for a job?" I asked a little louder this time since it seemed she had ignored my other questions. The nerve. No manners and downright rude besides.

She shrugged as she looked around as if to grab an answer from the air.

My special friend as well as love interest, Elmer McKinsey, known to me and all the other residents as Smiley, stopped his ogling and popped up from his seat. He scooted inside like a nervous sparrow, always one to avoid the slightest hint of a confrontation.

Pearl, my high school friend who rarely knew me or anyone else these days, floated from the porch with clippers in hand. She made a beeline for an unruly boxwood.

William brandished a cigar from his shirt pocket, unwrapped it, and bit the end off before spitting it into a pot of red geraniums. He thumped down the steps, apparently answering the call for a smoke off the premises.

All three managed to disappear in a half-blink, leaving me with this stranger.

Dee cleared a frog out of her throat and leaned closer.

"Owned my own business, years back. Had to give all that up while I lived in the *Big House*. Assigned to the laundry, of all things." She held out her hands as she eyed them. "They ain't never gonna be the same."

I gathered my knitting into my Walmart bag and hung it on the back of my rocker. Too many interruptions to make any headway today. I picked up my big, red purse, soft as a baby's behind, and hugged it to myself. Who was this woman who looked like a flower child, but had already lived long enough to serve time? Her heels jerked against a loose plank. Was she always this skittish?

"Why were you sent to prison?" The words burst out of my mouth before I could stop them and hung in the air. A tremor seized my insides. What on earth was wrong with me? Did I even have a right to know?

No answer. Those indigo eyes bore into mine.

My precious stretched and stood with a twist of her little tail. She gazed up at this Dee person. Miss Margaret was rarely wrong about anyone's character, but maybe her judgment had slipped since she had gotten older. I blew out a long breath. "We need to get back to the matter at hand," I said as I squeezed my purse tighter.

Dee raised her right hand. "According to the law, I'm not obligated to tell you, especially when I'm trying to get a job. Though a pitiful one it's sure to be."

Had a sneer passed over her face before it vanished? I decided not to press the issue.

She crossed her arms over her flat chest. "You profilin' me, old woman? Once a criminal always a criminal. Right? Never mind. I'm getting used to it in this hick town. I weren't no murderer, so put your mind to rest."

Determined not to let her intimidate me, I met her glare with one of my own.

Finally, she dropped her eyes as she squirmed in her seat. "If you must know, I was accused not only of harboring a fugitive, but being in cahoots with that low-life. Had no idea what he'd done or that he ran from the law. None of that mattered 'cause nobody believed me." Her attitude had switched quick as a flash. Maybe she was bi-polar. Or was she trying to gain sympathy when she had obviously made bad choices in her life? She crossed her legs, swinging her right one which revealed a snake tattoo that ran up her calf. It disappeared underneath her flowered skirt while suspicions about her honesty ran clear up to the top of my head and dug in their heels.

I pulled my eyes away from the snake. "Do you live at—"

"Yep. As you know, it used to be a funeral home before it became the Last Chance Pawn Shop. Now it's the House of Hope? Hope for *what* I'd like to know. Time will tell. Or maybe not? Might not stick around long enough to find out." She swung her snake leg faster while biting on a thumb cuticle.

I was more than a bit uncomfortable this close to a former criminal. Who had decided this girl had reformed, changed her ways, and maybe one day would turn into a law-abiding citizen? And how could I be sure? "Why do you want such a *pitiful* job, as you called it?" I asked as a prickly sweat broke out underneath my arms. I groped around in my purse for my funeral home fan but gave up the search.

Dee fluffed her hair, making her look like one of those wild hippies from Woodstock or some such place. A strange reaction to my question indeed. I glanced around. Since she made her appearance, nearly everyone had vanished. This girl apparently made an entire porch full of people uneasy. Only two people remained. Lollipop, so nicknamed because he stuffed his shirt pocket with Tootsie Pops, plus Francesca, our outspoken, wheelchair-bound resident. Neither would look my way.

Miss Margaret nosed her stuffed monkey over to Dee, who picked it up and tossed it down the porch. "Have to have a job if I want to stay here in Sweetbriar. Plain and simple. Making it in this Podunk town is my last chance. Even part-time would be a start. I'd be willin' to do anything else that needed doing when I wasn't fixin' nails. Except laundry. Had enough of that stinkin' duty to fill ten lifetimes."

My mind did a few flips searching for a response.

Miss Margaret dropped her monkey by Dee's feet. The girl looked down, smiled a crooked smile, and stood. "Maybe next time? Or maybe not?" She bent over and scratched behind my pig's ears. Then she held out her hand until I extended mine. We shook a second time. "You can let me know? Or not? Done my part. Figure the ball's in your court. You might hire me? But I'd bet you ain't. I can tell by the look frozen on your face plus the twitch in your jaw. Seen 'em before."

Unable to produce anything more than a polite smile, I had

to admit her attitude, plus her habit of speaking in questions, unnerved me. It was way past time for Dee to be on her way, but she pulled out a scrap piece of paper from her dress pocket. She held it out until I reached for it.

"My name and phone number. Zelda Dee Sizemore. Been walking the straight and narrow for nine months. I'll swear on a stack of Bibles I don't do drugs no more. Come away from prison with two things. How to look as innocent as a newborn and how to write poetry. You reckon all them days, not to mention them nights, locked up was worth it?"

She didn't wait for an answer—if she even wanted one—but thudded down the steps and scooted down the sidewalk until the sound of her wedge-heel sandals disappeared. A strange young woman with a sketchy past and a hostile edginess, not to mention her evasive way of talking.

Francesca flounced around in her wheelchair. Her tightly squeezed lips and puffed cheeks made her look like she might pop before she could spout her opinion. I didn't have to wait long. "Never trust anyone covered with tattoos. And did you see that snake on her leg?" She twisted around and stared toward where we had last seen Dee. "A rattlesnake. Gave me the heebie-jeebies. Her choice speaks volumes if you ask me."

"It was a corn snake," I said as I pushed myself upright. "Always had 'em in the barn. They eat mice and make good pets."

Had I defended this girl of a woman because I'd passed judgment on her but now felt guilty for doing so? For sure, Miss Margaret liked her. Claimed to be a poet of all things. Did she throw that in for good measure? What had she said about learning in prison how to appear innocent? Hadn't she served time for helping her boyfriend commit a crime and then hiding him to boot? Had she passed herself off as someone she wasn't? And what about the way she talked in questions? Oh dear, but didn't I do the same thing? No, I decided that was different. My questions were mostly in my mind.

"Ugh! Only good snake is a dead one," Francesca continued as she smoothed her pearls with fingers sparkling with diamonds, emeralds, and one large ruby. She shuddered before she dropped her ever-present tarot cards into one of many leather pouches that hung within her reach. She referred to her customized wheelchair as her Cadillac. One day I asked her why it wasn't motorized. After a rosy blush crept up her neck, she huffed and glared at me. "What I have or don't have and why is no concern of yours."

For once she was right, so I never brought the matter up again, although our retirement home gossips declared her no-count son had swindled her out of her money and left the country. "Left her poor but too proud to admit it," I had whispered to Charlie. He agreed.

Lollipop sauntered over. "Dee's pretty. I like her," he said around a sucker.

"Pish posh," Francesca said as she turned her wheelchair to face the house. She looked back. "Some people have no judgment. Besides, she's obviously a smoker. That's not allowed at the Manor, not even for my Willy. One of you needs to hold the door for me. This place ought to have a handicap opener like they have down at Belk's, like our new owner promised."

I flinched. That would be me.

Always anxious to please, Lollipop rushed over to hold the door for our grumpy friend.

"Henry ordered one. He'll install it as soon as it comes in," I said to her back. I could never manage this place without my son-in-law's practical help or his rock-solid advice, not to mention his financial investment . . . which neither of us had shared with my daughter, Betty Jo. Francesca waved a sparkling hand as Lollipop followed her inside.

I moved to the swing, my favorite place to ponder. Before being interrupted by this Zelda Dee, the dishonesty of our administrator and what to do about him had consumed me. I'd never fired anyone in my life. Charlie always handled any sticky issues with our farmhands, but like it or not I had to locate someone fit for such a job. And now, as if that weren't enough, an ex-convict had the gall to make me feel like a scumball because I didn't hire her on the spot as our manicurist. Why had I thought running Sweetbriar Manor would be a snap? A breeze? To my way of thinking, it was supposed to be as delightful as sharing a cup of herbal tea with Smiley in the middle of the night when neither of us could sleep.

Focus, Agnes, I told myself. Charlie shook his head with a silly grin on his face. He reminded me I had done it again. I'd attempted to corral a whole herd of buffalo when roping one hefty calf would have been enough. *Now* he decided to chime in.

Shirley would be delighted to be relieved of nail duty since she prepared three home-cooked meals each day, kept a sparkling-clean kitchen, plus grocery shopped within the Manor's tight budget. Maybe I should ignore any misgivings about hiring an ex-con.

Hmmm. Would Zelda Dee Sizemore be an answer to Shirley's prayer, or a mistake I couldn't afford to make?

CHAPTER TWO

That afternoon after Miss Margaret's constitutional, I got her settled in my room with my Philco tuned to our favorite Bluegrass station, Going 'Round the Mountain. Then I grabbed my cane, used only on occasion these days, and closed the door behind me as Bill Monroe belted out "Blue Moon of Kentucky." A cup of Earl Gray called my name.

I sat at the old workbench converted to an island and held my warm mug with both hands. The tightness in my neck eased a bit as Shirley slipped a Mississippi mud cake into the oven. I could taste it already.

The peaceful moment evaporated, however, as the overhead lights flickered and then went out altogether. Just like that. On a clear, sunny day. Shirley dropped a pot lid and threw her hands into the air. "Happy Halloween!" she shouted, which she was known to do whenever disaster struck.

I slid off my stool, hung my cane on my arm, and left the kitchen to find Mr. Lively. As long as he was my employee, he needed to tend to his duties.

He exited his windowless office with a flashlight and shut the door behind him. "No use trying to work in the dark."

"At least call the power company to report our outage."

He puffed out his chest. "Already did. We can expect our power to be restored within eighteen hours. No reason given, which is typical for these situations. We'd really be in a fix if a storm left us without power for a week or more. It could happen you know, especially during hurricane season. We need to talk about making some changes around here, including the purchase of a good-size generator. Which, I might add, you could afford if this place were managed correctly." He smacked the flashlight against his palm and grimaced like he had indigestion. Or maybe constipation.

"We need to talk. For certain." I straightened myself with

my cane and looked him square in the face. Well, as close as I could get. Managed correctly? The nerve of him. "We'll clear the air soon but not now. I'm too frazzled to think straight at the moment."

Not only that, I had to find a way to prove his thievery before I confronted him. The whole situation had me stumped. I had poured over the Manor's books, but saw nothing amiss. Yet the funds kept in a metal cashbox for small daily expenses, or ones that might pop up unannounced, had suddenly dwindled to nearly half of the five hundred dollars normally kept there. He was as slick as a greased pig at the county fair.

"Not as easy being in charge as you thought, is it?" He sounded too cocky to suit me. Was he getting ready to turn in his resignation? It would be welcomed. His bug eyes grew even bigger as he stared at me. I waited, determined not to answer his disrespectful question. "Appears to me you've taken on more than you can handle," he finally added as he plucked a thread from one of his leather suspenders.

A guitar battle rose from my purse, but more than a phone call was on my mind. I glared at this most irritating man. "I'll have you know anything you say or do during your working hours is my concern, which includes your attitude. I'm the owner of this establishment." I lifted my chin to show as much confidence as I could muster. Then I fished out my phone and raised it in the air. "My daughter." I hightailed myself toward my room.

By the time I'd slammed my door, Betty Jo agreed the outage was only a minor nuisance. As she chattered on with no end in sight, I said good-bye and pushed the red circle. Then I rubbed behind Miss Margaret's ears before the two of us left for the porch. "A mere inconvenience my foot," I said to Charlie as we moved down the hallway.

Late that afternoon from my rocker, I spotted Henry as he appeared in the opening of the Manor's ancient rock wall down near the street. He trudged up the narrow sidewalk fanning himself with his *Henry's Hardware* cap. His green plaid shirttail hung loose over grimy jeans.

"Whew," he said as he climbed the porch steps. "Seems like bags of mulch weigh more every spring, and nearly every customer needed theirs delivered today. Had to order another load."

"You work too hard," I said as I pushed up from my rocker to greet him. "You'll end up having a heart attack or a hernia. Maybe you and Betty Jo could take a vacation. A cruise would be nice."

His attention landed on Miss Margaret, snoring away, and his face beamed through the dirt and sweat. He wiped his face across his shirtsleeve and plopped his cap back onto his head. Miss Margaret spent most days at his hardware store and her evenings and weekends at Ben's Lama Farm. But she visited me two days a week at Sweetbriar Manor. The former rule of *no pets allowed* was abolished as soon as I became the owner.

When Henry whistled a short ditty, Miss Margaret's ears perked up. She opened one eye. He squatted and opened his arms. She stood, shook herself, and leaped toward him. Jealousy popped up inside me like dandelions after a rain before I remembered to thank the Lord someone loved my precious as much as I did. He stood and hugged her to his chest. She nuzzled underneath his chin while he relayed information about our power failure.

"Two blocks away on Fifth Avenue a dead oak tree bit the dust. Like that big one in your front yard. Have you seen about having it removed?"

I shook my head.

"No? If you call the Tried and True Tree Service, they'll give you a fair quote." He stroked Miss Margaret's head but couldn't calm her. "Anyway," he continued after dodging her slobbering mouth, "this one took out a transformer. Seems a gust of wind was all it took to bring it down at just the right, or wrong, time. We've had stronger winds for hours at a time that never budged it, and I reckon people figured it'd stand forever. Affected a whole section of businesses downtown, including . . ." He set a squirmy Miss Margaret onto the floor who raced to and fro across the porch, her clattering hoofs making a terrible racket. "Where was I? Yes, including my store," Henry said, raising his voice. "Even reached as far as Mike's garage across the street. Understand, it may take a while to fix. You folks gonna be okay for now?"

I nodded then caught Miss Margaret before she flew by us again. Her heartbeat thumped wildly against my arms. I stroked her back and whispered the 23rd Psalm in her ear before handing her back to Henry.

"Wish I knew how you do that, Mother Hopper."

Miss Margaret let out a great sigh before she closed her eyes.

"I've quoted a Psalm to her since she was a piglet. You'll learn your own way to calm her if you should need to. One thing's for certain. The two of you have a special bond I've not seen since Charlie was alive."

He smiled and turned to go. Then he stopped and looked back. "Are you sure . . ."

I waved him on his way. "Certainly. We'll make do. I'll call you if we run into any real trouble." Real trouble? Who was I kidding? I had no qualified, dependable, sociable, honest person to help me run Sweetbriar Manor. Charlie nudged me to tell Henry everything. Didn't he deserve to know? After all, this honorable man was my silent partner. So why didn't I stop him from leaving? Because I wanted to present him with a solution, not my problems. I sensed Charlie shaking his head, but I assured him I would seek some advice from two of my dearest friends, Shirley and, of course, Smiley—the man whose big brown eyes could melt a rock. As well as my heart.

Shirley tossed out a fallen cake, stuck three half-cooked stewing hens into the refrigerator as soon as they cooled, and served us peanut butter and banana sandwiches for supper. When we finished eating, with no television to watch, most of us turned in early.

I reminded everyone to raise their windows, as the night air was cooler than a closed-up room. But I didn't remind Francesca her bed would also be cooler with one person in it rather than two. No need. Every night at nine o'clock sharp, William left his room in his sock feet and tiptoed to hers. They thought I didn't know, but they hadn't fooled me. I spotted him one night as he edged his door shut with his shoes held in one hand. He glanced around, but I had stepped behind a cart stacked with magazines, newspapers, and books. Focused on getting to his sweetie, it was easy to follow him to her door, where he promptly disappeared.

We needed to address their situation. Soon. They had to

make their love for each other legal, but I would not judge them. William had grown children who had vowed to make their marriage difficult, if not impossible. All because his children feared they would lose their inheritance. Which surely couldn't be much since William had retired from thirty years as a taxi driver.

Francesca, on the other hand, had come from money, which was evidenced by her diamond rings and strings of real pearls. Gossip claimed her son had squandered her fortune through drinking and gambling, leaving her with a mere pittance—which was why she had moved to Sweetbriar Manor, the cheapest place she could find. She probably had no money to motorize her Cadillac either, but I would never bring that subject up again. I reminded her that if she hadn't come here she never would have met her William, a bear of a man who was also a Southern gentleman who worshipped his wheelchair-bound sweetie.

Smiley seemed unusually quiet as he walked me to my room. Tonight should've given me the perfect time to ask his advice before I fired Mr. Lively or hired anyone who had served time to do our nails, but he said he had a pounding headache. "Sis,"—his favorite name for me I never grew tired of hearing—"I'll see you in the morning." He laid his hand on my shoulder. "Too much happening around here, don'tcha know. Plain unsettling."

He had no idea.

As he turned and left me there, I stood at my door and watched him move like a whisper on his little bird legs until he disappeared around the corner. He would pass through the foyer and enter the hallway leading to his room. I sighed. Would he ever take me into his heart like I had welcomed him into mine? Or should I be thankful for his friendship and expect nothing more?

Instead of going in my room, I headed back toward the kitchen. Maybe Shirley would still be there. She had better advice for the lovelorn than Dear Abby. Not to mention she most likely knew how to best run a retirement home when I was beginning to doubt my own abilities. But it was not to be. As I stepped into the foyer, Jack, Shirley's fellow, who she called *Baby*, swooshed through the front door. He waved his cowboy hat and kept moving. One boot thumped along as he drug his stiff leg over the wooden floors. His long brown hair swished across the back of his denim shirt. Shirl's Jack was more handsome than the Marlboro Man.

Then in a flash, the two lovers appeared and disappeared in a whirlwind of his deep voice and her giggles rising like bubbles. They didn't think to shut the front door but sprinted to Jack's motor scooter, jumped on board, and putt-putted into the twilight. So much for talking.

As I gazed after them, Nellie climbed the front steps. She hadn't made an appearance all day, but that was nothing unusual. She edged past me reeking of grease, chili, and onions. Obviously, she had eaten at Blind George's Pool Hall. George claimed to have the best hot dogs in town. I had to agree. Nellie nearly stumbled as she shifted a shopping bag from one arm to the other. What had she stolen this time? Something metal clanged inside her bag. Even though I made sure she attended her counseling sessions, her strange habits hadn't improved.

Feeling discombobulated, and without creaming my face or brushing my teeth, I fumbled around in my darkening room and changed into one of Charlie's favorite Hawaiian shirts—bright orange decorated with hula girls—instead of the pair of fancy pajamas Betty Jo had given me for Mother's Day. They looked like a flower garden trimmed in lace and itched like the dickens.

Tonight I needed to feel Charlie's soft shirt next to my skin even though it no longer carried any trace of fresh-cut hay or his Lifebuoy soap. I reached for the shower cap that always hung on my bedpost. Leopard print with a rhinestone pin, it was a snazzy sale item from Stein-Mart. After slipping it over my curls, I crawled into bed, suddenly bone-tired.

Sleep visited in fits and starts until evidence of our restored power blasted forth from my radio as Merle Haggard belted out "The Fightin' Side of Me." I jumped up, turned off the music, and picked up my phone. Only ten o'clock. When I opened my door, the hallway was lit up like a starship. Televisions boomed from two different rooms, on different channels.

Shirley whooshed in the back door from her date and looked me up and down. "Honey, that's one sexy nightshirt. Plus your cap is the cat's meow."

"Thank you," I said as I felt the warmth of Charlie's presence.

The two of us made our rounds. We turned out any unnecessary lights as someone turned off the televisions. When we finished, we hugged and said our good-nights. Then I turned off my room's air conditioner to enjoy the quiet without it. *Ahhh.* With my window raised, the night's stiff breeze carried the aroma of sweet gardenias into my room. They reminded me of Charlie after he planted such bushes underneath our farmhouse bedroom window.

All seemed quiet and normal. Mr. Lively never made an appearance to help us set things in order. The man was worse than useless.

I crawled back into bed, but was suddenly assaulted by toe cramps. I bolted upright and tore open some packets of mustard from Bob's Burger Shack, kept on my bedside table for a quick medicinal cure. It always worked. When I slid back underneath the covers, I sank into a deep well of sleep until a distinctive smell tugged me upward. I sniffed. A whiff of . . . what, bacon? Morning already? Had I lost my mind? Maybe I was dreaming.

The distant wail of emergency vehicles pierced my foggy brain. Now on full alert, I jumped out of bed and ran to my window where a wind gust snapped my yellow-checked curtains like sails. A faint red glow pulsed against a dark sky, and I caught the distinct smell of smoke. My thoughts flashed back to the day Miss Margaret and I stood in my garden, raised our heads, and sniffed the air. We had no idea my kitchen curtains had blown against a pot of beans left on high. The fire spread quickly, and even though Sweetbriar's fire department came as soon as they could, my old farmhouse burned to the ground.

CHAPTER THREE

Sirens blared. A fire truck sped past the Manor, followed by an ambulance, a police car, and yet another fire truck. All headed toward Sweetbriar's downtown. What could be burning? Could it be the ancient First Baptist church with its outdated electrical wiring?

I had warned them about the stacks of hymnals stored in their cleaning supply closet. I even rescued a dozen of their discarded books we now used for our Sunday services led by the Salvation Army.

I grabbed my cane—not that I needed it—plus my phone before I threw open my door. Henry's phone was busy as was Betty Jo's, so I slipped mine inside Charlie's shirt pocket and gave it a pat.

Sleepy-eyed residents stumbled into the foyer. We bunched together in our rumpled nightclothes as voices murmured. *Did you hear the explosion? Loud enough to wake the dead. Must be a big one. Could you see the fire from your window? What can we do? Nothing is what. Absolutely nothing.*

Pray. For sure we could do that.

On the front porch we pushed a jumble of rockers out of our way to reach the railing. Hanging ferns, tossed by the wind, swung above our heads. No one spoke as we gazed toward the red glow against a dark sky. Everyone joined hands and huddled together. Smiley hadn't appeared yet, but I wasn't surprised. A headache that had sent him to bed early, plus the medicine he always took for such a doozy, had likely knocked him out for the night.

After a heartfelt prayer from Shirley and several "amens," she touched my arm. I turned toward a set of wide eyes. Her blonde hair stuck out in all directions, and red, baby-doll pajamas spilled from a blue silk kimono. "Jack called," she whispered in my good ear. "We can ride with him. He's determined to go see what's burning. Used to be a volunteer fireman you know."

No, I didn't know, but Jack could always surprise me. "On his scooter?" Impossible unless he carried us there one at a time. I shivered at the thought of Charlie's Hawaiian shirt billowed by the night air as we sped toward town.

"Produce truck," she said as she grabbed my hand. "Let's go."

We reached the street as Jack's hefty work truck with *Case's Produce* written across the doors in big white letters screeched to a halt. The old vehicle shuddered before it belched a cloud of exhaust. Jack leaned over and threw open the passenger door. Shirley sprang inside and hoisted me up. Before I could reach for the handle, Mr. Lively landed next to me, scooted close, and slammed the door. Why did he think he needed to go along? Totally out of character for him to concern himself about anyone in trouble.

The truck rumbled off. Mr. Lively shouted over the noise, "Head to the halfway house!"

"How do you know?" I asked.

"Police scanner. Handy device."

Shirley's robe fell open revealing her skimpy nightclothes. Mr. Lively leaned forward and stared as she grinned and winked at him. Jack shot him a seething look until he came to his senses and sat up as straight as a number two pencil. "Can't this jalopy go any faster?" he asked.

"Don't see you offering your fancy car," Jack spouted back. Mr. Lively's red convertible, with its protective cover he'd recently ordered from Amazon, stayed in the Manor's old one-car garage on the back of the property, except for Sunday afternoon outings—if the weather happened to be just right. If he had anything to do with it, his car would never feel a drop of rain or one scorching sunray. He loved that car more than life itself.

We rode in silence until Jack pulled into the town's only public parking lot, a block off Main Street. A cluster of emergency vehicles and a tangle of firehoses prevented us from getting any closer. We piled out and made our way to a crowd of townsfolk gathered in front of a stately house with tall columns and wraparound porches. Spotlights glared onto the butter-cream exterior and flickered across the blue porch ceilings as a stiff breeze sent tree shadows dancing over the House of Hope.

For a short moment, the image was surreal and even strangely beautiful. Wisps of smoke trailed from the first floor windows, then suddenly billowed out in black puffs. Bright orange flames licked their way upward. Sparks whirled into the dark sky, and some landed on the roof. A firefighter sprinted up a long ladder before disappearing inside a second-story window. Another one followed. We couldn't tear our eyes away. More sirens wailed in the distance. Time seemed to drag on forever until Jack shouted, "There! Look!"

A fireman's helmet, then his shoulder, appeared in the window. A body hung down his back like a ragdoll as he placed his boots on the ladder. A pair of women's shoes appeared to float from the sky. By the time he was halfway down, the other fireman emerged from the same window. He cradled a small, dark bundle.

As soon as the first boots touched the ground, paramedics rushed over, secured an oxygen mask onto a woman's face, then laid her on a gurney. The second fireman placed a wiggly black dog next to her. Tattooed arms reached out to pull the animal closer. A reporter from the *Timely News* zoomed his camera onto none other than Zelda Dee. When she spotted the newsman, she cursed, flayed her arms, and jerked off her mask.

A buxom woman in a long nightgown with a head full of curlers ran up to the reporter. She shoved him to the ground. "Don't you got no respect?" she shouted.

The growing crowd clapped and then turned silent. An EMS worker replaced Dee's mask and tried to comfort her as another man took the curly-haired animal from her arms. He turned to the crowd. In a flash, he shoved a squirming miniature poodle into the arms of Blind George. The two emergency responders then whisked a protesting Dee into an ambulance. Doors slammed and they sped away.

George held the dog away from his chest as pee streamed from the squiggly animal and splashed onto the ground. "Dang mutt. Always a nuisance."

A snicker escaped my lips, causing George to turn my way. His frown turned into one big grin. Before I could protest, the trembling little dog was thrust into my arms as George hightailed himself away from us. I didn't know a big man could move that fast.

"Wait!" I yelled, but I might as well have been whispering next to a thundering freight train. Now what? After a slight hesitation, I huddled over the shaking poodle and whispered a Psalm in his ear. Just like Miss Margaret, it worked. The tiny dog relaxed and began licking my fingers. I'll have to say his body against mine warmed me clear through.

Shirley and I stood barefoot on the grass, wet with dew. At least for now the wind had settled into occasional gusts. She draped her arm around me and pulled me close as she cooed over and petted the dog. Jack tried to drape his leather jacket around the three of us. It helped, but Charlie's shirt of hula-girls ended mid-thigh on my uncovered legs.

A sudden cool breeze made me tremble. Before I knew what was happening, Mr. Lively shifted the leather jacket away from me and onto Shirley. Then he plopped his sport coat onto my shoulders, still warm from his body. Even though I was flabbergasted he would do such a thing—plus it stank of moth-balls—I was grateful. Maybe he loved animals, and I just happened to be holding a cutie. Whatever the reason, I turned to thank him, but he had disappeared.

A nearby fireman removed his helmet as he leaned against a tall pine tree. I walked over to him. "Did everyone get out?"

"As far as we could tell." He wiped his face against his sleeve. "Chief says it's too dangerous to go back in. Could have another explosion worse than the first one. You didn't hear it from me, but this fire looks suspicious." He took a long drink from a water bottle.

In the next moment, windows popped. Tinkling glass covered the ground. The firefighter broke into a run toward the old house.

I returned to stand beside my friends.

"I'd wager somebody was cooking meth in there," Jack said in a low voice.

Neither Shirley nor I commented as we looked at him, but I filed his words away in the back of my mind. A drug operation inside Hope House? Did that cause the explosion?

Once a funeral home and then a pawn shop, the halfway house had become the place for young women seeking another chance in life. Where would they go now? Surely the prison system would find them another home. After all, it shouldn't be my concern. And what about Dee? Would she recover? I had witnessed a big chip on her shoulder, but if she didn't let her troubles pull her down, perhaps her spunk would serve her well. Had she returned to rescue her dog? And what did the fireman mean by *suspicious?*

Another firefighter connected a hose to a hydrant near us. "Get out of here! You're in the way!" he yelled. We backed up, but none of us mentioned leaving. We couldn't. The disaster continued to unfold before us and held us in its spell.

More fire trucks arrived from the neighboring towns of Lees' Villa and New Point. Firefighters rushed past us in their bulky coats. I spotted one as he climbed a ladder up to the roof, a hatchet in his hand. Another aimed water through a broken window. On the expansive wraparound porch, smoke swirled around a cluster of rockers the way questions continued to swirl in my mind. Was this night the beginning of the end for young women like Dee who had sought a second chance? I couldn't help but wonder what would happen to them or why I felt ashamed for not wanting them to relocate somewhere else in Sweetbriar. Wouldn't our town be much better off if they had to move on?

The night air snuck around the edges of Mr. Lively's tent-like jacket and swished clear to my armpits. I hugged the squirming dog closer.

Townspeople bunched together in the early morning darkness. We watched in stunned silence with our faces turned toward the crackling fire as three firemen carried a black body bag from around the back corner of the house. We let out a collective gasp, then a hush fell over us as they transported the bag down to an ambulance. When the vehicle pulled away, no lights flashed. No sirens wailed. No need to hurry.

Sheriff Caywood approached the crowd, and we gathered around him. His hands trembled as he pulled a handkerchief from a shirt pocket. He removed his hat and wiped his face. Then he took a deep breath and slowly blew it out. "All I can tell you folks is that someone has died here tonight, perhaps from smoke inhalation. The person's next of kin will be notified immediately. Until then, no name will be released. Tomorrow, an autopsy will be performed."

"Where was the body found?" someone asked.

The sheriff raised his hands. "No questions at this time.

We'll hold a press conference when we have more to say." He turned away and headed toward the fire chief who stood aside waiting for him.

Jack gathered Shirley and me close. "Overheard a couple of firemen talking. Seems Mary Wilson's the one who died," he whispered.

Mary had run the halfway house and was the one who named it the House of Hope. A great sadness filled my heart. Some gossip about town spoke of her unreasonable strict rules, plus her hateful temper toward her charges, but others said she was doing her job the best she knew how. I had no way to figure which scenario was true, or if the truth lay somewhere in between.

Movement from Blind George caught my eye as he tossed a bar towel over one shoulder. So he hadn't left the scene after all. I rushed over to return a dog that was not my responsibility.

He turned to me with a scowl. "Reckon we'll never know for certain."

"About what?" I lifted the squirming animal toward him.

George folded his arms across his ample belly, glared at me, and shook his head as my arms returned the dog to my chest. My face, neck, and ears were soon covered by slobber from a very wet tongue. George refused to take Dee's little pet, and I had no way to make him.

"What will we never know?" I asked again as I took a step back. My curiosity had been tweaked.

"If them women could've made it in our town. Or anywhere. Never had a chance. Now there's no one to run a halfway house in Sweetbriar." Somehow he also must've heard who had died in the fire. Probably by now everyone knew. He pulled his apron strings tighter and tied them in a knot.

"Dee didn't really want a job at the Manor anyway," I said, as if I needed to defend myself. A cool breeze found my neck even though I had turned up Mr. Lively's coat collar. "She was required to say she had applied for at least three positions so she could stay at the halfway house. Terrible attitude when I didn't hire her on the spot."

"Not how I heard it. Us ex-cons gotta stick together."

"You?"

He looked down at me with a scrunched up face. "I used to

be homeless to boot. Like your friend Josiah. Ain't you ever heard *judge not*?"

"Of course, but—"

"I'm going to the hospital. Check on Dee. Offer her a job if she gets to stay in town. Don't suppose you'd want to . . ."

I felt someone staring at me before a tiny woman jerked her head away, turned, and then dissolved into the crowd. I couldn't be sure, but she looked like our resident klepto. I knew Nellie well enough to know if she was trying to avoid me, she was guilty of something. What could she have stolen this time?

"Mother," Betty Jo called as she pushed her way past Blind George. I raised my hand to ask if I could ride with him to the hospital, but he ignored me and hurried away. Henry followed close behind my daughter. My family gathered around me.

"I need my coat back," Mr. Lively said. I jumped, not realizing he was nearby. "Terrible situation, but there's nothing I can do here," he added. "Sheriff ought to tell everyone to go home." Now he sounded more like the selfish man I knew.

I reluctantly shed the warm jacket and handed it over as Henry grabbed a blanket from an EMS worker and wrapped it around me. Mr. Lively dashed away without a backward glance.

"What on earth are you doing here, Mother?" Betty Jo's voice scolded me like an overprotective parent. "And what are you doing holding that stinky dog?"

"Long story." When a disaster occurs in a small town, it draws everyone like a magnet. Some out of curiosity, but most anxious to help.

Betty Jo leaned closer. "Mother, you've not heard a word I've said. We're headed to the First Baptist Church where the Red Cross is setting up a temporary shelter. We'll stop by the Manor first. You need to change into some decent clothes if you want to join us."

"You two go ahead. I'll come later."

Betty Jo scowled. "But how will you—"

"Mother Hopper will be fine," Henry said as he secured my blanket and leaned close to ruffle the dog's curls. "You can tell us the whole story later." He winked and gave me a quick hug. "Jack and Shirley said they'll look after your mother," he added to Betty Jo. "My, my," he said, shaking his head. "I dare say these young women being transported to the church are in shock after what they've witnessed. We're needed there now."

Betty Jo wasn't finished. "Mother has no business standing out here in the damp night air with no shoes on her feet. Mark my word. She'll end up sick. Then who do you think will take care of her?" Her eyes met mine before she lifted her chin and turned away.

Henry smiled slightly and shrugged. Then he cradled her elbow like the gentleman he was and led her down the sidewalk toward the parking lot.

After a bit, Shirley and Jack joined me. He lifted the poodle from my arms. I imagine it was to give them a rest.

"Dee's got no family," Shirley said, though I didn't know how she knew that. "Now the woman who was closest to being like her family has died," she continued as we watched the smoldering House of Hope. The fire had spread quickly throughout the old home. Before it was finished, only a skeleton would remain. Memories of watching my farmhouse burn to the ground washed over me like it happened yesterday instead of nearly two years ago. I pushed the sadness aside and swallowed the foul taste in my mouth.

I leaned close to Shirley. "How do you know about Dee?"

"After she asked you for a job, she showed up at the back door. Asked if I'd put in a good word for her. I didn't want to tell you this, but she also said you were . . . well, you were a hard woman who had no compassion in your heart. Of course, I told her she was wrong, and her thinking was all scrambled up in her head. She gave me a fearsome look, but then I asked her to step inside for a piece of my apple cake. Dee's rough around the edges for sure, but somehow after she sat down in my kitchen, we hit it off right away."

I pulled the blanket back onto my shoulders, feeling more than a little put out at her. "Why didn't you tell—"

"Didn't see the need. For certain, you've got enough on your plate with Mr. Lively acting like a horse's behind. I wouldn't put anything past that no-count. He bears watchin'."

Did Shirley know everything? She certainly had plenty of street smarts. I made a mental note to find out exactly what else she might know about Mr. Lively. "Blind George has gone to check on Dee," I said. "He's going to offer her a job, but does an ex-convict, and a young woman at that, have any business working in a pool hall?

Shirley didn't answer.

"Besides, unless someone looks after her little dog," I added, "which he won't do, it's going to end up in a shelter. George only welcomes those cats that hang out around his alley dumpster because they keep the rats away from his fine establishment."

Shirley turned to Jack. "You reckon we could go see how she's doing?"

He nodded, handed me the dog, and then hurried toward his work truck.

As the old jalopy chugged away from the curb headed toward the hospital, I bounced on the cracked leather seat and held on to the door handle. I waved to Mr. Lively when he looked up.

He threw his hand in the air. "Wait," he mouthed.

He would have to find another ride back to the Manor. *Oh my. His jacket.* I leaned over Shirley's lap toward Jack. "Stop! Turn around. Go back to Mr. Lively."

In short order, Jack made a screeching U-turn which tossed Shirley and me like straw hats on a windy day.

"This better be good, Miss Hops," he said as a grin overtook his frown. Jack was never out of sorts with me for more than a half-minute. Not in his nature to be ugly with anyone. Unless the sheriff tried to make eyes with his Shirl. Then he turned fierce as a bull ready to charge.

Jack's truck rumbled up to the curb where Mr. Lively remained as we had left him. His scowl fairly bristled with agitation. I opened the door and slid down to the pavement.

"I suppose you came back for this?" Mr. Lively asked with hitched up eyebrows as he pulled my cell phone out of his jacket pocket and held it out. "Mighty careless and forgetful these days, like most old folks. Could lead to paranoia, not to mention making false accusations."

"I . . . I'm sure you've left your cell phone somewhere before."

"Never saw the need for one. Should have known you weren't coming back for me."

"We're headed to the hospital." I slipped the phone back into Charlie's shirt pocket. "Maybe someone would carry you to the Manor if you asked *politely*. Or maybe a long walk back home would do him some good," I whispered to Charlie. My sweet departed agreed, as he most times did. "By the way," I called to Mr. Lively's back. "Seventy something is not old." I climbed into Jack's truck refusing Shirley's hand to hoist me upward.

Jack pulled up to Pardee, the new satellite hospital Sweetbriar citizens dearly loved. He held onto Coal—for that's what we were calling Dee's beloved pet—as Shirley and I jumped out of the truck and entered through the emergency room doors.

The woman at the desk wore a tight bun on top of her head and horn-rimmed glasses. She looked familiar. Then I remembered. She was the one who gave me a hard time when Smiley came to Mission Hospital with bronchitis that nearly turned into pneumonia, and I tried to pass myself off as his next of kin. Maybe she wouldn't recognize me. I scooted behind Shirley to let her do the talking.

Shirley leaned down to the small opening in the window. "Zelda Dee . . ." She turned to me. "Gee whiskers. What's her last name?"

"Sizemore," I whispered.

"What did you say?"

"Sizemore!"

Shirley faced the window again, but the receptionist leaned to the side where she caught me square in the eye. "You. Up to your old tricks I see. Obviously, neither of you are family. Wait here. I'll see what I can find out. If you see an old man who looks like a mangy pirate, tell him if he tries to enter our restricted area again I'm calling my supervisor. We've got our hands full right now, and we don't need people who can't follow the rules." She pushed back her chair, leaving her assistant in charge, and disappeared through a door behind her desk.

I moved to the waiting area where I could keep watch on the receptionist's return while Shirley joined Jack and the miniature poodle outside. Two EMS workers wheeled in a gurney. A soot-covered fireman lay on his back with his arm thrown over his pinched-up face. He groaned. As they sped past me, I noticed his right foot was twisted in the wrong direction. My belly did a flip-flop.

Minutes dragged by. During that time, a woman was admitted with a possible heart attack, and a scruffy man pulled up his shirt to show his knife wounds from a bar fight. The receptionist finally appeared, so I returned to the window. She frowned and pursed her lips. "You people need to go home. If you've got one. The young lady's in the process of being admitted, so you can't see her. I'm not authorized to tell you anything more. Now, clear out of here before I call security. We've got our hands full around here."

"You've got that right," I mumbled.

We had to leave, but before we did, I leaned down to the small opening once again. "Let Dee know Agnes Hopper will take care of her dog until she's discharged and can come get him. Agnes of Sweetbriar Manor. Do you understand what I'm saying?"

The woman huffed. "I'll see what I can do."

Blind George appeared beside me. "Deliver the message," he said in a gruff voice. "If you don't, and we got ways to find out, we're coming back to lodge a complaint. And we ain't leaving so easy the next time. Also, tell Dee she's promised a job. It's waiting for her at Blind George's. Got it?"

The woman's face turned white as a corpse. "Leave," she said through clinched teeth. "All of you crazy people. Now."

Once outside I scooped the dog from Jack's arms into mine. I sensed Charlie's smile with his *I knew you would* twinkle in his blue eyes. "Just because I'm taking care of her pet, temporarily mind you, doesn't mean I'm getting involved in her life. Absolutely not. That girl will do just fine on her own," I muttered under my breath. Who did I think I was fooling? Certainly not my Charlie. And probably not Jack or Shirl.

We left the hospital with a vow to return later in the day. The early morning sky of dark gray clouds, now streaked with shades of magenta, orange and cotton-candy pink, spoke of the Lord's creation as we headed to the First Baptist Church.

CHAPTER FOUR

Shirley and Jack dashed ahead and disappeared inside the church gym as Smiley eased down a carton of toilet paper onto the sidewalk and rushed over to me. He threw an arm around my shoulder, releasing a scent of his Old Spice as he ushered me up the stone steps. Even though I didn't need my friend's help, his firm grip was a comfort. The little poodle trembled in my arms.

"So sorry to hear about Mary Wilson. Terrible. Simply terrible," he said as he pulled me closer. "Where did that little thing come from?" he asked, nodding to my bundle.

"Belongs to Zelda Dee. That strange girl from the halfway house."

"But how come you . . . Never mind. I'm sure you'll fill me in later." He planted a kiss on my cheek. "For always trying to take care of someone else," he whispered. A tingle flew from my toes clear up to the top of my head. "Spiffy hat," he added with an eye roll followed by a grin.

"The latest style," I said, making a little bow. I had forgotten my shower cap was still there, but it was Smiley's kind words giving me credit with far more than I was due that caused my heart to spill over with happiness.

Together, we pushed open the doors and entered a gym full of shiny wood floors and tall windows painted a steel-gray. Rows of lights glared from metal cages across the high ceiling. At the far end of the room, Shirley and Pearl poured water into two commercial-sized aluminum coffee pots sitting on a rectangular table. Beyond them, a large opening in the wall revealed a kitchen buzzing with activity.

I turned to Smiley. "I kept looking, but I didn't see you anywhere at the fire. Were you there?"

"Nope. Slept through the whole thing. As did Francesca and William. By the time we were up and stirring about, the place was deserted."

"How did you know where to go?"

"Paperboy. *Timely News* hit the front porch at four-thirty sharp. By that time we were standing out there wondering what had burned and what we should do. He informed us it was the halfway house, and the Red Cross was setting up a shelter at First Baptist. We struck out for the church at a fast clip since that was closer than the Hope House. We figured we might be of some help. We hurried as fast as we could manage with Francesca's wheelchair. Do you realize the sidewalks in Sweetbriar are not handicap-friendly?"

"You walked to the church?"

"No other choice." He tipped the bill of his red baseball cap and winked.

We hugged each other as close as possible with a pup between us. "I'm glad you're here now," I said as his wispy hair tickled my nose.

Smiley had promised Henry he'd help unload meat, eggs, milk, and bread donated by our local Winn Dixie, due to arrive at the back door at any moment. When he rushed away, the urge hit me to make myself useful, but somehow I had taken on the job of caring for a frisky dog. Why had I done such a thing?

The church's spacious kitchen of industrial-sized stainless steel appliances included a giant gas stove. Shirley watched over bacon and sausage that sizzled in two enormous skillets. My stomach growled.

After searching inside several cabinets, I found a plastic bowl and drew some water from a faucet. I set Coal on the floor, placed the pan of water beside him, and knelt. My bad knee popped and groaned.

The dog whined and scooted closer to me. He wouldn't drink, so I sank onto the floor, took him onto my lap and whispered the 23rd Psalm. When he calmed down, I stirred the water with my fingers. He peered up at me and then finally lapped it up.

What in the world could I feed him? Maybe he had to have a special diet, like so many pets these days. Jack squatted down beside us. "Want me to watch him for a while, Miss Hops? Had a passel of dogs hanging around me all my life. Never killed a one."

I nodded, and he lifted the pup into his arms. "What will

you feed him?" I asked.

"I'll check the food pantry. Maybe we'll get lucky." He held Coal in the crook of one arm and helped me up with his other. They left in search of food.

I washed my hands, cracked eggs into an enormous mixing bowl, added milk, beat them, and then set the bowl aside for Shirley. She shooed me away. "Go sit down somewhere and catch your breath. You look plum tuckered out."

"Looks can be deceiving," I said, feeling a bit miffed. "I'm perfectly fine."

Tables pushed together in the gym would serve as a long buffet line. Paper plates, napkins, and plastic utensils lay scattered in piles. I sorted and organized the mess as the aroma of fried bacon and sausage drifted into the gym.

Shirley and Jack carried out platters of meat to the buffet. Someone had set up rows of tables, spread paper cloths over them, and surrounded them with folding chairs. I asked Jack about the dog, and he assured me Coal was fine. Betty Jo and Henry kept the serving dishes filled as people helped themselves to a breakfast fit for a king—including grits, gravy, biscuits, and local honey, plus the never-ending hot coffee.

Smiley carried over two plates of food to a table, set them down, and motioned for me to join him. He pulled out my chair before he settled into his. "I'm starving," he said. We both dug into our breakfast like farm hands after housing tobacco.

When someone whistled loud and clear, a hush fell over a gym full of people. Henry stood near the buffet table with his arms raised and his head bowed. "Good morning, Lord. We're thankful for our community coming together in this crisis as well as for the professional ones who risked their lives to save a young woman and her dog. Be with Mary Wilson's family and the women of Hope House as they grieve their loss. Thank you for this feast before us, the friends beside us, and the love between us. In the days to come, let us not forget the ones who are hurting and homeless. Amen."

Many "amens" were heard around the room. For sure, the person who had died in the fire was common knowledge. In spite of the tragedy, my breakfast on that windy May morning was the best I'd ever eaten in my entire life. Afterward, I helped Jack clear the tables until stomach cramps sent me in search of the ladies' room. Perhaps I had overindulged.

Henry left to help the Red Cross workers set up cots in Sunday school rooms located along both sides of the gym. They announced that showers were down a nearby hallway where soaps, shampoos and towels, plus clothes from the church closet waited for the women.

Before they hurried off to bathe, I asked a tall lanky woman with long, stringy hair if she had heard anything further about Dee.

"No," she said as she bunched her hair up high with her hands. "But she's as tough as an old chicken. If anyone can make it in this world, she will." She released her hair. It fell around a young face yet one as hard as flint. I saw Dee's face in her expression and wondered if serving time in prison did that to a person.

"I suppose you're right," I said at last as I shifted my weight off my bad knee. Dee would probably be just fine without any help from me. She, as well as every woman from Hope House, would survive on her own. I felt Charlie frown. Did I hear him moan his disapproval?

A silence fell upon us, and the woman turned to join her companions until I placed my hand on her arm. "I'm so sorry about Mary Wilson." I didn't know what else to say. "Where will you all go when you have to leave the church in a few days?"

She shrugged. Her eyes filled with tears as her face softened. "Don't know. Reckon we'll be scattered wherever they have a place to stick us. Nobody wants us around here no how."

My ears perked up. "Anyone in particular?" Did someone hate them enough to try to burn them out? No one, especially the sheriff, had mentioned arson, but a fireman had said the fire was suspicious.

"I'll swear I never said nothing," the woman mumbled as she studied her feet.

"Absolutely. We never talked." I led her into an offset where we slipped into an empty classroom.

She tucked her long brown hair behind her ears, where it didn't stay, and leaned closer. "The old woman next door always hollered at us whenever she saw us coming or going. And one time when she worked in her garden I seen her throw a rock at our house like she was pitching a fastball. If it had hit a window, it would've gone clean through it."

"Oh my. Nobody confronted her?" Surely some of the neighbors knew what was going on, but apparently no one had gotten involved. That's when it hit me square between the eyes. Was I the pot calling the kettle black?

She shook her head. "Maybe I was the only one who seen her, and I'm not about to take on trouble."

"What are some of the things she said?"

"Go back where you came from. We don't want you here You got no business ruining our town. Things such as that."

"It's not easy to leave the past behind, is it?"

"Maybe impossible. In this little town at least. We've even been harassed by the delinquent who showed up next door. Got no more manners than a billy goat." She stood straight and tall. Her brown eyes flashed.

"Someone's staying with Lucy?"

"A teenage boy's been hanging around for a week or more. Does tricks with his pocketknife and gives us the *once-over* ever chance he gets, if you get my drift. Must have raging hormones, but that ain't no excuse. Had a mind to set him straight a time or two. But as I said, I ain't itching to cause trouble."

"Oh my. You've had more to put up with than I thought. Did you get along with Mary Wilson? I heard she was tough."

She shrugged. "I ain't saying no more to nobody." She turned and headed toward the showers. As her bare feet thumped across the wood floor, my heart grew heavy. I had kept the prison system from buying Sweetbriar Manor when I bought the retirement home myself, but then hadn't I found another place for the women to live at a more reasonable price? Yes, only now the former pawnshop turned halfway house had burned, and they had no home. Plus, they had no one to run a halfway house even if they had a place to go. Why did I feel guilty about how things had turned out? I hadn't wished them any harm. But I hadn't exactly welcomed them either. No doubt about it, guilt is a terrible thing to carry.

I found Jack and inquired again about Dee's pet.

"Miss Hops, he's been fed, he's pooped, and he's now snoozing away on an old blanket from my truck in an empty storeroom. I'll check on him in a bit and take him for a walk if he's so inclined."

I reached up and hugged his neck. Couldn't help myself. Jack had shown his tender side, which happened more often now since he attended his AA meetings regular as clockwork.

Only eleven-thirty by the big gym clock, though it seemed like it should have been at least three in the afternoon. The sheriff appeared and asked to speak to me. In private. Dressed in a plaid shirt and those khaki pants fishermen wear, he had found the time to pin on his badge and put on his official hat, which he removed and carefully placed on a nearby table as he sat down. I pulled out a chair beside him and sank onto it.

Shirley, who has sharp ears and eyes, set two cups of coffee in front of us and leaned over to me. "If he gives you a hard time, holler for more hot coffee. I'll come running."

As she straightened up, Sheriff Caywood reached for her hand, but she was on the move and headed to the kitchen with Jack, whose eyes shot his rival poisoned arrows. The sheriff had declared his love for Shirley months ago after she and Jack had a humdinger of an argument and he left town. No one knew at the time he was an alcoholic and had gone to a rehab facility. Even so, Shirley never gave up on her Baby, and she never gave the sheriff any encouragement.

"Good strong coffee, don't you think?" I said as I sipped and eyed our sheriff. Hershel never answered, but out of the corner of my eye I saw him reach inside his shirt pocket. He produced his buckeye and rubbed it between his fingers and thumb while he watched the kitchen door, a habit of his when he was doing some serious thinking. Not about me—at least it seemed so at the moment—but probably about Shirl. He reminded me of a little boy with a crush on a girl who would never give him the time of day, good luck charm or not. I repeated my question.

"What?" he said with a jerk of his head. He turned toward me and placed a big hand on my shoulder. "Miss Agnes, I have to ask you some questions. It's my job."

"For heaven's sake. I know that, Hershel."

"Just so we're clear," he said as he dropped his buckeye into his pocket and gave it a pat. "Tell me what you've heard around town about the women at the halfway house, especially any suspicious activity that might have gone on there."

I squirmed in my chair. If a drug operation had been run out of there, I had no clue about it and for certain the sheriff didn't need to know Jack suspected the explosion had been caused by cooking meth, whatever that entailed. No need to bring Jack to the attention of our lawman. For more reasons than one.

He squinted at me over his coffee mug. "Do you realize you're wearing a shower cap?"

I reached up and touched it. "Oh my. I forgot. I always wear it to bed. Keeps my curls from becoming a scrambled mess come morning."

"Aren't you going to remove it?"

"Absolutely not. Sure as shootin' I'd catch a cold in this drafty old place. My mother always said to keep your head covered when the air's chilly and damp. Now, remind me again what you wanted to know." I tried to act normal, but my whole body felt like I'd taken on a high fever. His line of questioning had my nerves on edge.

"So, you don't know anything about illegal drugs being sold out of the Hope House?"

I shook my head. That was the absolute truth.

The sheriff shifted in his seat and laid a pencil on the table before he leaned toward me. "Okay. Some people in town haven't exactly welcomed these women. Do you know anything about that?"

Their next-door neighbor, Lucy, had called them names and thrown a rock at the halfway house at least once, but Hershel would want to know how I'd come by this information. I didn't want him to know I'd questioned one of the ladies since he took offense whenever he thought I was stepping into his territory. I shook my head and rummaged in my purse for my funeral home fan, which didn't seem to be there.

Those dark eyes held steady onto mine. "All I'm doing right now is routine work," he said after a long moment. "I have to cover all my bases or the whole investigation could be declared fraudulent. And since there's been a death, probably due to this fire, we have to consider the possibility it was set on purpose. Even though there's no indication of such at this time. You were there, in the crowd. Did you see or overhear anything that might shed some light?"

My right eye commenced twitching, a nervous habit whenever I was fixing to skirt the truth, which it seemed I was bound to do once again. "Not exactly." I gulped my coffee.

"Someone did say the explosion looked like someone had been cooking meth in the basement."

His brows shot up. "Who told you this?"

I shrugged. "Someone in the crowd." This was a white lie, or maybe it was a dirty, gray one. But he didn't need to focus his attention on Jack. Neither did I share that a firefighter had said the fire looked suspicious to him. Gee whiskers. My eye had a spasm. I prayed for forgiveness, but it didn't help one smidge or even half of one.

Sweetbriar's sheriff settled back in his chair with his coffee mug and seemed to be thinking. After a bit he set down his cup, retrieved his pencil, and rapped on the table, but he didn't produce a notebook or pad.

"Aren't you going to write anything down?" I asked.

He touched his temple with his pencil. "Photographic memory. When I get back to the office, I'll sort through what I need and file a report. Might become useful in the future, especially if I'm called to testify."

"Make sure you wear a fresh uniform," I said, nodding to his fishing clothes. "First impression makes a difference."

The sheriff threw down his pencil. When it rolled off the table and hit the floor, he took no notice. "Miss Agnes, this ain't no game we're playing. A woman has lost her life, and it seems the whole town knew her name before I could notify her kin. Thankfully, I was able to make the necessary calls before they got the word."

"I'm well aware this is serious. I didn't know Mary Wilson personally, but her death has left a great sadness in my heart. I understand she was a hard-working woman who tried to make a home for those girls, while at the same time she held them accountable for their choices. Not an easy task for anyone." I took in a quick breath. "Tell me one thing. Does the cause of this fire look suspicious to you?"

"Maybe. Maybe not. Hasn't been officially determined yet." Hershel stood and squared his hat onto his head. "Some things don't add up is all I can say. By the way, didn't you organize, not to mention *lead*, the protest parade against those women living in our town?" He took a step back and folded his arms across his chest.

"You best get your facts straight," I said as I got up and stepped toward him. "I didn't want the prison system to boot us out of the Manor so they could buy it and those women could live in it. That's the only reason we protested. Didn't I also find them another home?"

He sighed and tipped his hat ever so slightly before he turned away and headed toward the kitchen.

I sank back down onto my chair, suddenly weak-kneed. In the next moment, our illustrious sheriff bolted out of the kitchen in a huff. He marched across the gym and slammed through the double doors that lead to the welcome center. "Charlie," I whispered. "He's fired up after Shirley's cold shoulder, and I pity the next person he's set on questioning." Right on the money, Charlie agreed.

"Nothing worse than lukewarm coffee," I grumbled. I grabbed my mug and pushed myself up as Francesca wheeled herself toward me. Her white lacy robe flew around her like wings. She sported her multiple strands of pearls, earrings, and diamond rings as if she were fully dressed instead of in night clothes. Her eyes flashed. Red blotches had popped out on her cheeks. She stopped within an inch of running over my toes.

"The sheriff's questioning my Willy. Of all the audacity. Told me to leave them alone. Is that legal?"

I grabbed her trembling arms. "Settle down before you have a stroke. I'm sure he'll talk to everybody. It's routine. The facts will prove the fire was accidental, and he'll leave everyone alone." A knot settled in my stomach like a stone.

Francesca twisted her pearls into a knot. "My Willy's too good and kind and honest. He's bound to incriminate himself. I told him if he smoked his nasty cigar it would get him in trouble one day. Didn't I? He's already confessed to smoking in his room, plus he's burned holes in his sheets. He's even smoked over at the halfway house when he went to help those criminals with their computers, which I told him not to do. But did he listen? Of course not."

I kept my mouth shut, trying not to act surprised.

"Our mayor had no business allowing them to live in our town, especially Melba Lee or whatever she claims her name is. Well, that's one problem solved now, isn't it? I'm sorry Mary Wilson died. I'm even sorry their home burned to the ground, but the sooner the whole bunch clears out of our community the better."

Some of these same thoughts had popped into my head,

though I would never admit to such. Was I really a hard-hearted woman like Dee claimed?

Two young women with dripping wet hair, dressed in jeans and wrinkled shirts, stopped their chatter. As they stared at Francesca then me, one looked like she might burst into tears.

"Shhh," I whispered to my excited friend. "Keep your voice down."

I poured her a glass of orange juice from a nearby pitcher. "Sip on this. Take some deep breaths. While you're at it, pray for your Willy. And pray for some compassion in your heart." I left her there and headed toward the coffee urns, but guilt dogged my heels. What did the Bible say about removing the plank in your own eye so you could see the speck of sawdust in your neighbor's? For sure, each of us were on edge.

Hershel hung around the gym and talked to first one person, then another. He tried to catch Shirley's eye, but she never glanced his way. Finally, he left wearing a scowl. Mr. Lively hadn't appeared, and I breathed a sigh of relief. I had to deal with that whole situation, but right now my plate overflowed with fear and uncertainty. Had the Hope House been a drug house? If so, how had that happened right under our noses? And how many of the women were involved?

CHAPTER FIVE

My daughter declared she had other duties calling. "I've given enough of *my* time to the Red Cross. I'm worn to a frazzle. You ought to leave now too, Mother." We stood beside a drinking fountain in the church hallway near the side exit doors. "You look terrible," she added as she looked me over. "And that ridiculous shower cap doesn't help matters."

"Leopard prints have always been my favorite. And the rhinestone clasp sets the cap off. A fashion statement, don't you think?" I struck a bit of a pose. It was fun to mess with her. "Besides, I don't have a big enough pocket to stuff it in, and I certainly don't want to lose it." I bent over the fountain, gulped some foul-tasting water, and gagged.

Betty Jo just stood there with her hands on her hips.

I got hold of myself, wiped my chin with my hand, and turned to my daughter. "Would you stop by the Manor and bring me a change of clothes and my purse before you head home? Shouldn't take you long." Mr. Lively would have to hold down the fort, like it or not. An easy job since most of the residents were here. Oh my. That meant no one could keep an eye on the thief among us. I hoped Shirley had found a secure place for the cash box in her kitchen.

Henry informed Betty Jo he wasn't going anywhere. His assistant manager had opened up the hardware store after picking up Miss Margaret from Ben's Llama Farm.

Smiley became Henry's shadow, and the two men made an excellent team. They, along with a Red Cross worker, talked with each young woman and made a list of what she had lost in the fire and some of her immediate needs. I gave thanks for two of my favorite men, not counting Charlie of course.

The visible stress level surrounding the homeless women moved down a half-notch, even as they planned a memorial for Mary Wilson and questioned if they had any future in our town of Sweetbriar.

Betty Jo handed me my big red purse plus my favorite purple sweat suit and orange tennis shoes. "Walked past Mr. Lively napping on the front porch," she said. "Never moved a muscle until I slammed the front door on my way out. He's no asset to your business, to say the least."

If my daughter only knew.

After assuring her I would soon address a slack employee, I hurried away to the women's locker room, empty now except for the aroma of shampoo and soap clinging to the damp air. I tucked my shower cap into my handbag. Then I showered, towel-dried my hair, and dressed. Only my daughter had failed to include a bra. Charlie's Hawaiian shirt had suited me just fine without one. Hopefully, that piece of underwear could be deemed unnecessary in this crisis. What other choice did I have?

Henry left with a Red Cross worker and headed to the Dollar Store whose manager had donated many of the women's needed toiletries. Smiley stayed behind. As he restocked the buffet table with paper plates, napkins, and cups, he laughed and talked with two young women volunteers who were shameless flirts.

In the meantime, the Sweetbriar Women's Club delivered potato chips, luncheon meats, tomatoes, lettuce, cheese, and bread to the church kitchen, plus homemade potato salad, bean salad, and pound cakes. Shirley rounded up the Hope women—which is what she called them—into an assembly line. They made sandwiches for everyone, which included a dozen volunteers, five worn out firemen, and two homeless men who had hung around all morning outside the gym door.

After lunch I found Jack in the storeroom checking on Coal. "Could you carry me to the hospital?" I asked. "We ought to check on Dee's condition, and you know they won't tell us anything over the phone."

He stood up, dusted off his cowboy hat, and grinned. "On my scooter?"

"Thought you had the produce truck." It ran worse than a jolt-wagon, but at least it hadn't up and quit like his usual transportation was prone to do.

"Mr. Case needed it. Just lucky he gave me the day off." He shifted his weight off his stiff leg and held his cowboy hat with both hands while he waited.

"Scooter it is," I said as I secured my purse straps over my shoulder.

He planted his hat on his head and adjusted the brim, then eyed me. "Might do Dee a world of good if she could see Coal. Have to sneak the pup inside of course."

With the dog tucked inside my jacket, I zipped it and looped my purse straps across my chest before slipping my arms around Jack's waist. We sputtered down Washington Street and turned onto Main. Coal snuggled close to me without a whimper.

After Jack inquired at the front desk, we took the stairs to the third floor where I sank onto a bench and caught my breath. When I reached down to massage my bad knee, Coal squirmed around inside my jacket, and a warm wetness spread over my stomach. Gee whiskers. Now I'd smell worse than the county's animal shelter. "Let's go." I jumped up and limped down the hallway.

"Wait up, Miss Hops." Jack came alongside me. "Let me take him." When he lifted him from me, he wrinkled his nose and laughed.

It wasn't that funny, at least not to me. I shot Jack a look and entered Dee's room in front of him. We both stopped short. Hershel Caywood stood beside her bed. When he looked up and frowned, Jack tucked the dog underneath his arm and stepped back into the hallway.

Dee's face, pale as the sheets pulled up to her chin, scooted further down in the bed. She became nearly invisible, except for the oxygen tubing and a tuff of blue frizzed hair, until her dog whined and yapped. In an instant, Dee pushed herself up-right and threw back her covers. "Pepper?" she croaked. Jack entered with her pet. The little dog scrambled from Jack to her outstretched, tattooed arms. I zipped my jacket to contain some of the wetness and stink while Dee snuggled her face into the dog's curly fur. "Have you been a good boy? Who's been taking care of you?" When she looked up, her face was flushed with life as her eyebrows rose into peaks.

Pepper? So much for Coal. "We have," I said after a bit. "Me and Jack."

"You? Why you?" She glared at me.

Humph, I grumbled to Charlie. Still has that chip on her shoulder and seems it's growing. Some people don't know how to be grateful.

"We'll talk again soon," the sheriff said to Dee, interrupting my thoughts. With a clinched jaw, he dropped his buckeye into a shirt pocket and brushed past me. He had changed from his fishing clothes into a starched and creased uniform. Handsome, official, and serious. "Don't leave town," he ordered as he glanced back at Dee. "Do you understand?"

Her oxygen tube slipped from her nose. "Yeah, like I have a place to go. You would stop me if I did." A ragged cough stole her breath.

The sheriff made a quick exit as I pointed to her tube. She replaced it and sank onto her pillows with a sigh. Her blue hair looked electrified.

"Reckon I'll have to give up smokin'?" A ghost of a smile passed over her face as she closed her eyes. Her freckles looked dark against her skin, yet a contented smile grew as she ran her hands down Pepper's back. She opened her eyes and locked them onto mine. "You didn't answer my question. Why you?"

"Well . . . uh . . . Blind George couldn't take care of a dog with all those cats around his pool hall, so he handed him to me. Jack cottoned to the little fellow right off. He's the one you should thank." Why did I think I had to explain anything to her?

She nodded and turned to Jack. "Thank you," she whispered through tears that began to flow. That did it. Even though she hadn't included me, my heart softened, at least for the moment. I handed her a clean hanky from my purse.

"Now tell me, if you would, what on earth the sheriff was doing here," I said. "I'm not just being nosy. This could be important."

"You think?" She twirled a stray lock of hair around her finger.

Jack took Pepper for a walk. I pulled up a folding chair beside her bed.

"Sheriff says I'm a person of interest? All because I hate livin' in this hayseed town and told everybody so?" She scooted around in the bed and straightened the covers.

I leaned closer. "Is that all?"

"Reckon not. I was a plum fool to trust my boyfriend. Believed ever word he said. Jimmy's got six more years to serve time, and I ain't havin' nothin' to do with that varmint once he gets out." She folded her colorful arms across her chest as her studded nose flared, causing the ring below her eyebrow to dance.

"Sounds like a good idea. Why was he sent to prison?"

She took a deep breath. "Set fire to an airplane hangar. Said he thought the place was empty at the time, mind you. Turned out a janitor was inside a supply closet and barely escaped with . . ." A coughing spell wouldn't let her continue.

"With his life?" I said after she settled down. She nodded as a tear trailed down her cheek. She obviously still had feelings for her ex. This was not good. What else was she hiding? She closed her eyes, and we sat for awhile in silence. After she recovered, I tried again. "Why did your boyfriend do it?"

"He's not my boyfriend!" Dee shouted as one of her monitors squealed.

"My mistake. Simmer down." I stood and handed her a cup of water.

A nurse appeared and pushed me aside. "If this happens again, you'll have to leave."

"Just a few more minutes, and we promise to stay calm. Right, Dee?"

She nodded, but her eyes flashed daggers my way.

The nurse left in a huff.

I returned to my chair, wishing I hadn't left my cane at the church. "Now, tell me why this scoundrel committed arson."

"His instructor wouldn't let him finish his flying lessons 'cause he showed up drunk one day. He come by my place after he set the fire. I found him there when I come home from work, and he was hittin' the bottle again. I had no earthly idea what he'd done. Told me he had to lay low for a while 'cause he'd taken some food from a convenience store. The owner chased after him and nearly caught him. Jimmy said he was hungry and had no money. Said he spent his last dime on those lessons. And I believed the jerk."

Dee closed her eyes, and I wondered if she was through talking. I waited.

"After a couple of days," she finally continued in a near whisper, "I told him he was gonna have to move on. I wasn't puttin' up with his freeloadin' no more. Before long, the police showed up at my door. That's when I learned the truth. Reckon Jimmy decided it was payback time for kicking him out. He told the police I'd known about everything from the beginning and even helped him plan it all. Those stupid police believed his word over mine." She clasped her hands together and stared at the ceiling.

"Oh my," I said. "But what motive would the two of you possibly have to burn down the House of Hope? Every crime has to have a reason behind it. Besides that, arson hasn't even been proven yet."

Dee lifted her chin as her attitude flashed in her blue eyes. "Maybe the sheriff will give us a motive. Come up with his own. So he can say *case solved*."

"He says your boyfr . . . I mean Jimmy, helped you in this crime here in Sweetbriar?"

"He says being in prison don't stop a criminal from causin' trouble on the outside."

I agreed with Hershel but not out loud. "One more question." I stood and moved the folding chair back against the wall. "Did you get along with Mary Wilson?"

Dee grabbed a hairbrush from her nightstand and shook it at me. "I know why you're asking. You ain't foolin' me none." The tiny ring below her eyebrow quivered as her brush dropped onto the bed. When she looked up, her eyes had taken on a deep sadness. "She had her favorites, but I wasn't one of 'em. Reckon I spoke my mind too many times. I'd say we shared a mutual dislike for each other, but I never wanted her dead."

"Did you know about her doing drugs? Cooking meth in the basement?"

"All of us knew, but she threatened us if we told anyone. Said she'd take us down with her, and nobody would believe the innocence of an ex-con."

"So she blackmailed all of you."

"Sure did. Worked too."

I straightened my jacket and turned to go. "One way or another the truth will come out. You can count on it."

She tried to smile, but it was as pale as winter sunshine.

Jack returned with Pepper. After letting Dee fuss over her pet a little longer, we took the excited little animal and left the hospital. I filled Jack in on the way to the parking lot.

The sheriff had determined Dee was a person of interest, and I could see how he had come to his conclusions. If he knew she still had a tender spot for her former boyfriend, a convicted arsonist—plus feelings of hostility toward Mary Wilson—neither would be good. I was trying to stay objective about her possible involvement, but it was becoming more and more difficult.

Jack pulled into the circular driveway in front of the House of Hope, or what was left of it. We returned to the scene of the fire after promising to look for Dee's shoes. She swore they'd slipped off her feet as the fireman hoisted her down the ladder.

Jack cut off the motor and turned to me. "As sure as shootin', I've got a hunch nobody never started no fire. But our sheriff's convinced Dee's guilty of something. What if there's no evidence to prove she ain't done nothing wrong?" With no answer forthcoming from me, he shook his head. After I swung my leg around and stood, he did the same. "Ain't you gonna jump into the middle of this mess like you always do? And if you ain't, why not?"

I pulled my jacket tighter. "For one thing, Dee served time for aiding and abetting this Jimmy she denies is her boyfriend. She might have protested a little too much. The law's looking at Dee because of her link to an arsonist, for goodness sake. And what about her claim about being blackmailed so Mary Wilson could make and sell drugs? Do we just take her word? We've got to look at the facts. Period. With no emotional attachment."

Jack scowled at me. "Yes, but—"

"You want to follow your gut because you can relate to being an outsider, someone who doesn't belong. You know how that feels. Lonesome. Hurtful. Sometimes angry. I can tell by the way she talks that she's not from around here. Same as you. Same as me."

Jack's frown deepened. "You?" Pepper whimpered and squirmed until Jack set him on the ground with his leash secured in his hand. We continued to talk as the little dog found a nearby bush to relieve himself.

"My folks moved south from the mountains of Kentucky when I was four or five," I said. "I learned to rid myself of the twang in my speech, though every now and again it shines forth. But my momma and daddy? They suffered the most.

Town folks called them dumb hillbillies when they were two of the smartest people I've ever known."

"Rats," Jack said. "Some of the uppity-ups, like the ones who made fun of your folks, got no manners. As you well know, I'm an alcoholic, but there's those who look down their noses if they see me on the street. I've learned to tip my hat and smile real big. Gets 'em every time."

This hard-working guy, normally a man of few words, had shared his heart as well as his sense of humor. Francesca was one of those who didn't trust Jack to this day. But I hadn't behaved any better toward Dee when she showed up out of the blue and asked for a job. My first reaction had been to keep my distance, even to turn my back. Could I overcome my feelings of prejudice that I had only recently recognized as belonging to me? The sheriff apparently saw Dee as underhanded. The girlfriend of an arsonist who also took part in a drug operation. Guilty or not, the odds were stacking up against her. Especially if Sheriff Caywood discovered her affections for her boyfriend remained. Along with her feelings of hostility toward Mary Wilson.

Pepper tugged on his leash and barked at a squirrel.

"Let's focus on why we came here," I said.

"You got it," Jack said with a salute. "We need us a plan."

We gazed at the old building that leaned into itself and was charred as black as coal. Yellow tape stretched around the outside of the property while signs of *condemned* and *no trespassing* had been nailed to the fence posts as well as on the front door that had refused to collapse. In the distance, three men wearing rubber gloves and carrying plastic zipper bags poked through the rubble. With their eyes focused downward, they didn't seem to notice us.

"Gee whiskers," I said. "If we try to sneak past that tape, they'll spot us for sure." I squinted to read it. *Crime Scene. No Trespassing.* The sheriff's department had obviously purchased a supply with the correct wording instead of *Wet Paint* like they had used after I discovered Josiah's body dumped in Beulah Land Cemetery.

"Got it. Just leave it to me, Miss Hops," Jack said, bringing me back to our present dilemma. "Pepper and me'll go to the left behind those fellows. You duck on the other side of that big locust and turn right as soon as the commotion starts." He set

Pepper down on the ground and since there were plenty of squirrels in the front yard, he took after them with Jack not too far behind yelling for him to stop.

When I slipped from behind the locust, I ducked underneath the yellow tape and scooted to the right behind some chinaberry bushes. I was trespassing. Breaking the law. But the shoes seemed very important to a young woman who had come close to losing her life. Sneaking out from the bushes, I ran smack dab into an old man wearing bib overalls and a straw hat.

"What're you doing here?" he growled. "Can't you read?"

"Might ask you the same," I said.

"Asked you first." He peered down at me with his thumbs hooked underneath his waistband.

"Looking for some shoes. Pink wedge sandals. Could be burnt up, but thought I'd try. A young woman lost them last night, and she could sure use them about now." I didn't think I would actually find them, but we had promised to stop and look.

"I'll walk around with you a bit, but don't you touch nothing. I've been hired to keep folks away. We've got a job to do."

"Yes indeed. Let's start in the side yard if you don't mind." I hoped the shoes I had seen fall from the air last night were Dee's.

"Stay clear of the house. Least six feet back."

"This is going to be a waste of time," I whispered to Charlie. He told me not to be so sure. That's when I spotted them. One shoe underneath a laurel and the other in a clump of grass. "There," I said as I pointed ahead.

As the old man gathered the first one, smudged with soot and dirt, and moved forward to pick up the second, I spotted something as his big feet parted some tall grass. I bent down and slipped my fingers around it. When I stood upright, I met a pair of questioning eyes. "Never know when vertigo's gonna hit me," I said. "You ever have it?"

He shook his head and frowned.

"You're lucky," I chattered on. "It can land you flat on your back for a week. Why, I remember right before Christmas ... or was it Thanksgiving ..."

"Never mind," he said, pushing the shoes into my hands.

Thankfully, we soon parted ways, and I headed back to the

scooter. A cigarette lighter rested in a pocket of my jogging pants. I removed it and examined it closer. It was no ordinary lighter. Vintage. Silver with a flip top. Did it belong to Dee? She was a smoker, but could this lighter connect her to the crime?

Jack rounded up Pepper, and I held him in my arms while Jack attached the shoes to his bike with a cord. Then I handed the dog back and moved next door to Lucy's. Perhaps she had witnessed friction between Dee and Mary Wilson. What if she had? Was I trying to prove Dee was innocent or that she had a motive for burning down the Hope House? Maybe the sheriff was right in his suspicions.

Lucy's expansive front porch was filled with a jungle of ferns and other greenery. I pushed her doorbell three times before she threw open the door. "What do you want?" she blurted around a mouthful of food.

"I apologize for interrupting your lunch." I shifted weight off my bad knee.

She glared at me as she chewed and swallowed.

I had to think fast. "I'm with the town's planning committee. We're taking a survey of the neighbors to see what people would like to have built here when this awful place next door to you gets bulldozed." I took a deep breath and let it out slowly.

She wiped her mouth with the back of her hand. "You don't say. Funny thing no committee asked me before what I thought about convicts living in our neighborhood. Just moved 'em into that big old house. First a pawn shop and then a home for criminals." She shook her head. "Don't know what this world's coming to."

"I'll bet those women caused Mary Wilson all kinds of trouble." I hoped my supposed sympathy would lead her to share a specific incident.

"You wouldn't believe some of the language those women used. Not fit for a lady's ears."

"Such as . . ."

"Well, I couldn't exactly make out every word, and I'd never repeat it if I could, but they were always hollering at each other. And then they'd double over with laughter like they'd told some dirty joke. Disgraceful. The only time they acted decent was whenever their supervisor came around, which wasn't often enough to suit me."

"I suppose you're glad they're gone."

"You bet. Now they have nowhere to live in this town, so they'll have to move on."

"That's a relief, isn't it?" I leaned against the porch railing to rest my aching knee.

"Absolutely. Fire was a God-thing is my way of thinking. Judgment Day for no-count criminals. Now, what were you asking me before?"

A pimply-faced teenage boy appeared in the doorway with a pocketknife. He quickly closed it and shoved it into his jeans pocket. With a toss of his greasy hair, he swept past us. "See ya," he said with a wave of his hand as he bounded down the steps to a rusty old bike lying in the yard.

"Wait, Terry," Lucy said as she leaned over the porch railing. "Where you going? And when will you be back?"

"Around. Later." He sped down the street without a backward glance. We watched until the bike clickety-clicked around a corner.

"Sounds like he's got a loose spoke," I said.

"Lord a mercy," Lucy said, shaking her head. "Gave that boy some money to fix that bike. Bought a new knife instead."

When I cleared my throat, she glanced at me. The confused look on her face spoke volumes. Whoever this boy was, not only was he disrespectful, she had no control over him.

"Young people these days," I said. "They've got a mind of their own. I don't envy you having one around to look after. Is he your grandson here for a visit?"

"Terry belongs to my younger sister. Sent him here for the summer. Declared if he lived with his aunt in a small town it'd help his attitude. Hogwash." She turned to go inside but stopped to look back. "Would you like a cup of coffee?"

I wanted to say yes, but Jack was waiting. "Truly wish I could join you, but I'm on a tight schedule. Perhaps you have time for one more question?"

She nodded.

"What would you like to see built beside your property? Sheriff Caywood says the whole place will be demolished as soon as they determine what caused the fire. No need to keep an eyesore around any longer than necessary."

"Sheriff's a good man. He's got my vote next election. Tell your committee I'd like a nice park with a fountain and lots of flowers. And no riffraff like those awful women allowed within fifty miles of it."

"I'll let them know." I hurried to the street where Jack was seated on his scooter reviving the motor. "Where's Pepper?" I yelled over the noise.

"My jacket," he yelled back.

I jumped on the back and held on as we crept away like a slug. "Is this thing going to die?" I yelled in his ear.

"Nope."

I waved to Lucy who still stood on her porch. She didn't smile or wave in return. I hadn't gained any useful information that might help Dee or might incriminate her. The sheriff considered her a suspect. At this moment I was riding the fence, but some things were not in her favor. She had gone bonkers when I called her ex-fellow a boyfriend. Had he enlisted her to commit another crime like the sheriff supposed? He didn't have a motive, but she might. Exactly how much had she disliked Mary Wilson? Did she have reasons that she hadn't shared? Confusing thoughts and questions filled my head, not to be shared with anyone, especially Jack who seemed to have taken a liking to this mountain girl.

CHAPTER SIX

After a sudden shower, the afternoon turned steamy. I wished for my old gardening hat I'd worn on the farm. Outside the church's gym entrance Pepper sniffed through a patch of grass before he raised his leg. I stepped aside as Shirley exited the heavy doors and thumped down the steps.

"Whew," she huffed as she grabbed a dishtowel from her shoulder and fanned herself. "I'm ready for a bubble bath, a shampoo, and my Baby waiting to rub my swollen feet, plus other parts if he so chooses." She giggled and tapped my shoulder.

Jack appeared, encircled her waist, and kissed her behind her ear. "Maybe later," he whispered. "Scooter's running on fumes." With a pat on Shirley's behind, he said he was headed to the nearest gas station.

"I'm itching to shed this robe," Shirley said as she watched him leave. "But that old woman on her front porch over yonder would probably call the law." Her loose sash had allowed her red baby-doll pajamas to spill out of their silk covering.

I squinted up to her blond pouf highlighted by the sun. "Something's got to be done about the Hope women as long as they're still in our town. Seems they've had a rough go of things. And not only that. Our sheriff has jumped to conclusions about Dee. He's zeroed in on her before anything's been announced about the cause of the fire or about the drug activity going on."

"That Hershel Caywood. Always trying to make a name for himself. Thinks he's a hotshot detective. The talk around town is there's no evidence of arson whatsoever. The Hope women? Drugs or not, they're like a bunch of stray kittens nobody wants. Surely our community could step up to find a temporary solution." Shirley moved to a redbud's scrappy shade while Pepper stretched out underneath on a patch of damp earth.

I joined her, but no breeze stirred the air or her words hanging there. Apparently she hadn't thought this through. "In Sweetbriar? Our good mayor has never wanted them here in the first place. And didn't we have a protest parade to keep the prison system from buying our home?"

"Yes, but you found them the perfect place, and before we could turn around twice, that big old house was renovated for them. I think you could do it again."

"But no one wants them living in Sweetbriar."

"Name five people who would throw them out without a second thought."

Shirley didn't have to wait long. Four names came to me immediately. "Our mayor, Lucy, the sheriff, and Mr. Lively who once told me 'those women are no-good troublemakers. Always have been. Always will be.'"

"Only four? Piece of cake. Who you gonna work on first?"

"The mayor for sure, since he could sway our citizens one way or the other, but I haven't a clue how."

Shirley gave me a sweaty, perfumed hug. "Miss Hops," she said, using the name Jack liked to call me, "you got my confidence."

"Let's head inside," I said, wishing for some of that same confidence. Sweat trickled down my neck. "Jack's taking too long. Let's get something to drink." The panting dog stood and followed us.

In the kitchen, we gulped our water and watched Pepper lap his from a Tupperware bowl while my thoughts about the Hope women shaped into possibilities. Maybe I had come up with a solution, but could the mayor be convinced? I turned to Shirley. "I'm going to recommend those apartments in the Ancient Oak Elementary. I hear they're really nice, plus they have a community room for meetings and gatherings. Sounds ideal."

"Don't know of another place in town that would work, but are they ready for movin' in?"

"Not sure." I took out my phone and called Mayor Stone Phillips' office. His secretary, Miss Louise Smith, dashed my plans. "Thank you for the information," I said and hung up. "Three weeks until completion. We're back to square one, and I'm standing on it."

I had no choice but to take action. How could I live with myself if I did nothing? But where could the women possibly go? Who would take them in? Even temporarily.

I found two Hope women sweeping the gym when lunch was over. After securing a phone number from one, I placed a call. After I explained my idea, the prison warden was speechless. Then he doubted it would work. Finally, he was totally against it.

"What's *your* plan then?" I asked.

"Well, uh . . . they'll be placed in a holding facility in Memphis until we can find a permanent location. Not easy as you well know. May take a while."

"My idea has got to be a better choice." We discussed the situation a little further. "I'd send someone to take a look at those schoolhouse apartments before they get snatched up," I said. Maybe the renovations would be completed ahead of schedule. I sensed Charlie shaking his head.

"I'll get back to you on that," the warden said. "First priority is to hire someone to be in charge of those women. You sure you want 'em scattered all over town? They ain't exactly the cream of the crop. Mary Wilson filed complaints against nearly every one of 'em. Anybody gives any trouble, you call the sheriff. And then you call me."

After I assured him I would, I returned outside where Shirley waited on the now-shaded gym steps. A breeze stirred the air. "Right or wrong, I've set the wheels in motion and convinced the warden to go along." I bit into a big piece of lemon pound cake left over from lunch. "Now we've got to enlist six people to take an ex-con into their home for three weeks. Heavens to Betsy, I can't think of one person who would agree to such. Can you?"

"I would bet a bottle of my hair color, *Blonde Bombshell*, we'll figure somethin' out," Shirley said as Jack's scooter puttered up to the curb and promptly backfired.

Jack cut the motor, removed his cowboy hat, and ran his hand through his long hair. "Miss Hops, reckon I'd best take you home first. Maybe you can talk some sense into that crazy woman shouting and running around the Manor like someone possessed. I seen her from the street. Mr. Lively was running after her, but he was laggin' behind."

"Who are you talking about?"

"Nellie. That klepto-woman. That's who."

I caught her in my arms as she rounded the back corner of the Manor, sending us both into a hosta-edged flowerbed. We sat in the middle of broken begonias and impatiens as Nellie sobbed into her hands. When I reached over and rubbed her back to help sooth her unpredictable behavior, she lifted her head with no evidence of tears.

"I can't find Aunt Mildred. I've searched everywhere. Every nook and cranny."

We helped each other stand, and I managed to brush off some of the dirt and leaves clinging to our backsides.

Mr. Lively huffed past us and collapsed on the side porch steps. "Are you all right, Nellie?" he called out. For some odd reason, he seemed to care about her and her for him.

"We're fine," I hollered back with a wave, even though it was only Nellie he was concerned about. He pushed himself up from the steps and disappeared inside. I fished a clean hanky out of a pocket and held it out. She blew her nose and offered it back.

Yuk. I shook my head. "No, you keep it. Now, tell me about your Aunt Mildred." We climbed out of the flowerbed and sank down on an old garden bench that creaked in protest.

A dramatic sob caught in her throat. "I promised Auntie Pearl I would look after her, and now she's gone. Someone must've taken her. Why would anyone do such a thing?"

This woman was either totally crazy—as Francesca had determined and would take great delight in if she were here to document her point—or had merely acquired the habit of talking to deceased relatives like I did with my Charlie. I could never fault her for that.

I turned toward her and reached for her hand. "Tell me. About Aunt Mildred."

Nellie pressed my hanky to her nose. "She was the one person who loved me no matter what. Used to spend the summers with her. She lived alone. Could see into the future. And she talked to herself. People called her crazy and all sorts of other names. She was gifted, but no one appreciated her. She died back in 1965. A neighbor found her slumped in her porch swing. Had her cremated, and I've been in charge of her ever since. Now she's gone."

"Well now." I stood, much relieved. "I'm sure you'll find her. Is she in a box or perhaps an urn? Have you checked underneath your bed?" Nellie's room normally looked like it had been sucked up into the air and released by the Wicked Witch of the West. Aunt Mildred might never be found.

"Last time I checked she was in a Maxwell House coffee can. Her favorite brand." Her long chin hairs quivered. "What am I going to do? Auntie Pearl will never forgive me."

"I thought Minnie Pearl died."

"Those people can hold a grudge forever. Very unforgiving lot."

I pulled Nellie upright, then took her arm and led her back inside. We headed down the hallway toward her room. "Think where you last saw your Aunt Mildred and start there. Take your time. I'll stop by later. I'll bet the two of you will be talking up a storm."

"How did you know we—"

"Oh, I had a hunch. Now you go on." I shooed Nellie away on her mission. It seemed she had forgotten her tantrum of a few days ago when she stomped her foot and left the dining room in a huff. Refusing to admit to her kleptomania habits, plus her irrational behavior, might get the best of me yet. Could her Aunt Mildred be the key to her mixed-up mind? The only one who had loved Nellie and now she was gone? I made a mental note to ask her counselor.

Jack delivered Shirley to the Manor. As I gulped a glass of water while standing at the kitchen sink, she appeared dressed in jeans and T-shirt with her hair caught up in a red bandana. "Hot dogs, kraut, and baked beans for supper," she announced as she set to work. "Might have time to stir up a pineapple upside-down cake for dessert. How does that sound?" She looked at me with a big smile. That woman loved to cook better than anything.

"One of my favorites." I drained my glass and placed it in the sink. A comforting rest before dinner beckoned me. After changing my pee-soaked clothes, that is. The rank smell had increased considerably. As I moved through the dining room and into the foyer, Mr. Lively appeared. He closed his office door behind him.

"Since when are animals allowed in here?" he said with his nose in the air. "Smells like a kennel," he added as he wrinkled his nose.

"Spray some air freshener. Lavender would do the trick." I hurried to my room.

After slipping into a pair of loose-fitting bellbottom pants and a tie-dyed T-shirt, I sank into my rocker with a sigh. This had been a long, emotional, and upsetting day. My eyelids felt so very heavy...

I awoke with a jolt to my phone's guitar music. *What? Where am I?*

By the time my room came into focus, the phone lay still and quiet on top of my chest of drawers. Then it started up again. I grabbed it and answered. Blind George was on the other end. He had gone back to the hospital to check on Dee and discovered she had taken a turn for the worse.

"I'm on my way," I said, already in motion as I snatched up my purse from the floor. This time I remembered to grab my cane, which was leaning against the doorframe, and my red straw hat from a nearby hook. Then I stopped. What was I thinking? No one was around who could take me there, and eight blocks was a bit too far to walk. The only one around with a car was Mr. Lively. I headed for his office.

He grumbled and frowned his displeasure. "How do you expect me to get any work done around here?" He removed car keys from a desk drawer. "How bad is she?"

"Worse is all I know." We passed through the dining room, then the kitchen where Shirley turned toward us with eyes wide. "Dee. Call you later," I said with a quick wave. No time to explain as we flew out the back door headed for Mr. Lively's car sheltered in an old garage on the back of the property. I could hardly believe he was actually giving me a ride as I hurried to keep up with his long strides.

In his open convertible, the wind blew my hair in every direction and lifted it up until I felt like I could fly. We hadn't spoken since he told me to be certain to shake every speck of dirt off my shoes before getting into his prized, not to mention immaculate, possession.

A red light on Main brought us to a screeching stop. Mr. Lively turned to me with a scowl. "Just so you know, my office door has always been locked, according to your insistence if memory serves me right. You're the only other person with a key. I'll wager you've paid someone else besides the yard boy out of the cash box and forgot you did. I don't appreciate your unfounded accusations, and I'm looking for a job elsewhere."

The light turned green, and we took off with tires squealing. The silence between us turned as heavy as a wheelbarrow full of river stones. I had been certain he was a thief even though I had no concrete evidence. I'd thought the worst of him because I didn't like him. My thoughts tangled into their usual knot. If he hadn't taken the money, then who?

He pulled up to the hospital's entrance. With a few grunts and groans I managed to swing my legs around and push myself upright with the help of my cane. "Thanks for the lift." I slammed the door harder than I meant to.

He flinched like he'd been struck and then with a flick of his hand he was gone. I hurried inside. For sure we had to get to the bottom of this. Perhaps I'd made a mistake. But I still didn't like the man. He had always rubbed me the wrong way, like a piece of rough sandpaper.

Blind George, hands clasped behind him, paced in the hallway leading to intensive care. When he turned and spotted me, I thumped my way over to him as my knee protested my haste. "What happened?" I asked before he spoke. "When I saw Dee around lunchtime, she seemed fine. Well, not fine exactly. Her voice sounded raspy, and she had some coughing fits. But it didn't seem serious."

I looked up into George's unshaven face scrunched into a wad of wrinkles. He pulled the bar towel from his shoulder and wiped his sweaty brow. His bloodshot eyes flashed with . . . with what? Anger? "Doc says this can happen quick. She's on a ventilator. Possible pneumonia." He pounded his fist into an open palm. "She was alone. I should've never followed their stupid rules."

I knew George sympathized with her since he had also served some prison time years back, but this was more than that. He felt it was his duty to protect her. Maybe his reasons would come to light, but there was no need to press him now. He was stressed enough as it was. We walked down to a nearby waiting area where he flopped into a green vinyl armchair, sending it against the wall with a thud. Then he leaned forward with his arms on his knees, clasped his hands together, and stared at the floor. His lips moved. Perhaps in prayer. So I slipped back into the hallway and called Shirley. Nearly six o'clock according to my phone, and for sure I wouldn't be home for supper.

Five minutes later I returned to where I had left George. He was no longer there or anywhere around that I could see. How could a big man like him slip past me without being noticed? I headed for an exit door leading to the stairs. When I pushed it open, there he stood on a landing, gazing out a tall window. I walked over to him. The sunlight of late day had turned a scrubby vacant lot of weeds into a garden bathed in gold.

I placed my hand on his large, muscled arm. "I'll be glad to stay if you like."

He finally turned his head toward me and nodded.

"How about a cup of coffee?" I asked, not knowing what else to say to this man who had always faced life head-on with a no-nonsense confidence. "I've heard the café also makes a mean hamburger, and I'm starving. I'll get us both one and be back in no time."

"Just coffee," he said as he turned back to the window. "Thanks," he added. "For staying." The window had turned a soft pink as this burley man watched the setting sun. He obviously hadn't changed clothes or shaved since the fire, and he smelled worse than he looked. Here he was waiting for news about a young woman fighting for her life. I wanted to know more, to know why he cared so much, but I bit my tongue. Now was not the time.

In less than fifteen minutes I was back from the café. "It would be wasteful to throw one of these away," I said as I handed him a wrapped sandwich and sat the coffee carrier in the seat between us. He nodded, and we ate our supper in silence. I hoped Shirley saved me a piece of her cake.

"Reckon you're wondering why I care so much. About Dee." George wiped his sleeve across his mouth and gulped the last of the coffee.

"As a matter of fact . . ." I managed to say around a mouthful of greasy burger.

He balled the cup and burger wrappings in his big fists and leaned on his knees. "I had a daughter. Once. Had an attitude. Like Dee. Got into trouble. Drugs. Stealing from her own pa to feed her habit. No telling what else she done. I'll never know because I sent her away. Told her she was no longer welcome." He jumped up and thumped his trash into a recycle can. I waited without speaking until he finally sank into his chair again.

"What was your daughter's name?" I asked as I wrapped up my half-eaten burger, no longer hungry.

"Janie Elizabeth," he whispered as he stared into space.

"Did she die?"

He dipped his head. "Drugs. Alone. Like Dee."

"You're a good man, George."

The doctor appeared, and we both stood. "She's a fighter," he said. "I can't promise you anything, but I know that much."

"When will we know?" George asked.

"Sometime tomorrow, one way or the other."

We thanked him and he left. It was almost nine o'clock. "My bones are talking to me," I said. "Want to take a walk? A short one. Just to get some blood moving."

"Reckon so," he said. "No need for you to stay, though. Matter of fact, I could carry you home and be back here in no time."

"Maybe later." I took a minute to stretch my cranky back.

We ended up across the street from the hospital so George could grab a quick smoke. He threw a half-smoked cigarette into the gutter, took my arm, and we headed back. "How's that mutt of Dee's?" he asked as we rode the elevator to the second floor.

"I think he's . . ."

The doors swished open. Hershel, Shirley, and Jack stood in a cluster around a vending machine. They all looked up.

Jack spoke first. "Any word yet? Hadn't heard from you, and you didn't answer when Shirl called."

"Must've had my phone on silent. She's still critical, but we should know by tomorrow if she'll make it. According to the doctor, Dee's tough, and that's in her favor."

Everyone moved into the intensive-care waiting area. The sheriff sank into a chair, plopped his laptop onto an end table, and fished his buckeye out of his pocket. He rubbed his lucky charm and stared into space. Why had he stopped by? His suspect certainly wasn't going anywhere. Something had taken hold of him so much so that he seemed in a daze, not even flirting with Shirley. Which was totally unlike him.

Jack unwrapped a Hershey bar, and the chocolate aroma made my mouth water. Shirley took the seat next to me and put her arm around my shoulder. "Jack can run you home. Smiley's worried sick about you. I'll let you know if there's any change."

I shook my head. "Maybe later." I slipped out into the stairwell and made a phone call. Since Smiley didn't own a cellphone, William could inform him I was doing fine.

Jack and Shirley disappeared and returned with pillows and blankets. I made myself as comfortable as possible using an extra chair to prop up my feet. Shirley and the men scooted chairs around a coffee table. Jack produced a deck of cards and a quiet game of poker was soon underway. The expected fireworks between the two rivals for Shirley's affections didn't happen. Maybe concern for Dee had brought about an unspoken truce. For now anyway. My eyelids closed. Minutes crept into one hour and then two as I dozed in bits and pieces.

Voices called as if far away in a fog.

"Agnes, wake up."

"Sis. Sis, it's time to go home."

Shirley and Smiley stood over me. She was rubbing my back, and he was holding my hand in both of his. He grinned at me. "You'd sleep a sight better in your own bed, don'tcha know."

My friends gradually came into focus as I gazed at them. "Dee? Is she ..."

"The same," Shirley said. "We took a vote and decided we could call you as soon as we heard any more news. Besides, your snoring's interrupting our card game." She straightened up, sporting a wide grin.

I flopped my feet onto the floor. Smiley helped me stand. "That's ridiculous," I sputtered as my stiff neck protested. "I don't—"

"Sit back down a minute, Sis. I'll get that crick worked out." And in less than five minutes he did.

"How did you get here?" I asked as I reached for my cane and pushed myself upright.

"The short of the story is I rode on the back of Jack's scooter. More fun than I've had in a coon's age."

"But how—"

"Sheriff says he'll carry us back home. He's got to make his nightly rounds downtown anyway. Make sure everything's locked up tight."

On our way back to the Manor, Smiley said William's earlier assurances about my wellbeing hadn't satisfied him. He paced the floor worrying about me and finally used the house phone to call Shirley. They decided I had to get some rest in my own bed.

Smiley walked me to my room, and I gave him a big hug before he could scoot away. "Thank you for looking after me," I whispered as he disappeared around the corner. My heart filled with love for that scrawny little man. As soon as I closed my door, I slipped off my shoes and fell into bed. After a prayer for Dee, I sank into a welcomed sleep.

Morning sun streamed through my window. Nearly eight o'clock according to the clock-radio beside Charlie's picture. I jumped out of bed, grabbed my phone, and hurried to the kitchen for a cup of coffee.

"Three o'clock this morning, Dee made a turn for the better," Shirley said as she flipped sausage patties and then slipped a pan full of biscuits into the oven. "Not completely out of the woods yet, but improved."

"Thank the good Lord." I blew across my cup of hot coffee before sipping it. "When did you get home?"

"Jack dropped me off around three-thirty before he headed to his place."

"What about Hershel?"

"Funny you should ask. He returned an hour or so after he carried you and Smiley home. Before we left, he got a big cup of coffee and said he was going to stay a bit longer. Set up his computer and got involved with something. He never looked up when we said good-bye. Our good sheriff was not acting like himself last night. You reckon his investigation has proven Dee's guilt? At least in his mind?"

"Or her innocence. And now he's trying to figure out where to look next."

CHAPTER SEVEN

After breakfast I rescued Pepper from his beauty-parlor-safe room, which was actually the enclosed back porch next to the kitchen. It was also a lonesome place for a pup since it had high windows and no human presence. He danced around with excitement as I hooked his leash to his collar.

When we arrived on the Manor's front porch, it was deserted except for Smiley, slouched in a rocker with his eyes closed. The *Timely News* lay by his feet. I leaned over and tapped his shoulder. His eyes fluttered open.

"Walk uptown with us," I said, not really giving him a choice. "We need to talk with the mayor."

"We do?" Smiley yawned and stretched.

"On our way, you've got to help me decide how to present our case." Pepper tugged on his leash.

Smiley pushed himself up. "What case?"

I linked my arm in his. "Let's get cracking." We headed down the wheelchair ramp with the dog pulling ahead and urging us to step up our pace.

As soon as we walked inside Stone Phillips' office, his secretary, Miss Louise Smith, screwed up her face. "We only allow service dogs in this office, which obviously that little thing is not. It will have to leave." She smoothed her perfect hairdo while her manicured nails sparkled like a celebration.

"I see you've been to the Kut'N Loose," I said, trying to start a casual conversation.

She surveyed our little gathering over her glasses and didn't smile.

"I admire you for sticking to the rules," I added into the cold silence. "More employees ought to do the same, don't you agree?" Smiley and Pepper headed for the door. "Go visit Blind George. I'll meet you there when I'm finished."

I turned back to Louise. "I called for an appointment and,

according to my watch, I'm on the button."

"I do declare," she said with an actual smile. "I believe we have something in common."

"Yes indeed," I said as Louise stretched out her long, shapely legs revealing her bare feet. Rarely did I wear shoes when working inside my farmhouse. Gives a person more freedom and comfort too. But this was an office. "You must love working here."

"Oh my, yes. This place is like home." She pushed the intercom button and announced my presence.

"The mayor is fortunate to have you," I said as I moved toward his office.

Stone Phillips rose from behind his desk and bent forward. We shook hands.

"The residents of the House of Hope need your assistance," I announced without any idle chit-chat. "As you know, the Red Cross has arranged a temporary shelter for them in the church, but in a couple of days they will be homeless. We've got to do something, but I need your help." A twinge of lightheadedness called for a place to park myself, but I couldn't risk moving my head to look around. So, I leaned on the massive desk in front of me and pressed my hands onto the shiny wood.

"You don't say." He frowned as he plopped into his leather chair and rolled up to his desk. He leaned on his elbows, steepled his hands, and studied me. "You realize I promised our citizens that I would never allow a halfway house in Sweetbriar. Thought I could keep it out, but that didn't happen thanks to you. You understand what I'm saying?"

"Absolutely." I fixed my eyes on a moose head hanging on the wall behind him. When a dizzy spell hit out of the blue, any movement was risky. I slowly shifted my weight and leaned on my cane. Out of the corner of my eye I spotted the mayor leaving his chair and coming to stand by my side.

"Are you ill?" he asked. "You look mighty pale. Let me get you something to drink."

"Temporary sinking spell. Maybe if I could sit . . ."

He pushed a chair to the back of my legs. I sank onto soft leather as Louise appeared with a glass of water. She and the mayor watched me drink. As far as I could tell, my head was clearing, but I couldn't take any chances with sudden movements.

The mayor looked genuinely concerned. "Can I carry you home?"

"Maybe we should take you to the ER instead," Louise said.

"Thank you, but I'm perfectly fine. If I could just sit here a moment before leaving."

"Yes, yes of course. Louise, bring Miss Agnes another glass of water and some of those Girl Scout cookies you always have in your desk."

After a few moments of munching thin mint cookies and sipping water, I leaned back into the red leather chair. The mayor propped his backside against the front of his desk with his arms crossed and studied me. I locked eyes with him. "You don't have to look so worried. I'm fit as a fiddle. Let's return to the matter at hand."

He pushed off from his desk and returned to his chair. Some papers shuffled back and forth before he spoke. "Those women are not my problem. They had no business being any-where in Sweetbriar in the first place. I'm not obligated to pro-vide a shelter for them, even a temporary one. Our town can't be run like a charity."

"I couldn't agree more. Except for a tragic death, the fire worked in the town's favor. Sent them packing so to speak."

"You could say that." He returned to me, placed his hand underneath my arm, helped me stand, and moved me toward his office door.

I loosened myself from his grasp and turned toward him. "With election year fast approaching, your approval rating would soar if you could show the town your compassionate side." Surely he had one. I was counting on it.

"You don't say. And how do you think I could accomplish that?"

"Appeal to our citizens to shelter six homeless women for two, maybe three weeks. Think of the positive publicity our town would receive, plus you would be hailed as a hero. I know a reporter with the *Timely News* who would love such a story. And William, who is a computer whiz, could share it on social media."

"Hmmm." He rubbed his chin. "You say this is temporary?"

"The prison warden has assured me that by the end of three weeks, or even sooner, a permanent location will have been secured." No need to mention that the Ancient Oak Apartments at the edge of town were a good possibility. He'd find out soon enough.

Louise handed me some cookies wrapped in a tissue. "You don't have trouble with your sugar, do you?"

"Never have," I said, thanking her with my best smile. I loved Girl Scout cookies.

"Have it checked anyway. Blood pressure too. Could be it's too low or even too high. My grandmother used to have a dizzy head. Put her flat on her back for days. Had that kind of trouble all her life."

"And how long was that?"

"Ninety-five, almost ninety-six."

"Well, there you go." I turned to the mayor who had edged back to his office door. "What if the town council stood behind you and supported your offer to lend a helping hand to these women?"

"Next to impossible." In two big strides he stood in front of me and held out his hand. "Pull that off, and you've got a deal." We shook on it.

I left with my cookies and headed to Blind George's place. *Now what, Charlie*, I mused. Betty Jo was a member of the town council as well as president of the Women's Club, but she could either be of no help whatsoever or a stumbling block. The Hope House women might have one or two more days to camp out in the church gym. That didn't give me much time. I kept asking myself why I was getting deeper and deeper into the middle of things. If I did nothing, the women would soon leave Sweetbriar and many people, including the mayor, would breathe a sigh of relief. But could I live with my guilt?

My trek to Blind George's pool hall transpired as fast as my gimpy knee and recovering head would allow. Not only had George served prison time, our mayor had harassed him because of it. Stone Phillips had an unsavory pattern of behavior toward all ex-cons. There was no doubt to the prejudices of our city official. I had once thought he was an okay guy. Not the most upstanding man in our small town, but mediocre. But I had come to realize his integrity had more holes in it than an old screen door. Charlie agreed. Now I had to persuade such a man to show some compassion for six women who had served time and were struggling to start over in Sweetbriar. And meanwhile I had to confront my own uncertainties toward these women. Especially Dee.

Midafternoon at Blind George's, the quiet darkness smelled of boiled peanuts, a sweet aroma to a Southerner. George dipped a strainer into a steaming pot and filled a tin bucket with his specialty. I climbed onto a stool. "I understand Dee's turned the corner, even improving some."

"Sure is." George handed me a small sack of hot peanuts. "They wouldn't let me see her, but I'm going back this afternoon and staying 'til they do."

"She's lucky to have you in her corner, especially with Sheriff Caywood breathing down her neck."

"You got that right, Granny."

"All the Hope women could use your help right now." I pulled out a peanut and blew away the steam.

"How's that?"

"They need places to stay for a couple of weeks. When they leave the church, if they don't have anywhere to go, they'll be placed in a holding facility back in Tennessee."

George frowned. "We can't let that happen."

"Exactly. Let's think of who in Sweetbriar would have enough empathy to open their home to an . . ."

"Ex-con."

I nodded. Unfortunately, that's how most folks would see them. And I had to count myself among them.

"Where's Pepper and Smiley?" I asked. "Thought they'd be here."

"Gone for a walk. Reckon them two hot dogs that little dog gobbled up didn't set right." He wiped his hands on his apron and set a stack of napkins in front of me. "Your boyfriend says you've been visiting the mayor."

"He ever toss some stumbling blocks your way? Make it hard for you to run a small business?" I popped another shell open and sucked out the salty goodness.

"Made some *suggestions* about upgrading my fine establishment. Said if I didn't I could lose my liquor license."

"Is that all?"

"Come to think of it, he added 'or worse.' What could be worse than not being able to drink a cold beer with these boiled peanuts? Salt, peanuts, and beer go together like a hot dog, chili, and onions. You thirsty, Granny?"

"How about a cherry Coke?"

"You got it." He filled an old-fashioned glass with ice and fountain Coke before adding a generous squirt of cherry juice and setting it in front of me. "You say the Hope House women ain't got nowhere to go once they have to leave the church?"

"Yep. We've got to put our plan into action. And quick."

"We? What plan?"

"Since you seem to have a heart for these women, especially Dee—what with offering her a job and all—maybe you can help us out." I added another peanut shell to a growing pile.

"You got my attention. What can I do?"

"I've got an idea or two that might work."

"Let's hear 'em," he said as he attacked the counter with a wet, sour-smelling rag.

Turned out George nodded his approval for only one location for one of the women and shook his head as I suggested two other places. He was no help whatsoever. When did this unkempt man get so particular? I counted out some change from my coin purse.

"No charge, Granny. Today's on me. Did you say if somebody was to take in one of these women, the prison would pay 'em room and board?"

"Certainly. And the arrangement would be temporary. Two to three weeks at the most. A month tops."

"You know I've got an apartment upstairs. If I remember right, you considered it yourself at one time."

I had taken a look when I had thought about leaving the Manor for a place of my own, but it was ugly and downright depressing, so I hadn't ever considered it. "I'm not sure if a place over a pool hall would be approved. No offence, you understand."

"No offence taken, but you let me know if you come up short."

Smiley and Pepper returned, and the three of us headed back to the Manor. The dog trotted along beside us instead of tugging on his leash. I slipped my hand inside Smiley's. What should have been a gentle, contented moment was not, all because of the turmoil going on inside my head. And it was not my vertigo acting up this time.

We stopped to rest on a bench in front of Rodeo Rags

where the owner always left a dish of fresh water for any animals walking by. Pepper drank his fill and then stretched out by our feet.

After I shared the mayor's reaction to my visit, I fished Louise Smith's card out of my purse and handed it to Smiley. "Well, what do you think?" I asked after a time of silence. "Should I ask her to help us?"

"The mayor's like a sheet hanging on a clothesline." Smiley waved the card back and forth.

"How do you figure?"

"However the wind blows, the sheet's gonna flap that way."

I took the card and returned it to my purse. "You didn't answer me. Should I call her? She could be helpful if she's a mind to."

"Or not. Old maids are always loyal to their boss. Protect his opinions with her life."

"I think you're wrong. She said ex-cons needed a way to put their life back on the right track, and she didn't agree with her boss's narrow-minded, judgmental stance."

"And you believe her?" He squinted at me and shifted in his seat.

"Don't have a reason not to." I reached down and rubbed Pepper behind his ears. One thing I did know for certain. Stone Phillips was unstable. No backbone. Plus, he had a hatred for the former convicts living in our town. Who knew what evil lurked in his heart? And Smiley was probably right about his secretary protecting him.

An unsteady, disheveled old man shuffled toward us. Pepper jumped up, tugged on his leash, and whined as the man approached our bench and stood closer than necessary. He stunk worse than a meat market's dumpster. In July. Smiley scooped up Pepper, whose whine had turned to yapping, and hurried off without a backward glance.

"You got my spot," the man said in a slurred voice. He hovered overhead.

I scooted away from him and stood. "This bench is public property." I moved a few steps back.

"Mayor told me it's mine. His word's good as g . . . gold." He plopped down and gazed up at me through bloodshot eyes.

By all that is sensible, I should have moved on, but something about him held me there.

"Don't remember me, do ya?" He reached out and tried to touch my arm. I stared at his long, dirty fingernails and took another step back. Who was he? Then it came to me.

This man had approached me once before in Blind George's. He had been a friend of Josiah's and wanted to help me solve his murder. When his hand fell away, I sat down beside him.

He stared off into the distance. "Somethin' you oughta know."

As I waited for him to continue, the deputy sheriff stepped out of the Kut'N Loose Salon brushing off his uniform. Larry glanced up and headed our way. I needed to be quick.

"Tell me." I leaned closer and held my breath.

"Nobody believes nothin' I say." He jerked his head toward the deputy who was nearly upon us.

I looked into his eyes. "You know where I live. Knock on the back door. Tonight. Whatever Shirley's cooking, you can have your fill."

He nodded.

"Well, well, well." Hershel's deputy approached the bench with a smirk. "Loitering again are we? I know your game, you old bum. Out looking for a free meal and a bed tonight, are we? Time to move along. Go back down to the river or wherever it is you people live. You're stinking up the whole town."

It was all I could do to bite my tongue.

The homeless man pushed himself up and grimaced with each slow step. He moved on down the street as if he were a hundred years old, yet his long brown hair and straggly beard had no trace of gray. A lump rose in my throat as I watched him leave. I hoped he would show up tonight for a good meal.

"Maybe he'll stay down there where he belongs," Larry said as he hitched up his pants. "What tall tale was he feeding you, Miss Agnes?"

"Said the mayor gave him this bench to use any time he chose."

Larry threw back his head and laughed. "That's a good one. You stay clear of that lunatic. You hear? Crazy as a bed bug, like most of them trash."

I had to get away before I spoke my mind to our officer of the law. Had the old man seen something or someone the night of the fire that would clear Dee of any suspicion? Maybe he'd been in a stupor and imagined it. Must've gone to the sheriff with some information, but they hadn't believed him. Did any of this involve the mayor who thought he could bribe the man with a bench of his own—which the deputy thought was a laughing matter?

I could only pray he would knock on our back door tonight, not only for food, but with some valuable information.

CHAPTER EIGHT

When at last I approached Sweetbriar Manor, Smiley slouched against the ancient stonewall, his eyes half shut. Pepper rested by his feet. Smiley's naptimes, regular as clockwork, had been gobbled up by assisting me whenever I asked. Maybe I had become too demanding of my obliging companion.

Pepper spotted me, strained against his leash, and danced on his hind legs. Instantly alert, Smiley pushed himself off the wall and scooped the frisky dog into his arms.

Thoughts of Mayor Stone Phillips and his secretary Miss Louise Smith—as well as the homeless man and our cocky, inept deputy—danced in my mind. Not to mention Lucy, who lived next door to the charred halfway house and would certainly protest if I found a way for the *ex-cons* to remain in Sweetbriar. Geeze Louise. I was in a barrel of pickles. And not sweet ones either.

An old, yellow taxicab parked alongside the street gradually came into focus.

William squatted beside a front fender holding a can of wax and a rag. So this was how he planned to win Francesca's heart. He stood when he saw us approaching, grinning around his cigar stub.

"Whatcha think, Red?" he said as he threw his arms out wide. "Ain't she a beaut? Upholstery needs a little mending, but otherwise she's clean as a whistle."

"Where did you find her?"

"Mike's been on the lookout for months. He's had her in his garage a week checking her out. Runs like a top." He squinted at the hood and applied more wax.

I hadn't been inside Mike's Motor Service across the street since the day the owner of Boss's Pawnshop was arrested for Josiah's murder. I shuddered at the thought of nearly being kidnapped. Or worse.

"Did you hear me, Red?"

I shook my head. What had William been saying? I couldn't concern myself with him and his problems right now. I had bigger issues shouting for attention.

Not to be deterred, William continued full speed ahead. He looked at me and then Smiley and back again. "The two of you keep this a secret until I get my driver's license. Mike says he'll take me. He says to study the book, but I can pull it up on my computer. Actually no need. Ought to know all the rules after driving my own cab for thirty years in New Orleans." He leaned further over the hood top with his polishing rag.

"Your car's in a no parking zone," Smiley said as he joined us.

"Meter Maid'll have it towed for sure," I added.

"No worries. I'm gonna take it back over to Mike's soon. She'll stay there until I'm legal." He stuck his cigar stub behind his ear. "Got it all figured out. I'll cruise with my sweetie pie over to Black Beard's Island about sunset when the time's right. Perfect location for a proposal."

I walked over and held out my hand. "Congratulations. I'm so happy for—"

Before I could finish, he grabbed me in a bear hug. Then he thumped Smiley on his back. "About time you and Red got hitched. Don't know whatcha waitin' for."

Smiley sputtered and stammered and ducked his head.

I gave William's arm a playful slap. "Your wedding's more than enough right now. We're too busy. Right, Smiley?"

He didn't speak. Just studied me with his big brown eyes until a horn tooted from a passing car and broke the spell. We managed to leave William and continue up the hill to our home with Pepper urging us on.

"Sis," Smiley said as he stopped on the front porch. "We need to talk. Wait right here." He sounded serious. He hurried to the front door with Pepper and released him inside. When he stood in front of me again, he wouldn't look me in the eye, but studied his sandals, which he always wore with black dress socks. One unruly sock had collapsed around his ankle and held my gaze.

"Well?" I straightened myself to my full height with my cane's help. "I'm listening."

He finally raised his head and looked into my eyes. "You've

been my friend since your first day here," he whispered. "Nothing on this earth's better than a good friend."

"Yes indeed, but—"

"I made a promise to my Lucinda." He stepped to the side and clasped his hands behind his back.

What on earth was he talking about? And what does that have to do with . . . I sucked in my breath. This could not be good.

"Promised I'd never get hitched again."

His words stole my breath. Either his dying wife had demanded he never remarry or he had volunteered. My knees felt as weak as overcooked macaroni, and my heart thumped in my ears. I placed my hands on his shoulders. "Look at me," I pleaded.

When he did, his eyes had filled to the brim. I let my breath out slowly. Somehow we had to find a way to move forward with our lives. I understood about promises and had made some to Charlie, but not one to never love another person.

"Can we sit?" I asked.

We managed to find the swing and sink into it.

I turned to him and took his hands in mine. "We will always be close no matter what. Right?"

He nodded as he took out a handkerchief and dabbed at his eyes.

I lightly poked his chest. "What gave you the idea I wanted to marry you anyway?" *Lord*, I prayed, *help me speak to this adorable man without scaring him off.* I had to slow down or risk losing the one I wanted to spend the rest of my days with. But without marriage?

"Sis, I'm sorry. I thought you—"

"Sam Abenda, you're the best thing that's happened to me since my Charlie, but I don't plan on giving up my freedom for any man anytime soon."

His bushy eyebrows twitched. "You mean it? Whew! That's a relief, don'tcha know. What I mean is . . ."

I hugged him around his neck, planted a kiss on his cheek, and resisted the urge to do more. "I know what you mean. We can talk more later, but only if you want to. For now, my good Watson, let's focus on our mission. Six homeless women need our help. Who in Sweetbriar would volunteer to take one in?"

He stood and offered me his arm. The sparkle had returned

to his brown eyes. "You can count on me," he said as he tipped his baseball cap and winked. "I've got an idea or two we need to consider."

We turned to go inside when something on the far side of the porch caught my eye. A shopping bag from the Red Dress Boutique, my daughter's favorite shop, sat on a rocker.

"You go ahead," I said to Smiley. "I'll be in directly."

"Sure thing, Sis. Looks like someone's got a surprise package." He gave a little salute before walking away with a spring in his step. I smiled in spite of any misgivings about our future together.

A note taped to the bag confirmed my suspicions. My daughter, who had never learned to sew a stitch, always relied on me for alterations on new purchases, as well as on old clothes that no longer fit. *Mother*, she wrote, *I'll pick these up in a couple of days. Instructions are pinned to each garment. Maybe they'll give you something to do with your idle time. BJ.*

I fumbled around in my purse until I found a pen, turned the note over and wrote, *Take these to Sunshine Cleaners. I hear they have a new lady who is a sewing wizard. I have no idle time. Mother.*

I moved the bag to a bench by the front door, undercover in case of rain, and where Betty Jo would spot it when she returned. "Idle time, my foot," I grumbled to Charlie as I entered the Manor's foyer.

I stopped short, trying to focus my eyes after leaving the bright sunlight. Mr. Lively stood outside his office door with a tattered suitcase sitting by his feet. How long had he been packed? And why was he leaving now? He held out a set of keys. "I won't be needing these." He dropped them and I caught them in midair.

I shifted my weight onto my good knee and peered up at him. "But you agreed to—"

"I've been asked, no begged, to close down a retirement home in the mountains of North Carolina before they call in the law. Far away from here, and that will suit me just fine." He picked up his suitcase and stepped closer. "The residents are putting up a fight, threatening a hunger strike, and refusing to leave the place. Sounds like a worse situation than Sweetbriar Manor, if that could be possible, but it comes with excellent benefits."

We remained in the expansive foyer between the grandfather clock and a ghastly bulldog statue that had stood guard since my first day at the Manor. I decided to confront the issue with Mr. Lively head on. "Since you've continued to deny you had anything to do with the money missing from the cash box, I'd like for you to stay long enough to expose the real thief. Do you think you could do that?"

His bug eyes widened as his mouth dropped open for the briefest moment before he straightened his face back to normal. My instincts told me he could be as guilty as sin, but I had no proof, no reason to force him to stay. If I gave him enough rope perhaps he would hang himself.

He puffed his chest against his red suspenders. "This place is run loose as a goose. If you know what I mean. No rules or regulations to keep order."

My whole body bristled, but I clamped my mouth shut.

With his suitcase resting on the floor in front of him, he stuck a hand inside his pants pocket, pulled out a quarter, flipped it in the air, and slapped it onto the back of his left hand. "I'm heads and you're tails," he said. Then he repeated the action.

What was I thinking? A fox couldn't guard a hen house. Maybe he would turn down my offer and leave regardless of how the flip turned out.

The grandfather clock struck four times, vibrating like the lowest piano key. Mr. Lively continued to flip his quarter. "Three out of five," he said as he dropped his money back into his pocket. "You won. I'll stay and flush out your thief in six months or less."

"No, in thirty days we'll talk about how things are going." I shifted my big purse to my other arm. He cocked his head and opened his mouth but didn't speak. We shook hands. "I'll mark the date on my calendar," I added. "But during that time, if either of us is unhappy for any reason, you'll leave Sweetbriar Manor. Maybe they'll hold your North Carolina job for the thirty days. Just in case."

He nodded halfheartedly. Was he feeding me a line about having another job offer?

After our exchange, the man surprised me by gripping my free hand and pumping it. Totally insincere and unnecessary. I took a step back and held my breath, hoping he didn't get the urge to hug me. He didn't. Instead, he turned, grabbed his suit-case, and bounded upstairs to his living quarters.

A sinking feeling told me I'd made a huge blunder. What would my Charlie have advised? I could sense him once again shaking his head, which it seemed he was doing more often than not here lately, but I ignored his obvious disapproval. I was desperate for someone to run this place, and I would give this latest development my best shot. I called Henry to inform him Mr. Lively would, at least for the next thirty days, remain as our administrator. I didn't share anything about the missing money.

When William returned from leaving his taxi at Mike's I enlisted him to cart the ugly bulldog statue to the basement. My second executive decision. He bent down and squinted at the animal, removed his ever-present cigar stub from his mouth, and gave it the once over. "Red, I can sell this thing on eBay. No sense stashing it away."

Since he was a master of such things, and I was still learn-ing how to use my cell phone, I made another decision. "Go for it. Whatever it brings, we'll split the profit."

With our deal struck, he took some pictures. Leaving the statue at its post, he hurried toward his room and his laptop. He looked as happy as a barefooted boy skipping down a sandy road.

After supper, I shared with Shirley everything that had hap-pened.

"Law, honey," she said. "If Mr. Lively ain't our thief then reckon who is? I would bet my last dime it's him. I don't trust him. No siree. But he's not the only one in this town's got me riled. Never trusted that mayor of ours either. Ridin' his bike all hours of the night, plus he's made no bones about not wantin' those *ex*-cons in our town."

I shrugged. "He was certainly upset when I left his office earlier."

"Law have mercy." Shirley said as she turned on the dish-washer and untied her apron. "This kitchen's closed 'til morn-in'."

"Think I'll stay here a while in case *someone* knocks on the back door," I said.

"Plenty of leftover chicken and dumplings if he does. Want me to send Smiley to check on you? Might get lonesome."

"Brought my knitting to keep me company. Besides, Smiley's working on a new painting in Pearl's room, and he's excited about a chance to make some progress. He's promised me I can see it soon." Thanks to Pearl, Smiley had discovered a talent he had never considered. At one time I'd been consumed by jealousy, but finally realized their teacher-student relationship had enriched both lives, and I asked their forgiveness.

I chose a stool at the island and pulled a lime-green afghan out of my Walmart bag. "Helps me think, and I've got a right smart of that to do."

"For me it's washing a sink full of dishes or peeling ten pounds of potatoes. And I do plenty of both."

"For sure," I said. Shirley left the kitchen as I took up my needles and went to work. Juanita, the young mother who lived in my rental house, would soon have a splash of color on her drab sofa. I wished I could do more to help her and her toddler, but for now this would have to do. That's when an idea hit me like a lightning bolt out of a clear blue sky. My little rental house located in a low-rent district of Sweetbriar called The Bottom, had two bedrooms. Juanita and her toddler only needed one. Would she consider taking in one of the women? She could certainly use some extra money, but would she be too scared? I'd go visit her as soon as possible and find out.

As I worked on the afghan, Smiley's promise to never marry kept popping up in my mind while I puzzled over who could be a thief among us. When the grandfather clock struck eleven, I laid my knitting down with a sigh. Between dropping stitches and correcting them, I had made little progress.

And there had been no knock on the kitchen door.

Early the next morning, the aroma of fresh coffee and fried sausage drew me into the dining room where people had begun to gather.

Shirley stuck her head around the kitchen door and motioned for me. "Go look on the back steps."

The homeless man was sopping up the last of his gravy with a biscuit. His dish looked clean enough to set in a cabinet. He grinned and handed me his plate. "That was worth a hundred-dollar bill. If I had one I'd gladly give it to the cook."

Shirley poked her head out the backdoor, handed him a paper sack, and took the plate. "Something for the road, Tom."

His eyes filled up and spilled over. He wiped his nose on his sleeve. "Much obliged, ma'am," he said, but Shirley had already disappeared inside. He rolled his sack down tight and held it in both hands as I sat down beside him.

"So, your name's Tom. Nice to meet you. Now that you've had a good breakfast, can you tell me what you saw? Was it the night of the fire?"

"Yep. Hadn't finished my usual bottle of wine neither, so I was sober. Didn't dream it or imagine it neither, but nobody believes me."

"You mean the sheriff and his deputy?"

"Right. Behind the halfway house is where I sometimes sleep. There's an old sassafras tree back there that nobody has bothered to trim, so the suckers has come up from the ground like a big bush."

"How do you know so much about trees?"

"Used to be a gardener." He chuckled. "Years ago."

"Go on," I urged.

"Well, I was fixin' to settle down for the night. Not sure about the time, but it was a right smart after midnight because it'd been a while since the courthouse clock had struck twelve times. Spread my coat out for my bed and sat down on it to keep it from blowing away. It was real windy that night if you remember. Anyway, I raised my bottle for a swig when I seen someone creeping around the back of the house."

I stood and reached into my pocket. After handing him a peppermint, I unwrapped one for myself. The mint couldn't disguise his foul smell, but I sat down beside him once again. "A man or a woman?" I asked as he sucked on his candy and stared into space.

"Ain't sure," he finally said. "Not much moonlight, but the figure wasn't real big, so it could've been a woman. Wore a coat, or maybe it was a jacket with a hood."

"What did this person do?" I stretched my stiff legs out in front of me.

"Slipped behind some bushes next to the house and disappeared. I waited with my eyes peeled. Then all of a sudden he or she jumped on a bicycle and was gone. I thought all this goings-on was none of my business so I tried to get some shut-eye. Then an explosion shook me awake and lit up the sky. Next thing I knew, flames was running up the backside of that old house. All hell broke loose. People was hollering, and the sirens was squealing. I got myself away from there quick as I could."

"Oh my. Will you come back and tell me if you remember anything else?" My feet were beginning to cramp, so I made circles with them to get my blood moving.

"Can I get me another hundred dollar dinner?" He looked at me and grinned, revealing a gold tooth that sparkled from his grimy mouth.

"Anytime. We'll be expecting you whenever you're hungry. New information or no information. You got it."

We stood and he steadied himself. "There is one more thing."

I waited while he coughed and spit out a glob of mucus. "That bicycle was old."

"How do you know?"

"Made a terrible racket."

"Thank you," I said to the man whose coat sleeves were slick with dirt and grim. "You've been more help than you know." Mayor Phillips was known to ride through the streets of town when he couldn't sleep, but his bike was probably new and expensive and quiet as a whisper. He might use some underhanded, legal way to rid the town of ex-criminals, but someone else had to have been behind the halfway house and ridden away on an old bike. But who?

Tom held his bag of food to his chest and shuffled down the sidewalk. He only made it a few steps before turning back toward me. "I'll never forget what you did for Josiah. Best friend I ever had."

"He was my husband's friend too. And mine."

"Friends are meant to look after friends," Tom said as he disappeared around the side of the Manor.

Indeed. I could see my Charlie nodding and feel the warmth of his smile.

CHAPTER NINE

Henry dropped off Miss Margaret for a visit while he helped organize the memorial for Mary Wilson. A distant cousin had arrived from Michigan, but Mary had no other relatives, as well as practically no money, so the Salvation Army stepped up to help. I always knew those folks were worth their salt.

"No need for Miss Margaret to lie around the store feeling all sad and lonesome while I'm gone. I could be tied up most of the day. Coming over here will perk her right up." Henry squatted down and told her good-bye.

After he left, Miss Margaret sniffed and rooted around three times, her usual routine, before settling onto her pillow by my feet. Soon, her eyelids twitched, and her long lashes danced. A sure sign she was dreaming. I reached down and stroked her smooth back, hoping her dream was a good one. Henry and I had agreed she would stay at the Manor on Tuesdays and Thursdays from eight-thirty to five-thirty, even though he didn't like giving up her company at his hardware store for even those two days. But today was Wednesday. A bonus.

When I stopped by his store one morning to state my case for her to visit on a regular basis, he thumped a bag of fertilizer onto the counter and agreed. "You're right, Mother Hopper, her sweet presence will be good for the residents."

Before I became the new owner, pets of any kind had been banned at the Manor. Now we had Pepper, temporarily, and Miss Margaret part-time.

Francesca, always the one to push the boundaries, rolled her wheelchair over to my rocker. "Whatever is good for the goose ought to be good for the gander. Right?" She fingered her pearls, and her eyes flitted over my precious before she turned a soft gaze on me. I knew what she meant. She didn't know how to be coy. Not her nature.

"Spit it out," I said as I recounted my stiches. This afghan had a new design, and I had to concentrate.

"Since your pig is more often than not hanging around, the rest of us can also have pets. Am I right?"

"Two days a week is not often." I couldn't let every resident have a pet or we would soon be overrun with animals. When I reached a stopping place, I tied off my yarn and set my knitting aside. We needed to talk this thing through. "Tell me what you have in mind."

"A stunning Persian is pinning away at The Barking Hound. Someone dropped her off like a piece of garbage. I want to give her a home." Francesca twisted her pearls into a knot as her face flushed a rosy pink. I was amazed she would think about anyone or anything except herself, but somehow a homeless cat had captured her heart.

But I had to be practical. "What if someone living here is allergic to cats? If so, would you agree to find her a good home somewhere else? I think the librarian, Thelma Watson, has a dozen or more."

"A Persian can't live with a herd, but I'll agree to find her a proper home." Francesca eased back in her wheelchair, but only for a moment until she gripped her chair arms and pulled herself forward. Her ring-studded fingers sparkled. "When are you going to ask everyone?"

I smiled in spite of myself. She was ready to do battle. For a cat. "As soon as everyone gathers for lunch. Is that soon enough?"

"I suppose," she said in a flat tone, but she couldn't hide the hint of a smile nor the twinkle in her eyes.

Persians. Didn't that breed have long hair that would shed and blow all over the place, into corners, underneath the old Southern huntboard, into the kitchen, and eventually into our food? I nearly gagged at the thought.

Nellie didn't appear for lunch, which was not unusual, but somehow I had an uneasy feeling. What if she were traipsing all over town looking for Aunt Mildred? In case she hadn't heard or paid any attention to the lunch buzzer, I went to her room before taking one bite of my taco salad, which was not easy.

I knocked on her door then opened it and peeked inside. Her room looked like a twister had set down in the middle of it all. A top dresser drawer hung open showing a mix of panties and scarves, with a long, black skirt spilling over the edge. As I turned to go I nearly tripped over a heap of something on the floor. I picked up a black hoodie and threw it over a chair. "How can anyone live in all this clutter, Charlie?" He had no answer.

Objects lined up across her wide windowsill caught my attention. I walked over to get a closer look. A row of four bronze vases held faded, plastic flowers. All roses, they were in various shades of red to dirty pink. Did Nellie take them from the cemetery or did each vase represent one of her dead aunts? Maybe I had something else to share with her counselor. I scanned the room for a coffee can. When I didn't see one, I returned to the dining room and my salad.

Shirley came by our table and refreshed our iced tea.

"Have you seen Nellie lately?" I asked around a mouthful of lettuce, beans, and guacamole.

She set the tea pitcher on the table and picked up a napkin from the floor. After Smiley claimed it and thanked her, she turned to me. "Law, Miss Agnes, I was fixin' to let you know she come into my kitchen askin' to search my pantry. Something about Maxwell House coffee, which I don't use. I finally showed her all I had was Folgers. Next thing I know, Nellie says she's got to go to Beulah Cemetery."

"Did she say anything about her Aunt Mildred?"

"Believe she did mention that name. Is she buried at Beulah?"

I shook my head. "I'm not sure where she might be."

With the Manor's residents having no objections to a cat and no allergies, Francesca and William headed to The Barking Hound without finishing their lunch.

Smiley, Shirley, and I discussed who might take a woman from the halfway house into their home while we put away leftovers and washed the dishes. Certainly not Lucy who lived next door to the Hope House, outspoken in her feelings of hostility toward the women. Lucy probably had a circle of friends she could bend to her way of thinking, plus she had done nothing to discourage her nephew from leering at the women whenever he got the chance.

Shirley tackled a big pot with a Brillo pad. "Raging hormones are not an excuse for a teenage boy's behavior. Next thing you know he'll be a man with no respect for a female."

"Amen." I slid a container of bean salad into the refrigerator. "Surely we can come up with some people in Sweetbriar who are good Samaritans. Smiley, have you thought of anyone?"

"Yep."

"Well, are you going to share with us?"

"Blind George."

"Why him?"

"Desperate times call for desperate measures, don'tcha know."

We finished our kitchen chores and moved to the front porch to soak up some warm sunshine while we continued talking. Yes, Blind George had an apartment above his pool hall. He had offered it, but most likely none of the women would agree to live there. It was bound to be dirty, smelly, and rat-infested like it had been when I thought I had to get away from the Manor and live on my own. I shivered at the thought of setting foot in that place again.

We were interrupted as William pushed Francesca up the handicap ramp. The Persian, introduced as Her Majesty, was curled on my friend's lap. I had to admit the cat looked as regal as her name. William said to expect a delivery soon of cat food, toys, and a self-cleaning litter box. He had ordered everything online.

In all of the excitement over the cat and our lingering discussion over anyone willing to live in a squalid apartment, thoughts about the whereabouts of Nellie and Aunt Mildred continued to fade.

Smiley, who had no regard for cats, left for his afternoon nap. The new cat parents left to get their *child* settled into William's room. Shirley headed for the pantry to finish her weekly grocery list, and I called the owner of the Abide-A-While Motel outside of town. After I explained the situation, the nice young man said he was nearly booked up with the start of tourist season, but he had one room he would rent to one of the Hope Women if she didn't smoke or use drugs. I hurried to find Shirley to tell her the good news but stopped in the foyer as Mr. Lively's voice drifted from his office. It reminded me to inform him to expect William's delivery sometime tomorrow.

I raised my hand to knock on his office door that had not been completely closed. He was talking on the phone, and I couldn't help but stand there and listen.

"Sugar," he said with a chuckle, "she's totally senile and clueless, like most old people. Why, she probably wouldn't miss a couple of Gs, but we'll have to be patient. A little at a time will have to do. That's right. It'll be in your account come morning."

Of all the nerve. *Sugar?* Probably a girlfriend and his cohort in crime. Was this the same woman he had been friendly with the night of the fire? How long had this been going on? And of all things, I had encouraged him to shift the blame for stealing onto someone else. No wonder he was so eager to stay.

I spun around and hightailed it away from there as Pepper zipped past me in a black streak chased by Her Majesty. Suddenly, the dog came to a screeching halt and faced his stalker. After a standoff of hissing and growling, the two animals resumed the chase. It hadn't taken long for the cat to make her presence known.

Feeling completely unnerved, I hurried to my room and flopped into my crooked rocker. The mere thought of accusing Mr. Lively caused my stomach to churn. I didn't have any actual proof he was stealing. He had *sounded* guilty, but it would be a he-said-she-said kind of thing. What if he denied any wrongdoing and named someone who was innocent?

Maybe I should ask Sheriff Caywood's advice before taking action. After all, he did know the ins and outs of the law, even if he sometimes ignored it. Or maybe I'd contact an auditor first. What would my dear Charlie do?

I leaned back in my chair and envisioned sitting on our back porch steps with my husband after supper. He would light his pipe before we talked about our day. A habit of his I adored, not to mention the sweet aroma of his cherry-blend tobacco. Sometimes we would listen to the katydids and crickets. Many nights we would gaze at the stars or watch the lightning bugs along the wood's edge before either of us spoke. I strained to hear some of Charlie's wisdom to help me through this crisis, but none came. This had never happened before. Not that I would always hear him speak since he had passed, but I would know his words in my heart.

"Charles Eugene Hopper, I need your help here," I said to his picture sitting on my chest of drawers. He smiled at me from his Ford 8N. Nothing came to mind. With a deep sigh I pushed myself upright and returned to my retirement home duties. My Sweetbriar Manor residents didn't need to know anything was out of kilter. This whole sordid affair concerning Mr. Lively was my responsibility and mine alone, yet no solution presented itself. Maybe a long walk would clear my head.

I moved down the hall and stopped at the sitting room where I found Smiley. "Going for a walk. Would you like to come along?" I asked him as he jiggled the *Timely News* to reveal the comics page.

He straightened the newspaper and looked up from his favorite chair. "Got a most worrisome corn on my right foot. Acting up somethin' fierce. Surely wish I could. Good news is this here corn won't stop me from working on my painting with Pearl. No sireee."

"Maybe you should see a doctor. Healthy feet are important to your whole body."

"I stay away from doctors. Sure as the sun rises in the east they'll find something else wrong and start messing with it. Besides, I'm using my granny's remedy for corns, and that'll cure it. Guaranteed."

Since there was no use in any more discussion, and I didn't want more information about an ancient cure that apparently hadn't worked, I gathered my cane and my purse and straightened my wide-brimmed straw hat. I left him to his newspaper and headed to my yellow rental house where Juanita and her toddler, Frankie, lived. Today was her day off, and I had checked to make sure she'd be home.

Their little house, located a block or so from The Bottom, had two bedrooms, one bathroom, a kitchen and a living room. Would she be willing to move her son into her bedroom and allow a woman, a stranger, to move into the other?

I ambled along since the heat and humidity tried to outdo each other, making a brisk walk impossible. Now and then a twinge in my bad knee made me question the wisdom of walking to Juanita's, but a phone call could never hold a candle to talking with someone in person. Not to mention the absurdity of trying to text a complicated discussion.

"These young folks have no idea what they're missing," I grumbled to Charlie. "Why, pretty soon they'll forget how to have a real conversation with a real person they can reach out and touch or hug or kiss." Charlie agreed. I could hear him say, "You got that right, pumpkin."

By the time I arrived, the sun had risen high overhead and

sweat had soaked the back of my cotton shirt as well as underneath my armpits. I could feel trickles run from my forehead, down my neck, and gather between my breasts. A least a breeze cooled me when it touched all that wetness.

As soon as I leaned on the squeaky yard gate, Juanita turned from cleaning the front porch windows and rushed toward me. Frankie looked up momentarily from shoveling dirt into his toy dump truck.

"Come sit a spell," Juanita said as she opened the gate. "I've been watching for you. Lemonade?"

I removed my hat and fanned myself. Frankie tottered over and hugged my legs before returning to more important matters. By the time Juanita appeared with two frosty glasses and a sippy cup, I had settled onto the porch swing and had somewhat recovered.

After I explained the reason for my visit and assured her none of the women were murderers, or sex offenders, or hardened criminals, Juanita said, "You can count on me to give a helping hand. Where would I be today if you hadn't let us live in this house? We could be out on the street, that's where. When can I expect her? I'll need to air the bedroom and wash the sheets. And Frankie's been sleeping with me lately anyhow. Been waking up afraid of the dark. Does this woman like kids? How old is she? What's her name?"

"Hold on," I said with a laugh. "I don't know who she is yet, but I'll make sure she likes kids, even one who might disturb her rest."

"It'll be mighty nice to have an adult's company for a change," Juanita added in a soft voice. "Someone to talk with. Gets lonesome around here sometimes." She jumped up and reached for my empty glass. "Merciful heavens, Miss Agnes. What am I saying? I've got no call to feel sorry for myself."

She rushed inside before I could respond. When she returned, I thanked her for opening her home and her heart and tried to reassure her that the Lord knew and cared about everything going on in her life.

After another glass of lemonade and a visit to her bathroom, I left and headed to Jack's employer. Thankfully, Case's Produce was just a block and a half away. Juanita had once lived in the trailer behind the produce stand after Frankie was born. She assured me Mr. Case had spruced the place up, but she didn't think he had found a renter yet. It had two bed-rooms, and I planned to see if it was a fit place for two of the Hope women.

Jack glanced up from arranging cartons of blueberries next to bundles of leaf lettuce. He smiled his usual crooked grin. "Miss Hops. What brings you to our neighborhood?"

"I'm here on a mission."

He raised his tee shirt and wiped his face. "Don't surprise me a bit. What can we help you with?"

"Mr. Case around?"

"Nope. Gone to pick up a load of strawberries. First of the season."

"Do you know if he's rented his trailer?"

"Nope. Saw a man looking at it yesterday though."

I would have to move fast. "Do you have a key?"

"Nope. It's unlocked. What you got up that sleeve of yours?"

After I explained, we walked behind the produce stand and went inside the trailer, leaving the door open since the air in-side was as hot as a tobacco field in August. We couldn't stay long, but from what I could tell the place was presentable and clean, although it lacked anything to give it a homey feel. No pictures on the walls, no throw pillows on the sofa, no curtains at the windows. If this place were available, surely it would do for two or three weeks. Even though it was located in a rough part of town, I knew Mr. Case would look out for the women, plus he kept a guard dog around at night. I took out my phone and snapped some quick photos.

"Tell Mr. Case I was sorry to miss him. Ask him to call me when he returns."

"Yes, ma'am." Jack gave me a mock salute and a grin. "My young helper can hold down the fort while I carry you home if you'd like."

I hugged his sweaty neck. Jack revved up his scooter, and off we went to the Manor. I held on to Jack's waistband with one hand and smacked my other hand on top of my hat.

If Mr. Case's trailer could house two women, Juanita's one, and the Abide-A-While Motel one, we still needed a place for two more. The only other option I could think of was the apart-ment above Blind George's fine establishment. I shuddered at the thought.

CHAPTER TEN

Mr. Case called after supper and agreed to help out. He promised the rent would be reasonable. Then I called the women's prison and spoke to the warden, agreeing to send pictures of the trailer and of Juanita's house that I had on my phone from before I'd bought the place. And I gave him the website of the motel. "We now have a place for four of the women. By tomorrow I should have rooms for the other two." The warden would have to settle on the various rental agreements, and I hoped Mr. Case wouldn't turn greedy and leave two of the women out in the cold—or rather out on the hot, steamy streets of Sweetbriar. Two more rooms. Could I deliver?

Shirley said Nellie had returned from her trip to Beulah Cemetery, so I decided to go check on her. At first her room seemed empty until the distinct sound of a match struck against a rough surface released a puff of sulfur. Nellie's eyes glistened as she touched the match flame to a tall candle. Then she leaned past a frayed wicker chair and stuck the candle into a star-shaped holder perched on top of a stack of magazines.

With a toss of her stringy hair, she glared at me. "What do you want?"

How could anyone, even Nellie, be totally clueless to the dangers of an open flame? For a moment panic seized me, but I took a deep breath and swallowed my fears. "No one can have candles in their room," I said as calmly as possible, resisting the urge to yell at this woman. "Maybe all of our residents need to review the rules. Shirley has permission to use candles in the dining room, but she puts 'em in jars of sand."

Nellie's body stiffened, but she didn't speak or offer to blow out the flame.

"Did you find Aunt Mildred?" I asked, hoping to distract her. I glanced around the room, but spotted no evidence that she had. Six bronze vases were lined up across her windowsill.

Earlier hadn't there been four? Had she taken two more from the cemetery?

Her eyes followed my gaze and locked onto the faded flowers. "Auntie Pearl will never forgive me," she whispered.

Seeing my chance, I grabbed the candle—as well as a box of matches sitting on her dresser—and rushed out of her room. While at a half-run with my bad knee protesting, I blew out the candle. I stopped for a moment and glanced behind me. No sign of Nellie, but I could hear her hollering before something shattered against her door. Pitching a pure hissy fit. She could have more matches as well as candles.

I pulled out my phone and called Hershel.

A lot of good that did. Deputy Larry said the sheriff left this morning on another fishing trip, this time to the Mt. Pisgah Mountains in North Carolina. I never understood how he could leave such an incompetent man in charge.

My only other option was to enlist Mr. Lively's help since, for some odd reason, Nellie liked the man. After setting the matches and candle on my dresser, I locked my door, climbed the stairs to his living quarters, and knocked.

"Come in," he barked.

He met me holding a drink that reeked of whiskey. "Can I pour you a shot? Or a double? Might be just what you need."

I took a step back. "What I need is some backup before Nellie burns the place down. And I don't need an employee who drinks on the job." Or steals for his *sugar*, though I pushed that worrisome thought out of my mind.

"What are you spouting off about?" He set his drink down and turned toward me. "I'm officially off the clock, and a drink helps me relax after a crazy day like today. Nellie? She's got some weird habits, but I don't think she'd set anything on fire. At least not on purpose."

"On purpose or not, her love of matches is dangerous. Can you come up with a reason to get her out of her room so I can search it?"

He cut his eyes at me, then walked to the window and pushed the sash up higher. "You got a warrant?"

"A warrant? You know I don't."

"Then I can't help you." He reached for his drink.

"Can't or won't?"

He finished his drink, sighed, and set the glass down. "Tell you what I will do. I'll talk to the woman. Obviously, you're not the one who knows how."

I didn't put up an argument, so Mr. Lively followed me back to Nellie's room.

While she shot daggers at me, he talked to this crazy woman like she was the Queen of Sheba. I had no idea he could be such a charmer, but then what did I really know about this man? I certainly didn't know until now that he liked his whiskey.

Nellie handed him another box of kitchen matches and five candles. Oh my. I hoped she had turned over her entire stash.

I told Mr. Lively to hide the matches and candles, then went to my room. As fast as my legs would allow, I returned to Nellie's room and placed a large flashlight in her hand. "This'll give you far more light than any candle to search for Aunt Mildred, but see that you return it. Belonged to my Charlie, and I don't want to lose it."

She nodded, clicked it on, and headed for her closet. Maybe Aunt Mildred would keep her out of trouble for a while.

Then I scooted to Smiley's room. He finally opened his door in blue pajamas covered with pink flamingos. His unbuttoned top revealed a scrawny chest covered in white fuzz that looked as soft as goose down. I resisted the urge to lay my hand on it.

"Sis," he said, bringing my eyes up to his big brown ones. "What's wrong?" He took a step back. "Come in."

He buttoned his pajamas as I tried to control my thoughts.

After we settled ourselves on his loveseat, he turned to me and covered my hands with his. *Oh my.*

"Now, tell me everything."

Everything? Certainly not everything that was bubbling up in my heart at the moment. Not yet. I gazed at his wrinkled, sun-spotted hands that looked much like my own, only his had specks of yellow and blue paint. His discovery of creative talents warmed my soul. Was I too old and foolish to allow myself to fall for this man? I swallowed the lump in my throat—along with my obvious affection for him—and began.

"Nellie's a firebug right under our noses. And Mr. Lively's a no-count crook. And every Hope woman might have, if we're lucky, a temporary place to live except for two. We could find a place for one, but Shirley heard gossip when she stopped by the Kut'N Loose that Dee's not welcome in Sweetbriar. It's possible nobody will take her in when she gets released from the hospital in a few days . . . if she keeps improving. This is thanks to the sheriff who still thinks she had something to do with the fire, even though arson hasn't been proven and such talk has gotten all over town so nobody except Blind George wants anything to do with her and . . ."

I rambled on and on, airing all my concerns to my reliable, listening friend, even if I didn't always agree with his advice. He nodded a time or two, but never commented. Afterward, we sat in silence except for the ticking of his camelback clock perched on his roll-top desk. After a loud click we looked toward the sound as the clock struck ten times and ended with a shudder.

"Harriet needs a good oiling, but whenever I think of it I don't have the time and whenever I have the time I don't think of it, don'tcha know." Smiley winked in my direction before he turned silent again.

"You named your clock Harriet?"

"Suits her, don'tcha think? When we, my Lucinda and I, had a half-dozen clocks, we named 'em so whenever one needed winding or worked on, we didn't have to explain which one we were talking about. Harriet's the only one I brought with me, though I do miss Velma and Martha and—"

"All female?"

He nodded with a faraway look. "My Lucinda's idea."

I grabbed the pillow behind my back, fluffed it, and returned it to the right spot before eyeing him with a steady gaze. He rubbed his chin and sighed. I had to get him away from dwelling on the past. I shifted in my seat and cleared my throat. "I need you to focus here. Let's start with Nellie. Tell me what you think."

"I've wondered about Nellie myself. Not only does she have a fondness for matches and such, she can't seem to keep herself from stealing, Mostly little things of no value. Just the same, she's got no business taking what isn't hers. She's one strange woman. And to top it all off, she talks to her Aunt Mildred and Auntie Pearl like they're not dead a'tall."

I shifted in my seat. No need to remind him of my conversations with Charlie. "Should I ask her to find another place to live?"

He stood and helped me up. "Don't make a hasty decision about her yet. Don't we all have peculiar habits? Quirks that no one else understands? Nellie's might be a bit over the top, but she's got one thing going for her."

"And what might that be?"

He slipped on his robe and tied the sash. "She ain't dull, and ya never know what she's gonna do next. Adds a little excitement around here. And we could use some of that."

"What about Mr. Lively? Do you think he's a thief? And Dee? What if I can't find her a place to stay?"

He opened his door and held it for me. "How about a cup of peppermint tea? Might help settle the nerves."

"My nerves are fine," I said as we entered the hallway that led to the dining room. He lifted my hand and linked my arm with his.

"Well?" I asked when we reached the foyer in silence. We stopped beside the grandfather clock.

"You're not gonna like this, but your evidence against Mr. Lively is circumstantial, although any unruly behavior of his doesn't surprise me. He's an unhappy man, unsuited for his job. Probably feels trapped. But would he steal money from you? I have my doubts."

So nothing was solved concerning Nellie, Mr. Lively, or a place for two Hope women. But somehow the load I carried now felt more like a pillowcase of feathers rather than one filled with bricks. In my mind, I skipped toward the kitchen.

Over a steaming cup of peppermint tea with lots of sourwood honey, Smiley shared his thoughts about Zelda Dee Sizemore. "That girl is scared, and somehow in her short life she has turned bitter and don't trust nobody."

I took a sip of my tea. "All of that may be true, but how is it my problem? If I hired her to work here, even part-time, she would bring all her troubles with her. Right? There's a reason no one in town has offered to take her in."

"Didn't Blind George say she could work nights at his pool hall and live in his upstairs apartment?"

"Sure did. He's gone overboard, because not only did he once serve time himself, he had a wayward daughter who died soon after he booted her out of their house. He's become very protective of Dee."

Smiley shrugged. "Seems to me the problem's solved."

"She might work at the pool hall, but even though his apartment's roomy enough to house two of the women, nobody's hankering to have Dee as a roommate. So there you have it. Not even her own prison mates want her. Back to square one."

"What will she do?"

"Don't know. We certainly can't offer her a place to live for two or three weeks, even if I'd consider such a thing. We have no extra space."

"And time's running out. Would the warden send her somewhere other than Sweetbriar?" Smiley frowned as he scratched his head.

"Not if the sheriff has any say in the matter. He wants her nearby. Talk around town—which includes the ladies who frequent the Kut'N Loose—says even our fire chief disagrees with Sheriff Caywood's suspicions of Dee. She did serve time for assisting her boyfriend, a convicted arsonist."

"Maybe she was wrongly accused."

"That's what she claims. But don't all criminals declare they're innocent?"

The teakettle began to whistle, and I rushed to lift it from the stove before the sound turned loud and shrill and hurt my ears. Smiley added fresh teabags to our mugs as I poured steaming water into them and then set the kettle on a hotplate.

"Tell me something." I climbed onto my stool. "How come you pointed out the good in everybody I've mentioned tonight? Not only that, you've ignored some obvious faults that are bound to cause trouble sooner or later. We've got to open our eyes to the facts, like them or not."

"As well as opening our hearts. Sometimes we see what we want to see. My granny believed in me when nobody else did, and that's why I became the top Fuller Brush salesman five years in a row. After that, I had enough money saved to open my own furniture store. When I get to heaven she's the first person I want to call on."

"I'm sure your granny was a wonderful person, and you owe a lot to her. But your situation doesn't apply here."

"I always say the proof is in the pudding."

"Exactly," I said, feeling miffed by his Pollyanna attitude. It was a good thing one of us had a realistic outlook.

The next morning I plucked the *Timely News* out of a Camilla bush. After the town's newspaper became a weekly one instead of a daily edition, our new delivery boy seemed to favor the bushes clustered at the corner of the house.

The front page was filled with pictures of the fire and the rescue of Dee and Pepper, plus it included a side shot of the crowd of townspeople. I looked closer at the people bunched together with their faces turned upward. One old woman's face glowed with an enormous grin as if she were watching a circus performance. No mistake. It was Nellie.

Later that day I reached for Smiley's hand as we climbed the steps to Mayor Phillips' office. If he would back our plan to house the Hope Women in Sweetbriar for two or three weeks, it might help convince someone to step up and do their part.

"But why would he do such a thing?" Smiley asked as we stood on a small landing before going inside. "He never wanted them here in the first place."

"No, but if he showed them a little compassion now that their home burned and they lost everything, his popularity would rise to the top."

"I don't know . . ."

I put my hand around his bent elbow. "Let me do the talking. And we're not going to mention they could become permanent residents once Ancient Oaks Elementary becomes a modern apartment building."

"You got it, Sis." Smiley pushed on the heavy wooden door and held it open. We approached the receptionist, Miss Louise, and asked to speak with our mayor.

"What do you mean he's gone," I said, my voice rising into a squeak. "When will he be back?"

Before she could answer, Louise sneezed three times and grabbed some tissue from a box sitting on her desk. She honked into a handful and tossed them into a wastebasket.

"Bad cold?" I asked.

She shook her head. "Allergies. The South is a danger to my health." She sneezed again while we waited. "Out of town two and a half days," she said at last. "Small town convention in Newsome, Kentucky." Louise powdered her nose and freshened her lipstick.

"I'm sure he has a phone with him," I said as Smiley found a nearby chair and slumped into it.

"He's not to be disturbed except in case of an emergency," she said while blotting her lipstick. "Which I suspect this is not.

Maybe I can help you."

"Can you ask him to call me when he returns? I have a matter that needs his attention."

"I'll pass your message along, but these days with all that's going on around here, he gets distracted and might forget. It's a thousand wonders he remembers anything. Not only does he have *do*-mestic troubles, the townsfolk can be a thorn in his flesh whenever he has done his level best to clean up Sweetbriar. Make it a decent place to live. Tried his best to keep those women convicts out of here. He's too good for this town, and nobody appreciates him." She sniffed, sneezed, and pressed a tissue to her reddened nose.

"You don't say." One thing I now understood. Miss Louise Smith was in love with her boss, and she would do whatever it took to protect him. I would bet my last nickel she would never give him my message. Smiley was right on the money about this one. It looked like we would have to forge ahead without his help.

I coughed a little to clear my throat. "One more question, if you don't mind. "The mayor rides a spiffy bike. Do you know where he bought it? I'm thinking of taking up the habit myself." Smiley's head jerked up as he stared at me, eyes wide.

"Same place I bought mine," she said. "Bike Awhile over near Orangeville. Got me a brand-spanking-new one, but our mayor has to watch his money, what with having to pay alimony and all, so he bought a used one."

That got my attention. "He did? Have any trouble with it?"

"Sometimes sounds a little rough, but after he tinkers with it a bit, it can take a notion to run smooth as a silk ribbon."

"You don't say. How long have you been riding?"

"Took it up a few months ago. Good for the thighs and the buns. You might try one of those tricycles for older adults. Cumbersome but safer."

I thanked her as she handed me the bike shop's phone number.

Once outside, Smiley turned to me. "I didn't know you wanted a bicycle, Sis."

"Never rode one in my life and don't intend to start now."

I felt ashamed of our townspeople while guilt continued to nip at my heels. No one had offered Dee a temporary place to stay. Rumors of the sheriff continuing to question her about the fire had cast a wide shadow over her. Since one of the Hope women had agreed to stay in Blind George's apartment, Dee was the only one left homeless, so I stepped up to the plate. Seems I didn't have much choice in the matter. I could see my Charlie grin and nod. "Yep. I knew you would," he'd say.

That night, Shirley asked me to join her in the kitchen for the last two pieces of lemon pie. She always made it with sour cream, sugar, and eggs, plus real lemon juice, then grated the lemon rind and piled it all in a graham cracker crust. With the pie on Blue Willow dessert plates, a glass of sweet tea for Shirley and a cup of hot tea for myself, we parked ourselves onto the island's barstools.

"I understand Dee's comin' to the Manor for a couple of weeks. Shirley lifted a forkful of pie up to her mouth where it quickly disappeared. "Hmmm. Best one yet," she said with her eyes closed.

"No one in the whole town wanted to take her in, plus the only resident in the Manor who will have her as a roommate is crazy Nellie. Why did I ever step foot into the middle of this gigantic mess?"

"Because you're not a hard-hearted woman like Dee once accused you of being."

CHAPTER ELEVEN

On Friday afternoon a gray Honda Accord arrived at Sweetbriar Manor driven by a Salvation Army volunteer. Dee stepped out from the passenger's door. She clutched a paper grocery bag that probably held all her meager belongings. She looked like a scrawny refugee. Her drab green dress was at least two sizes too big, and her wiry hair was in desperate need of a good brushing. And her shoes? She didn't have any on her feet. Where were the wedge-heeled sandals I'd rescued after the fire?

I went down to where she stood as the Honda drove away. "Shirley's got lunch ready. You hungry?"

Dee shrugged and looked away.

"Well, I'm starving." I turned and climbed the porch steps hoping she would follow. Who was this timid woman? I had expected the same sassy attitude as before when she expected me to hire her on the spot as our manicurist.

I heard her pad up the steps behind me. Then she stopped on the porch, unrolled her bag, removed her shoes, and slipped them on—sooty, pink wedge sandals.

The dining room was quiet, the residents waiting with anxious expressions. Every eye watched as we took our seats. Shirley had placed a chair for Dee between Smiley and me, at least for today. Whispered conversations sprouted up all around the room. "Enough of this," I whispered to Charlie as I stood and clinked my spoon against my tea glass.

"Listen up, everyone. Sweetbriar Manor has a guest for two weeks or so. We will help her feel at home as long as she's here. That's all I have to say on the matter. Is that clear?" A few nods and grumbles were the only answers except for my big-hearted Smiley.

"Absolutely, Sis," he said with a full salute, after which he gave Dee a warm smile. She actually smiled back . . . I think.

Pepper whimpered from the beauty shop next door to the kitchen. Dee pushed back her chair.

"After lunch," I said. "He's doing just fine you know. Everybody has spoiled him rotten."

"No animals allowed in the dining room during meals," Francesca said with a toss of her head. "Not even Her Majesty."

My fork slipped and clattered onto my plate. "You did close William's door, didn't you?"

"I know the rules around this place." Francesca lifted her chin and squinted her eyes at me. I had to bite my tongue. Her cat was always appearing underfoot in the kitchen where it was not supposed to be. Or if Her Majesty escaped to the outside, she would return with a prize—a mole, a baby squirrel, or a bird—and cry by the back door until someone let her in. I regretted giving in to Francesca's demands for a pet.

I turned to Dee. "Don't worry about Pepper. He's got food, water, and his favorite old blanket. He probably heard your voice. I know you're anxious to see him."

She nodded as her eyes filled with tears, then she leaned over her plate and picked at her food. When lunch was nearly over, she turned toward me. "Miss Agnes, I uh—"

"Just so you know," Francesca interrupted as she squirmed in her wheelchair and gave me a haughty look. "I'll be moving in with William. Permanently," she added with her nose in the air. "You can put *her* in my room. It makes no difference to me who might *contaminate* my room since I won't be there." Her eyes landed on Dee and stayed there.

My grumpy friend was angry. The queen of our retirement home felt threatened. Gee whiskers. She didn't know I had a place for Dee already, and it was not *her* room.

William stood and leaned over to my good ear. "Don't worry, Red," he whispered. "This time next week we'll be engaged. And the week after that, Mr. and Mrs. My plan's coming together."

I sure hoped he knew what he was talking about.

Earlier, Nellie had come to me adamant about Dee being her roommate, and since Dee didn't object, I agreed to that arrangement. Maybe the two of them would accomplish some housecleaning and find Aunt Mildred. Or maybe Pepper could sniff her out of the piles of clutter.

When I left the dining room, Dee waited for me in the foyer. "Miss Agnes, I wanted to thank you for helping us out, plus taking care of Pepper. Don't know what we would've—"

"Everybody needs a hand-up now and again. When you get settled maybe we can talk about the night of the fire. Confidentially of course. Maybe you'll remember something that would help to clear you. Anything."

"I'll try. The whole thing's a jumbled mess in my brain." She shook her head and left me to reclaim her little dog.

Whew. Everyone had a place in Sweetbriar to call home, at least for a while. The warden had said two weeks or three at the most. The former elementary school was close to becoming apartments that would suit their needs, and I hoped the prison system would give its approval. Maybe it was a good thing the mayor had been out of town when the arrangements were made. Now it was too late for him to interfere.

That afternoon, Mr. Lively appeared and stopped me in the foyer. "Do you realize we have run out of hot water? You're going to have to put a time limit on the residents' showers. Our water bill is going to be out of sight."

"I'll consider it. Let's go to your office where we can talk."

I had forgotten his workspace was cramped and dark. On top of a filing cabinet, the globs inside a lava lamp continuously rose and flopped back down. Mr. Lively sat at his desk and clicked on a gooseneck lamp. I squinted at the glare as I scooted a chair over and sat down across from him.

"We need to get some things straight to my satisfaction or we need to part ways, as we agreed when I asked you to stay for the next thirty days," I said in my best schoolteacher voice. Even though I had never had the opportunity to become a teacher, I'd heard plenty in the classroom when called down for talking or daydreaming. Seemed I was good at both.

"I never agreed to supervise an ex-con." He nervously straightened a stack of papers on his desk.

"I'm not asking you to do that. Dee's my responsibility. That's not what I want to talk to you about. Someone called *sugar* is on my mind and why you're sending her money."

"I have no idea what you're talking about. You're crazy and paranoid besides."

"I'll overlook those remarks for now. Let's start over. Who

is this sugar?"

"None of your business. It's personal."

"Whoever she is, did you have to resort to stealing for her?"

"Maybe I've done a little arm twisting and hinted at a little blackmail, but I'm no thief. I've got my eye on someone who might fit that bill, however. Isn't that what you asked me to do?"

I scooted a little closer. "I'm listening."

"Not ready to lay my cards on the table just yet. I plan to have all the facts before I accuse anyone, unlike some people."

Heat rose up my neck until my ears burned. I loosened my collar before I stood and pushed back my chair. Was he speaking the truth or feeding me a line? "Do you have the Manor's financial reports ready? I need to know where we stand and if we need to make any adjustments."

"Close to finished. I can tell you right now this place is operating on shaky ground. Not only do you need a budget, which is impossible when we're feeding extra people gratis, like that smelly homeless man always hanging around the kitchen door. And now we've taken in this Dee person. This place requires management skills. Sound business sense."

Heat burst from my body worse than those hot flashes of years ago. As much as I didn't like it, I never could manage money very well, and probably never would. Charlie was the one who kept me out of trouble all of our fifty-three years together. I needed a business-savvy person to run this place, but not someone with absolutely no compassion for a fellow man or woman.

I glared at this infuriating man. "We have one extra resident here. Temporarily. That shouldn't break us. And like you said yourself, personal affairs are just that. Personal."

He shrugged and shuffled some papers. Then he looked up and squinted. "I have one piece of advice. Talk to whoever's in charge of these women. The two of you need to set a time for Dee's departure. By the way, I've gotten another job offer, and a good one, better than the one in North Carolina. It's in Nevada. I'll be leaving in less than three weeks, so that should make you happy."

It should have but didn't. If he had stolen money from the cash box and then moved, I'd never be able to charge him with the crime. If he was innocent, as he claimed, who had taken the money? Would I ever find out? He said he was fairly certain of the thief but wasn't ready to share his information.

Humph. I was in over my curly red head.

"Our engagement's off before there ever was one," William said the following morning as he stared at his plate of scrambled eggs, bacon, and grits. Most of the residents had eaten and left the dining room. Our table was empty except for the two of us. Francesca hadn't made an appearance.

"Oh my. What happened?" I turned toward the big man with slumped shoulders and wild, uncombed hair. Totally unlike him.

William looked up. His mournful eyes had dark smudges underneath them. "She mustn't know."

"Of course not." I rose from my seat and scooted a chair close to his.

He pushed his plate aside, propped his elbows on the table, and clasped his hands together. "I failed the driver's test," he mumbled.

I poked him with my elbow. "So did I first time around. It's not the end of the world. Parallel parking's always a doozy. Practice a bit and take it again. You'll pass, I'm sure."

"The written test," William said as he turned his face toward mine.

"Oh. When can you try again?"

"Next week. Studying the book this time. Online. And that's the rub."

"How so?"

"My sweetie pie yelled at me. Said, 'You're spending more time with your computer than you are with me! That thing's taken over, and I'm not going to put up with it any longer. Is that clear?'"

A catch in my back set me on my feet. "Don't worry." I twisted and stretched. "I'm still here."

William cradled his head in his hands and didn't speak.

Why couldn't people just be honest with each other? Charlie and I had been like open books. No secrets between us. But Smiley was a different story. Why had I hidden my heart from him? And why hadn't William declared to Francesca that his love for her was the incentive behind his actions?

I turned my chair to face him and sat, rubbing my back with one hand. He raised his head. "Now tell me," I said. "How did things end between the two of you?"

William ran his fingers through his hair. "Francesca insisted I move her and Her Majesty out of my room, which I did. Back into her old room since it hadn't been contaminated by an ex-con like she figured it would be. Said she's staging a hunger strike until you make that criminal and her mutt leave our home. Her words, not mine."

Sounds just like Diamond Lil—my pet name for her that no one else knew about. "Where's Francesca now?"

"Front porch. Mad as a hornet." He pushed back from the table. We headed to the porch, but I had trouble keeping pace with his long legs.

"Slow down," I said. "Tell me what else is going on."

He stopped and faced me. "It's like this, Red. With Francesca out of my room, I can use my computer anytime I want, but I can't concentrate. Be a miracle if I pass that test."

"You've got to change your plan and get her behind you. If she knew—"

"Won't work. She won't even speak to me, and you know that's next to impossible for my gal."

"What if we . . ."

As he leaned his big frame down, his ear near my mouth, I shared my plan. William suddenly grabbed me and lifted me into the air. "When?" he asked as he set me on my feet and steadied me from toppling over. I stretched and twisted around a bit. Somehow my back felt better than it had after visiting the chiropractor.

"How about right before suppertime?" I asked, returning to the task at hand. "I'll ask Shirley to pack a picnic basket. You get Mike to drive your car over here and park it on the street, in the shade of course. You have her ring, don't you?"

He looked at me like a deer caught in headlights. "Ring? Looked on Amazon but haven't ordered it yet. What am I gonna do?"

"Can't be anything ordinary. You know how she loves jewelry."

William frowned, stuck his cigar stub in his mouth, and stomped away. "Won't work. Not enough time. I knew it."

I caught up to him. "How about Polly's Jewel Box? It's going out of business. Everything's on sale."

William stopped short.

I peered at my watch. "Polly opens in thirty minutes."

"You'll help me pick it out. Right?"

I agreed, and we headed for the front door. When we reached the porch, Francesca was nowhere in sight.

"Might be best to leave her be and let her simmer down," I whispered to Charlie. I could see him grinning no matter what I said or didn't say for this was his favorite time of the day, when the morning sun stretched across our freshly plowed fields pulling little puffs of moisture into the air.

"Give me five minutes to stop in the ladies room, William. I'll meet you at the back door. We don't want to confront you-know-who just yet."

He grabbed me in a bear hug before I could escape. "I knew you would, Red. I can always count on you."

Francesca suddenly appeared in front of us with Her Majesty perched on her lap. "So this is what it's come to. With my best friend. I might have known." She jerked her chair around and sped toward the dining room as fast as she could make her wheels spin. Her hunger strike must've been over.

"Now what?" William said with a sigh.

"Let's go ahead with our plans. Somehow, I'll get her to your car tonight." I had no idea how at this moment.

Had she called me her best friend? I didn't even know she liked me.

CHAPTER TWELVE

William and I left for downtown with Pepper on his leash, after rescuing him from Her Majesty. Dee seemed perfectly content to remain on the front porch. Smiley had scooted his rocker close to hers, and their chatter sounded lighthearted. I reminded myself to thank him when we returned. For sure she needed to rest, but she needed someone's company even more.

While William and I were downtown, I planned to stop at Henry's Hardware to introduce the miniature poodle to Miss Margaret. I felt confident the two animals would take to each other. This could make a difference since my precious would be visiting the Manor twice a week, if not more. They both had the same even temperament, not like the high-strung Persian. Our home had gone from no pets to two and an occasional three. That should be our limit.

"What did . . . you find out . . . about the small town mayor's . . . convention in Kentucky?" I managed to puff out as we practically broke into a jog in front of the Kut'N Loose.

"It's legit all right, but the agenda sounds more like a vacation, including a trip to the spring races in Lexington, which I figured was why he hadn't returned yet."

I stopped to catch my breath. "And I guess we're paying for all the fun he's having."

William seemed to notice I was no longer beside him and turned back. "Nope." He joined me on a Charleston-style bench, a recent addition along Main Street.

"Well, who is?"

"Don't know, but we'd better not be paying anything. He's not there."

"Not there? How do you know?"

"I called the place. Asked to speak to our good mayor. Said we had us an emergency situation here in Sweetbriar. Guess I sounded official enough. Lady checked and said he wasn't registered. I acted all upset and asked her to take another look. She did and came back with the same answer."

Even though every Hope House woman had a temporary place to stay—no thanks to Stone Phillips—I wanted to convince him to support the arrangement. The right newspaper coverage might put him and our town in a good, positive light. But how could I talk to him if he couldn't be reached?

We stood and continued down the sidewalk . . . a bit slower this time.

When we stopped in front of the Jewel Box, I shooed William toward the door. "You need to look first by yourself. I'll be back before you know it."

He removed his cigar stub, started to say something, but then stuck it back into his mouth and went inside.

After Pepper found a bush to his liking, we returned to the Jewel Box. He lay by my feet as William studied three rings lying on a piece of black velvet. "I can't decide which would suit her best," he said. "What do you think?"

"Knowing Francesca, I would say the biggest one. If you can afford it, that is."

William frowned and rubbed the back of his neck. "Might have to take out a loan. Fixing up that taxi is costing more than I figured."

"Never start a marriage in debt," I said as I eyed the ring choices. "Which one is in your budget?"

He picked up a small, plain solitaire. It looked lost in his big hand.

"Does it have to be a diamond?" I looked at the shop's owner. "What other stones are available?"

The jeweler's face lit up like the Fourth of July. He disappeared into the back of the store and returned with a white gift box. He opened it and removed a ring, which he then laid on another piece of black velvet. "Just got this in."

It was large, silver, and showy, with a pink center stone cut into the shape of a flower.

"How much," William asked as he held the ring up to the light and studied it.

"For you, only one hundred nineteen dollars." The jeweler rocked on his heels and smiled.

William grinned. "I'll take it."

"Tell us about it first," I said. "It's unusual."

"Certainly. This is called a Lady Rose Ring fashioned after the one worn by Lady Rose in Downton Abbey. If you will notice, a genuine white topaz rests in the center of the rose."

"Perfect," I said, admiring the ring. Not only does it look like Francesca, Lady Rose is her favorite character in the series."

William frowned. "She is? What series?"

I punched his arm. "You should stay awake more often when she's watching her shows."

"Whatever you say, Red." He turned to the jeweler. "Can you gift wrap this with a big pink bow?"

"Delighted. Congratulations. You made an excellent choice."

William laid two one-hundred-dollar bills on the counter. After he received his change and his package, he slipped the box into his pocket. "Thanks, Red. Now you've got to deliver her to my car without letting her know why. I'm sure you can do it. I'll be waiting there at six o'clock sharp. Do you think we'll be able to see the sunset from there?"

"I don't think that will matter. You lovebirds probably won't be interested in eating either, but I'll have Shirley pack a picnic supper for you just the same."

Pepper wanted to dally along, but I picked up my pace toward home. We would visit Henry and Miss Margaret another day.

"Where do you think the mayor's gone?" I asked William as Sweetbriar Manor came into view.

"I'll bet he has a girlfriend," William said. Then he stopped and stared at the sidewalk. "What if she turns me down?" He removed his cigar stub and flung it into a row of prickly bushes. He grabbed my arms and bent down to my face. "What will I do? My life won't be worth a plug nickel."

I sighed. Forget the mayor. William was only interested in one thing at the moment. "You're the best thing that could happen to her," I told him. "Plus, she's going to love your car, the romantic picnic, and especially the ring."

We slipped in the back door in case Francesca should be roaming the halls.

Shirley looked at William's purchase with a big grin on her face. As soon as he left to shave and shower, I put the kettle on for tea. My confidante and I had to figure out how we were going to pull this off, but first I asked her if she had any insight into Mayor Phillips' disappearance.

"He has a girlfriend," she said without hesitation. "Or he could have a whole other family somewhere, another life separate from the one in Sweetbriar. I've read about such things in *True Life Magazine.*"

"Do you think Louise Smith knows where he is and is covering for him?"

Shirley reached for two cups and the tea bags. "Have you ever been to a town meeting and seen how she looks at him? I'd say she'd do anything for that man."

Nellie burst into the kitchen through the swinging door. "Blind George's cleaning woman says she spotted a coffee can underneath some bushes, but she can't remember what kind or exactly where. I need help." With her straggly hair and dirty clothes, this wisp of a woman looked as though she'd been tromping through the woods all day. Shirley led her to a stool while I brought her a glass of water.

"Take a swallow. Then tell us what happened," I said.

Her hands shook, but she managed. "I looked behind all the rose bushes." She took another sip of water, then began to shiver.

"If you find a coffee can, how will you know it's the one with Aunt Mildred's ashes? What if it's empty?"

Nellie looked at me before a flood of tears started. This time they were real. I fished in my purse for a hanky, but came up short and grabbed a paper towel instead.

Shirley shook her head, then turned her attention to putting finishing touches on the engagement basket for William and Francesca, which included winding tiny artificial roses around the handle. Packed inside were heart-shaped cucumber sandwiches, chicken wings, potato salad, and chocolate cupcakes with sprinkles on top of pink icing. Somehow she had found paper napkins and plates left from Valentine's Day to tuck beside the food, along with some plastic cups and forks.

While Nellie tried to get hold of herself, an idea formed. I took one of her hands in both of mine. "You stay right where you are and talk to Shirley. I'll be back directly."

In the hallway, I ran into William, who smelled like he'd taken a bath in Brut aftershave. He sported a brand new cigar stuck behind his ear, but hadn't taken time to dry his hair—which now dripped water onto his pink cotton shirt. My *best* friend had better love this man or I'd bonk her over her head with . . . with my cane or a broom or anything I could get hold of.

"Where ya going in such a hurry?" he said with a beaming grin.

"Something I've got to do. My, you look spiffy. Have you checked with Mike? Does he know when to bring your car over? Shirley's chilling some champagne she found in the pantry. Do you have the ring? You haven't lost it have you?" I was rattling on, but in all the excitement I couldn't help myself.

"Easy there." He placed a big hand on my shoulder. "You'd think you were the one proposing here. Or are you afraid you can't get my gal to show up? I have no doubt you'll do it. Right?"

I scooted away before we wasted any more time. After I determined Francesca's whereabouts, I planned to send Nellie to beg for her help, the only possibility I could conjure up to get her out of the Manor. Since the two women had a mutual dislike for each other, the plan might fall apart, but I had to try.

About thirty minutes before Shirley called us to supper, I pulled back a dining room curtain and peeked out the window. William's yellow cab was parked where it should be. It sparkled from his cleaning and polishing as if ready for a vintage car show.

Apparently, Jack had been enlisted to help William. The two men were busy loading the back seat with roses Pearl had gathered from our yard, the picnic basket, and a bottle of champagne. I hoped William had remembered the ring.

I turned toward the sound of two women coming down the hall. As usual, Francesca was fussing. "I don't see why I'm the one who has to go with you. This is ridiculous. Aunt Mildred's gone. The sooner you accept that, the better off you'll be."

"Miss Agnes says you have the eyes of an eagle, and since your eyes are lower to the ground than mine, you'll spot what we're looking for—sure as I'm Minnie Pearl's cousin, twice removed." Nellie was playing her part to the hilt, but her acting threatened to go overboard. If it made Francesca suspicious, she'd balk. The two women had always rubbed each other the wrong way, but Nellie had agreed to my plan because of William. It seemed our crazy resident liked the men—William, Smiley, and even Mr. Lively. I was never sure how she felt about Lollipop. But then maybe they were too much alike.

"Well, let's make this quick," Francesca groused. "I haven't eaten in two days, and Shirley's fried chicken smells like heaven." The two women moved toward the kitchen where they would exit the back door, then move down a ramp and onto the sidewalk leading to the street. William waited in his cab beyond the boxwood hedge and the old stonewall.

Sweetbriar residents watched out the window. In fact, we were all there with our noses pressed against any window we could find. Smiley beside me. Shirley and Lollipop and Pearl, plus Jack who slipped beside her at the last moment. Like family, we had gathered to witness what I prayed would be a tender moment.

William got out of his cab holding the roses as the women neared. We couldn't hear what was being said, but in the next moment Francesca threw up her arms. William handed the flowers to Nellie and leaned toward his intended. She pulled him close. Nellie jumped up and down and hollered and ran inside the house still clutching the roses. She didn't mention anything about not finding a coffee can. Apparently, helping with the surprise had created the right diversion.

William opened the car's passenger door, then carried Francesca over to it and got her settled. He collapsed her wheelchair, slipped it into the back floorboard, and turned to the house with a thumbs-up. Everyone cheered, including Nellie.

Now, if he could pass his driver's test, he and his sweetie could really go places.

CHAPTER THIRTEEN

Smiley and I waited on the swing for the sound of a wheelchair coming up the handicap ramp. The evening air had cooled, and a breeze stirred the ferns hanging above the front porch railings. He pushed the light button on his Timex watch. "Whatcha think they're doing? It's going on nine o'clock."

"Hopefully, they're engaged by now, but if it were me, my bladder never would've lasted this long."

An engine started. Headlights flickered on. William's taxi pulled away from the curb. "What's he thinking?" I dashed for the porch railing.

Smiley rushed to my side. "Looks like he's leaving."

By the time we reached the Manor's front yard and peered around a Magnolia tree, the taxi's taillights were tiny red dots. We watched until they disappeared beyond Sweetbriar's last streetlight.

"Oh my. What if he has an accident or gets stopped for a traffic violation?"

Smiley slipped his arm around my shoulder. "Don't worry, Sis. Maybe they're taking a spin around the block. Wherever they've gone, this proves one thing."

I leaned into him as we turned to walk back to the porch. "And what might that be?"

"Love is stronger than any law, don'tcha know."

Or maybe any promise made to a dying spouse? A selfish spouse, I might've added, but I kept my thoughts to myself.

Smiley lifted an afghan from his rocker and spread it over our laps as we sat on the swing. With pillows stuffed behind us, we made ourselves comfortable.

"I knew you weren't going to bed with those two gallivanting around," he said. "Might as well wait with you."

"What if they don't come back?"

"You worry too much. Scooch closer. Rest your head on my

shoulder."

I did just that and shut my eyes. Had he forgotten the promise he made to his Lucinda? Or did he think since marriage was off the table he could be freer with his feelings for me? Never mind the why, I was going to enjoy the moment. The warmth from his body and the scent of his Old Spice made me wish we were in that taxi driving away somewhere. Anywhere.

Smiley began snoring, soft at first and then as loud as an old tractor. His head dropped over on top of mine, and it felt as heavy as a bucket of coal. After a bit, I heard a low rumble out on the street and then brakes squeaking.

I eased Smiley away, stood, and peered toward the sound. Yep. The taxi had returned. I slipped a pillow underneath Smiley's head as he grumbled and opened his eyes before closing them again. I pulled the afghan up and tucked it around him. No need to wake him until it was time to go inside. I hurried down the wheelchair ramp. Private engagement party or not, I had to know the outcome.

I opened the driver's door. "What were you two thinking, driving off without a license?" Not what I had planned on saying, but it popped out before I could stop it.

"You see, it's like this, Red. The Dairy Queen was calling us. For their restrooms and for vanilla cones double-dipped in chocolate. So we took a vote and decided to take a chance. And here we are, back where we started from. No harm done."

Francesca leaned over William and flashed her new ring. "It's the very one worn on Downton Abbey. Guaranteed. Don't know how my Willy could afford such an extravagance, but isn't it stunning?"

William reached for her hand. "Only the very best for you, my love."

I straightened up to relieve the crick in my neck and then peeked inside again. "Do the two of you plan to come inside tonight?" They looked at me like it was midafternoon and I had asked a most ridiculous question.

Francesca giggled like a teenager. I'd never heard such a sound from her before. "We might." She giggled some more. "And we might stay right here until the sun rises over Mike's Garage."

William pulled out his cell phone. "If we get into any trouble, I'll call or text you."

With that pronouncement, we said our good-nights. I made my way back to lead Smiley to his bed. Otherwise, he would be sleeping in the swing and, come morning, he'd be covered with dew. I might be the owner of our retirement home, but at this moment I felt like a housemother watching over her charges.

Our two friends had committed to marriage, but no place or date had been set. That I knew of anyway. I hoped they would at least wait for William to pass his driver's test.

After leaving Smiley in his room, I walked to mine, stretched out across my bed fully clothed, and gave in to sleep.

Guitar music jolted me awake. For a moment I thought my radio had come on. What time was it anyway? I peeked at my phone. William was calling. At three a.m.

Now I was wide awake.

"We got us a situation," William said in a loud whisper.

"Are you all right? Is—"

"We're fine. Wait ten minutes and call the sheriff."

"What? The sher . . . why?"

"We saw someone creeping around outside the Manor. Wore a hooded jacket. Had to be up to no good. Locked the cab doors, started the motor, and then flashed my lights. Whoever it was biked off down the street in a hurry. We're coming inside. Francesca says the world's changing, and we're not even safe in Sweetbriar these days."

"And why do you want me to wait ten minutes?"

"Maybe twelve. We need time to get inside. No need for us to get caught up in someone else's shenanigans."

"But what am I supposed to tell the sheriff?"

"You'll figure that out. You got our confidence."

"Do you need help with . . ." But he had already hung up.

I grabbed a quilt. No need for Francesca to get chilled from the night air.

As soon as they were inside and William's door shut, I called Hershel. He was not happy to be awakened, but I relayed all I knew from William's observations. A man or woman in a dark hoodie had been spotted close to the Manor, perhaps even peering in a window or two. Then he or she disappeared on a bike. Like I expected, the sheriff asked me a dozen questions. Then he wanted to know what I was doing up at this ungodly hour.

"Sometimes I don't sleep well, and I pace the floor. All hours of the night." This was true, though not in this instance.

Finally, he sighed. "Let's see if we can get some shuteye until daylight."

"Daylight? Aren't you coming over now?"

"Anybody hurt? Anything broken into? Anything stolen?"

"No. Not as far as I can tell."

"Probably some homeless person looking for a place to sleep. Nothing to it except your imagination. See you in the morning."

Humph. I'd never seen a homeless person ride a bicycle. Especially in the middle of the night.

Of course I couldn't quiet my brain enough to go back to sleep. This could be the same person seen behind the House of Hope before the explosion. No way to tell. But then again anyone could wear a hooded jacket. Or did William say it was a raincoat? On a spring night with no rain? Sometimes a homeless person would wear everything he owned to keep his possessions from being stolen. Maybe the sheriff was right, and this person was trying to find a place to spend a few hours.

I dozed in my rocker until some loud wrens outside my window announced the break of day. I slipped into my tennis shoes, laced them tight, and left my room before anyone stirred.

What I found on the back patio left me more puzzled. I didn't touch anything but immediately called the sheriff again. This time he said he would be right over.

And he was.

"Looks like someone was interrupted," he said.

"We stared at a heaped up pile of sticks and newspapers with charred edges. I wasn't going to volunteer that William and Francesca were the ones who had probably frightened this person away. No need to turn attention in the wrong direction.

Shirley popped her head out the door. "Hot coffee anyone?" She signaled me with a roll of her eyes to follow her back inside, which I started to do.

"Wait." Hershel said, putting his hand on my arm. "Go around to the front door. Investigators are on their way. We don't want any evidence disturbed."

"Is this how the other fire started?"

He grunted. "Can't answer that."

"Ongoing investigation?"

"Exactly."

Lost in a whirlwind of thoughts, I followed the walkway that led around the Manor to the front porch. It seemed unlikely that an arsonist had paid us a visit since any attempts to start a fire were on the patio and at least four feet away from the house.

But a worrisome thought nagged at me. William's description of a person messing around our home was the same as the one the homeless man had given me about seeing someone at the House of Hope. As vague and sketchy as both accounts were, they seemed to be the same. Why would anyone target a retirement home? Was someone trying to send a message to me? Perhaps it was a warning to unwanted ex-cons and to anyone who might offer them shelter in our town. And that would include me.

Shirley met me at the front door wearing a flour-dusted apron and clutching a rolling pin. I had forgotten this was the morning for sausage, biscuits, and gravy. "I tried to stop her," Shirley announced, "but she's stronger than she looks, besides being touched in the head." Long curls had escaped her hairnet, and her face was flushed from a hot kitchen. Or frustration. Or both.

"Nellie?"

She nodded. "Come on back. I've got to get the biscuits in the oven. You can stir the gravy." Shirl used an ancient baking powder can to cut the biscuits and line them onto baking sheets while I stirred the thick white gravy full of crumbled sausage.

I could see Hershel through the back screen door talking with a man who jotted down something on a clipboard. I wanted to know what they were saying, but I've never been good at reading lips.

"Did you hear what I said?" Shirley asked.

"Uh, not exactly. Could you repeat it?"

"Nellie told me she's catching the bus to Folly Beach. Says her Auntie Pearl told her that Aunt Mildred would be waiting for her there. Even Dee couldn't get her to change her mind. So she went with her, along with that little dog. They're over at Mike's waiting for the bus. Talk about crazy. For once, Francesca is right. That Nellie is nothing but trouble."

"Oh my. The sheriff could spot Dee boarding a bus when he told her not to leave town. No telling what he'd do. Do you think they've gone yet?"

"Don't know, but I can't leave my biscuits to find out."

"After the investigator leaves, invite the sheriff inside for a cup of coffee. Maybe he'll share some information with you." I poked my head into the dining room long enough to enlist Lollipop's help in the kitchen. Then I dodged through people who were headed for their favorite breakfast and slipped out the front door.

I reached Mike's Motor Service just as the bus pulled away. Nellie waved from the window. Dee and Pepper stood underneath the Stagecoach Express sign. I rushed over to them.

"I tried to stop her, Miss Agnes. I did. She wouldn't listen."

After I spoke to Pepper and rubbed him behind his ears, we headed back to the Manor. "Once Nellie gets something stuck in her head, it's there to stay. Like her habit of taking things that don't belong to her. Anything of yours missing since you moved in?"

"Come to think of it . . . a small notebook I scribble things down in. Some hair clasps. And a picture of my granny. About all that was saved from the fire. Grieve over that picture the most, but seeing as Nellie's room is a total train wreck most of the time . . . well, I figured my things were in there somewhere."

"Maybe they are. Are you willing to let me help you look? While she's gone would be the perfect time."

"I don't know. Don't like to be messing with another person's stuff."

"How else are you going to find out if your granny's picture is somewhere in that room? Maybe we'll even find her Aunt Mildred."

She agreed, and we headed back to the Manor. If Nellie traveled all the way to Folly Beach and did whatever she thought she had to do and then rode back, she'd be gone until seven o'clock tonight when the last bus pulled into Mike's Garage. No need for us to hurry.

"Let's have some breakfast first," I said as we entered the foyer, now filled with the aroma of sausage and biscuits. Dee took Pepper to leave him in Nellie's room while I scooted through the dining room, into the kitchen, then out the back door. Shirley and Hershel were standing on the patio talking.

"What's the verdict?" I asked as I joined them.

Shirley rolled her eyes. "Some people refuse to see what's plain as day. I've got my duties to see about instead of wasting time." She huffed past us with a twist of her behind and a toss of her blond pouf.

The sheriff frowned as the screen door slammed and shook. He continued to stare as if waiting for Shirley to return.

I coughed to get his attention. "What did the inspector say?"

"We determined this was merely some homeless person looking for shelter, like I said earlier. Probably checked to see if any doors were left unlocked. When that didn't happen, this person, probably a man, tried to start a fire to take the chill off."

"It wasn't that cold last night."

"Heavy dew. He . . . or she . . . was trying to make some coffee in an old can we found underneath some bushes. Something must've interrupted him. Never got it made."

"Maxwell House?"

The sheriff squinted at me. "How did you know that?"

"Just a hunch. So, where's the can now?"

"Gone to the lab. It'll be dusted for fingerprints, but I would bet this person isn't in any database. Unless he's a real criminal. Which I doubt. No need for you and Shirley to jump to any conclusions about a possible fire meant to harm the Manor. Didn't happen."

"That's certainly a relief, isn't it? Any leads on the other fire? Surely you have some suspects."

"Now, Miss Agnes, you know I can't share any information about that."

I didn't expect him to, but thought I'd stir the pot. "Since we seem to have someone wandering around here during the night, are you going to patrol the area more closely? What if a resident can't sleep and walks outside for some fresh air?"

"Not advisable in any neighborhood. Have to use common sense."

He wouldn't be sending around his deputy—or anyone else for that matter—to check on us. Too bad. Well, at least I tried.

I left the sheriff poking around in the backyard and went inside. If human ashes were actually inside that can, the lab would prove it, and the sheriff would want to know whose they were and how they got there. Had he discovered Aunt Mildred? Too many loose ends were making me dizzy. Maybe a sausage biscuit with gravy would help.

"Lord have mercy!" Shirley said after I shared with her about how William's romantic evening had come to an end.

I decided to wait on the report about the contents of a coffee can before saying anything else.

"My kitchen could've burned to a crisp last night. And Mr. Lively asleep upstairs," she added after returning to the stove.

"I don't think there was any danger to our home. At least not according to Hershel. Where is Mr. Lively by the way?"

"Went inside his office and shut the door. Asked me to bring his breakfast and a fresh pot of coffee. Said he had work to do before he left this lunatic place. Didn't say if he meant the Manor or the town. Have you fired him yet?"

"He saved me the trouble. Said he was accepting another job offer in Nevada or some such place."

"How will he get references?"

"I'm sure he'll manage to come up with some good ones, even if he has to make them up himself."

Shirley sniffed. "Whenever he goes, it's not soon enough to suit me. Have you found anyone to replace him?"

"Got some ideas. I'll run them by you and Smiley later. As well as Henry. He's got to be a part of this."

"Indeed. Besides being your partner, he's a smart businessman and has a kind heart. The perfect combination."

"Exactly." Yes, my dear son-in-law knew how to make a good living with his hardware store while he treated his customers and employees with respect. Mr. Lively and I had gotten off on the wrong foot in the very beginning, but allowing him to stay had not corrected our problems. It boiled down to trust. Neither of us trusted the other, and that was not likely to change.

Shirley fixed me a plate and poured some coffee in a Kut'N Loose mug. I sat on a stool at the kitchen island while she wiped down the stovetop that was now splattered with sausage grease.

"William's the one who scared the person off last night," I said between bites.

Shirley turned from the stove and faced me. "You tell William to come see me. Need to thank him proper. What's his favorite cake?"

"Italian cream for sure," I said without hesitation. "Just keep this whole thing quiet. Nobody needs to know William spotted someone messing around or that whoever it was tried to start a fire on the patio. Not only do we not want to worry everyone, the sheriff is apt to turn his attention to William and find out he was driving last night without a license."

"Seems he's lookin' at Dee now more than anyone—which is ridiculous. He asked me if she ever slipped outside during the night and roamed around or would anybody know it if she did? Of course I never shared with him that Nellie was known to do that sort of thing. Mark my word, he's trying to pin something on Dee. He's full of baloney is my way of thinking." Shirley lifted a hefty breakfast tray and headed to Mr. Lively's office.

I quickly ate my breakfast, washed it down with two mugs of hot coffee, then headed to Nellie's room.

CHAPTER FOURTEEN

When I opened Nellie's door, Pepper bounced over for some loving. Dee was sitting in the middle of the floor writing in a notebook. She looked up and smiled.

"You found it?"

"Sure did. In the bottom of my own laundry basket that nice man from the Dollar Store give me. Reckon it fell out of the sweatshirt I was wearing the night of the fire. Man does it stink. Looked everywhere I could think of before I found it. Nellie had stuck my hair clasps in one of her shoes, as well as some shampoo and a bar of soap the Red Cross give me. But you'll never guess what I found in the back corner of the closet, on Nellie's side."

I pushed aside a pile of clothes and sat on her bed while Pepper crawled up on Dee's lap. She stroked the dog's back as she looked up with deep wrinkles across her forehead. "Three coffee cans. Same brand she's been looking for. These were unopened."

"Oh my. What on earth?" I could not imagine what Nellie had been thinking. No one could know the mind of a crazy woman, but I was beginning to think Aunt Mildred's ashes had been lost years ago. "Did you find your picture?"

"That's the best part. Reckon I'd stuck it inside my notebook for safekeeping and then plumb forgot."

I glanced around the messy room. "Anything else you've thought of? You know I'm going to have to confront Nellie about taking your things." I nodded toward the cemetery vases lined up across the windowsill. "By the way, has she said anything about those? Where she got them or why she has them?"

Dee shook her head. "I've always said it's best not to mess in anybody else's business? Secrets. We all got 'em."

"Maybe we should find you another place to sleep."

"No, I've kind of settled in here. Don't say nothin' to Nellie just yet. About stealing. My dear granny had the same sort of problems. Our kin overlooked it because she never did no harm to nobody. Nellie and me took to each other right off. She's my friend, and I don't have many of those."

Nellie rarely had a fondness for anyone—except William, who had defended her against Francesca's sharp tongue, plus Mr. Lively for whatever reason I couldn't fathom. And Smiley was a friend to everyone, so that didn't count. Now, a bond had formed between these two women. I stood to go. "You realize Nellie needs to get some help."

Dee nodded her agreement. Then she tore a page out of her notebook and handed it to me. "Wrote this about my granny a while back. For a class when I was in the big house."

I took the paper and read it out loud, the best way for poetry.

Blue
Who'd you talk to if you could, but you can't no more
'cause they gone? Gone on to the other side or gone on
with their lives and, plain and simple, left you behind?
A woman from the outside that come to teach us how to
write poetry—if you can believe it—asked that question.
Locked up in here all these days and nights with nothing
but washing dirty laundry to occupy my waking hours
I was way ahead of her on that one. Granny.
I'd talk to Granny. Hear her talk. Laugh.
Write a memory, the woman said.
First thing that come to mind was me climbing
into Daddy's truck headed out to the cemetery
to bury Granny. We stopped to pick up Papa,
and I snatched pansies from the yard.
I helped plant them before she died.
The blues were her favorite.
At her graveside, the preacher read Scripture
while I pictured the Ball jar on her kitchen table,
the clear glass jar filled with pansies . . . purple,
orange, yellow, white, and blue.

The blues will always be my favorite . . . blue, like her eyes.

"Wish I had known her," I said. "You must've loved her

very much."

She swiped at a stray tear as she handed me a picture, a black-and-white photo of a shriveled-up little woman smoking a pipe and wearing a long, print dress. Dee hugged Pepper to her chest. "She was my rock."

The bedroom door swung open, and Francesca rolled herself inside. "Have you seen Her Majesty?" She wrinkled her nose. "Phew. What's that smell?"

"This room could use some fresh air." I walked over and raised the window.

"It's that dog," Francesca said, pointing to Pepper. "He needs a bath."

"I thought you were searching for your cat," I said. "Check the living room. She likes to stretch out on the floor where it's been warmed by the sun. Over beyond the piano."

"If I can't find her, you'll hear from me."

"I'm sure," I mumbled as the wheelchair backed out of the room. I held the poem out to Dee. "Say, would you mind if I made a copy of this? The office has a machine. I can bring it right back."

"Sure. If you forget, it's all in my head anyhow."

"Do you want me to help you straighten up this mess?"

She shook her head. "Don't have to be at work 'til noon? Nothing else to do. Besides, got some brand new words rolling around in my hollow brain. Maybe a poem. Sometimes they come to me when I'm doing something else."

"I know exactly what you mean." Maybe if I took up my neglected knitting, I'd figure out some of my personal as well as business problems that were more irritating than a drippy faucet in the middle of the night.

As I turned to leave, something caught my eye. A black jacket had been thrown over the back of a chair. Dee was busy attaching Pepper's walking leash and had her back to me, so I took a good look. Yes, it had a hood. Did it belong to Nellie or Dee?

"I've got some extra hangers in my closet. Looks like you could use some," I said as I nodded toward a pile of garments underneath the one in question.

Dee stared as if it were some foreign object she'd never noticed until now. She glanced up. "I'm . . . I'm certain we got plenty. Sure as shootin' we do? Yep." Pepper tugged on his leash, and the two headed out the door. I followed behind them, but Dee turned around and locked the door. Then she and her dog hurried toward the exit.

I watched them until they disappeared outside. What had just happened? Dee seemed to overreact when she focused on the jacket. It could be *the* jacket someone had worn behind the halfway house the night of the fire. Then again, maybe I was the one who had overreacted. There was no way I could know for sure.

Lost in my tangled thoughts, I bumped into a skinny man wearing a suit and tie. "Can I help you?" I asked after apologizing for not paying attention.

He stuck out his hand. "Tom Huggins. Parole officer sent to keep a lid on things down here. Starting with a drug test in the sitting room. I've called all the women to meet me here before they head to work. My assistant's picking up anyone who can't get a ride if they live too far to walk. None of 'em knew we were coming. They have tricks to show they're clean, so we have to keep a step or two ahead of 'em."

"Are drugs a big problem?" I asked.

"Can be. And they can not only ruin the women's future, but mine as well."

"What do you mean?"

"If drugs were to become a big issue, I would lose my job, plus any future halfway house wouldn't happen. Between you and me, we had planned a search of the House of Hope before it burned to the ground."

"Why? Did you suspect drug activity?"

"Received a call. Even though our plans fell through, the head honcho is mighty grateful to that person. Mighty grateful."

I headed to my room with a bushel of new questions. Who had called in a tip? The man wouldn't share a name. One person immediately popped into my head. Stone Phillips. He probably had access to all the secrets and sins of the ex-convicts he had come in contact with.

The night of the fire, Jack attributed the explosion to someone cooking meth in the basement of the Hope House. How did that happen unless their supervisor, Mary Wilson, was more than lax with drug checks. Maybe she stayed in the building too long trying to dispose of drug evidence.

The parole officer shared more than he should have. Someone had alerted the authorities about drug activities at the halfway house.

A loud knock on my bedroom door interrupted my scrambled thoughts. "Coming," I called as I threw open my door.

Mr. Lively stood there with a self-satisfied grin across his face. He rocked on his heels. "Found your thief. Someone you'd never suspect." He looked up and down the hall then back at me.

"Well, are you going to tell me or not?"

He leaned forward. "Your loony buddy," he whispered as he rolled his eyes toward Pearl's door.

"What? You're mistaken. She would never—"

"How do you think she's suddenly gotten all those art supplies delivered by Amazon? William probably ordered them from his computer since he's the only one around here with such skills. Except myself of course. Pearl's always lived on a tight shoestring, and now she's gotten three deliveries from some shop in Atlanta. I would bet she's spent at least two hundred dollars. Isn't that how much was missing? Now, what are you going to do about it?"

"This is truly a shock." I held on to the doorknob for support. "Going to take some thought. I'll let you know what I decide."

"Well, I suggest you don't delay. If she gets away with this, she'll find a way to continue stealing."

I thanked him for his help. As soon as he departed, grumbling to himself, I called Henry. He agreed Pearl was as innocent as fresh fallen snow. She could no more steal money from anyone than could John the Baptist—who was content to live on wild honey and locust in the wilderness. Had Mr. Lively set her up? He was right about one thing. She had limited funds. Because she did, unknown to her, I had adjusted her rent payments. She certainly didn't have the means to buy new art supplies.

Henry and I were both puzzled, but we agreed I had to talk with my old high school buddy. Then we addressed another issue. We worded a help-wanted ad for the *Timely News: Administrator for Sweetbriar Manor, a folksy retirement home offering a sophisticated salary including room and board. Only those qualified need inquire. In person.*

A few minutes later I knocked on Pearl's door. She proudly

showed me her new brushes, an array of oil paints, and a stack of canvases in multiple sizes. She said she had found the money one morning stuffed in a compartment of her easel tray. She never questioned where it came from or how it got there. "Like manna from heaven," she said.

"How did you order your supplies?"

"William of course. One click, and everything showed up the next day. Like magic."

I hugged this childlike woman. "That's really nice, Pearl. I'm happy for you." I left her as she turned her attention to the beginning of a new creation.

Pearl was not the guilty one, but neither was Mr. Lively, since whoever had taken the money had a big heart. Did I really want to find our Robin Hood?

The residents had all gathered on the front porch. It was almost suppertime as Dee straggled up the sidewalk from her job at Blind George's. She had recently increased her working hours since she had insisted she had fully recovered from her bout with pneumonia. Her pale face told a different story as she pulled against the handrail and climbed the porch steps.

"Are you feeling okay? Putting in too many hours?" I asked. "Maybe you ought to rethink that."

"I'm fine. Had a run-in with the sheriff. He stops in most afternoons for a Coke and peanuts. Reckon we caused some customers to up and leave. George said I needed to go home. Cool off. Sheriff's the one who started it. Ain't fair. I needed them tips too."

"What caused the argument?"

"Told me he had evidence I stayed in touch with my ex-boyfriend, and he had phone records to prove it."

"Is he right?"

"Yes, but not for the reasons he's thinking. I'd been trying to convince my ex he had to get some help. He's angry at the world. Like I used to be. I know what that's like."

Had Dee really changed that much in a short time? Only two weeks ago she had appeared on my porch and expected me to hire her on the spot, all the while sporting a big chip on her shoulder.

Shirley joined us on the porch. "Henry just called. He's

been trying to get ahold of you. Said to let you know that termites have been discovered in some of the schoolhouse apartments. They'll have to replace any infected wood and then treat the whole building. Seems the Hope women'll not be moving there as soon as planned."

"Humph," Francesca said. She twisted around in her seat and rolled her eyes. "I saw this coming," she fairly hissed.

William jumped up and offered his rocker to Dee. She crumpled into it with a sigh.

When Shirley opened the front door to return inside, Pepper dashed outside and headed for his owner. Dee scooped him up and tried to snuggle him close, but he twisted and squirmed to get free.

I hadn't noticed anyone coming, but there he was, big as life. Sheriff Hershel Caywood stood on the porch in the middle of us as the frisky dog growled and pranced around the officer's pant legs.

The sheriff eyed Dee as I pushed up from my rocker and positioned myself between them. "You're just the man I was coming to see," I said, turning to him. "You've saved me a trip. Has the lab determined the contents of the coffee can?"

He stared at me with a puzzled look.

"The Maxwell House can you found on the back patio. What was inside?"

"Oh. That," he said as he shooed the dog with his hat. "Nothing but dirt and some fertilizer. Maybe your gardener left it."

"Most likely it's from Pearl's gardening." I was glad to know the sheriff hadn't found Aunt Mildred. He'd probably be looking for a murder suspect. I shifted my weight to steady myself. "Won't you stay for supper? Pork chops, rice, and gravy tonight. One of Shirley's specialties."

"Can't," he said. "Here on business." He ran his hand through his hair before replacing his hat. "I need you to step aside."

"I'm inclined to stay right where I am." I felt a lot less brave than I sounded.

William rattled Her Majesty's treat bag and enticed Pepper into his arms.

Smiley sucked in his breath as he jumped up, but instead of disappearing inside like I expected, he stood by my side. He was joined by William with a firm grip on the poodle. Then Nellie, who looked as satisfied as a preacher after Sunday dinner, situated herself beside Dee. She folded her arms across her chest and grinned. Her mood swings were a puzzle since they often didn't fit the occasion.

The sheriff scanned our gathering before he grimaced, squeezed his eyes shut, and rubbed the back of his neck. With a groan, he bent forward and looked me square in the eyes. "Miss Agnes, I don't want no trouble."

"Neither do we. I suggest you leave before you have to call for backup."

"I'm not here to arrest anybody. Not today anyway." He looked at Dee. "I have a few questions to ask this young lady."

I glanced her way, and she nodded her consent. "Not without all of us being present," I said.

I motioned for Hershel to sit in my rocker, which he did but not without muttering under his breath. He took off his hat and fanned himself. The underarms of his shirt were ringed with sweat.

Smiley took Pepper for a walk as Dee sat down across from the sheriff. She swung her snake-decorated leg and chewed on a thumbnail. Her self-confident attitude was gone, and she looked like a scared little girl caught red-handed. What did the sheriff know that we didn't? Was this young woman guilty of something? Then I remembered seeing him ducking into his office on my way to Henry's store. Not alone either. A woman accompanied the sheriff. *Irene.* What was she doing back in Sweetbriar? She had once worked for the prison system before being fired. She must've given the sheriff some incriminating evidence against Dee. Such as keeping in touch with an arsonist. Or possibly helping to run a meth lab.

I walked over and stood beside Dee. Guilty of something or not, she deserved fair treatment. Nellie moved to her other side.

The sheriff took out a folded handkerchief and wiped his forehead. Then he fixed his eyes on Dee. "Tell me about the night of the fire."

I put my hand on her shoulder. I had no evidence for or against her, but I had a strong hunch she was not an arsonist or a drug dealer.

Dee sucked in her breath. "Not much to tell. Some loud

noise woke me up, I reckon. Maybe it was the explosion. Couldn't find Pepper. He had wandered off down the hall, like he does sometimes. Had to crawl on my knees. Smoke everywhere. Couldn't breathe. But I had to find him."

"So, you're claiming you were in your room, not the basement? How long would it take you to run up two flights of stairs to search for your dog? Two minutes? Three?"

"I didn't say anything about being in the basement." Dee twisted in her rocker and pulled her dress over her knees.

I stepped forward and stood as straight as I could. "If you're not here to make an arrest, I suggest you leave now."

He reached in a pocket and pulled out a package of Spearmint. He opened it, unwrapped a stick, folded it, and slipped it into his mouth. Finally, he stood. "I'll be back. You can count on it."

"And you can count on me to be in your office soon. Seems we have a lot to talk about," I said with as much confidence as I could muster.

He looked at me long and hard. Then his eyes swept over the porch gathering. "Don't none of you people stand in the way of this investigation or you'll be facing jail time." He turned to Dee. "And don't you even think of leaving town or ... or ..."

Dee turned her back on him, but I heard her plain as day. "Or you'll sic the mayor on me. He's meaner than a polecat and stinks twice as bad."

No worse than Irene, but if the two of them were in cahoots, we were in for double trouble. As soon as the sheriff left, I once again took out my phone and called Henry.

Everyone, except Francesca, gathered around to offer support.

"That small-town lawman don't scare me none," Dee said as she flipped her frizzed, blue hair behind her back. She rose from her seat and straightened her dress. "He's not gonna pin nothing on me." She seemed to have recovered her attitude. I hoped she was as innocent as she claimed.

After nearly everyone drifted away, I walked over to her. "Did you come across a woman by the name of Irene when you were serving time? It seems she's turned up in Sweetbriar."

"Irene? Sure. She made it a point to have all of us cross her path. She dug up every mistake or run-in we had with the law and held it over our heads."

"But why?"

"So we'd do her bidding. If she fancied a steak, we swiped it from the kitchen. If she wanted some weed, we found someone who could get it for her. If we refused, which I did once, she threatened to go to the warden whenever it was time for parole and list the reasons why it should be denied. She kept her word, and my time was extended three months."

"Did you know she had once planned to run the halfway house in Sweetbriar, only her cohort is serving time himself?"

"Yeah, I heard something like that."

"Why do you think she's here now? What possible reason could she have?"

"I don't know, but that woman's evil deep in her heart. She won't stop until she ruins any chance for us to turn our lives around. The women are afraid of her. Not just a little bit, but scared stiff. Mark my word. Irene's here to cause trouble. Not just for me but for everyone living at the Hope House. Did you know she and Mary Wilson were big buddies?"

"Had no idea. Do you think the two of them had some drug dealing going on?"

"Wouldn't surprise me none. And now she's convinced the sheriff that I'm the guilty one. Of what? Don't know how Irene done it, but since I ain't been arrested yet, he must not have much evidence to go on?"

"Sounds reasonable. But there has to be a motive, and for the life of me I can't figure one out for Irene."

"Meanness is probably enough reason. That woman is as mean as the devil hisself."

William returned with Pepper and handed him to Dee. We all said our good-byes and went our separate ways.

Mr. Lively wasn't in his office, so I used my key to let myself inside. While I made a copy of Dee's poem, I made a mental note to ask her more about her granny. Her words had brought back memories of my own ma-maw who had practically raised me in the hills of Kentucky, only two counties over from Dee's kinfolk.

As I left the office and closed the door behind me, Francesca blocked my way. "I understand Zelda Dee is a poet," she said in a voice dripping with honey. "Could I see what she's written?" She smiled and held out her hand.

"Certainly." I handed her a copy of *Blue,* though I was surprised she had an interest.

A moment later, she looked up. "You realize I'm a handwriting expert. This poem proves what I thought all along."

I snatched it out of her hands. "Did you even read the words?"

"That's not the important thing here." Francesca straightened herself in her wheelchair and brushed off her skirt. "Don't you want to know?"

"Not interested." I squeezed past her chair and headed back to the porch. "I have more important things on my mind."

She zipped along beside me. "Her pointed letters show she's aggressive."

I kept walking, but Francesca was being as bull-headed as ever. "Her words are slanted one way in the beginning and another way toward the end." Her voice rose with each word.

I stopped and faced her. "So?"

Francesca threw up her hands. "That means she's a liar."

"Is that a fact? Anything else?" I shook Dee's poem in front of her face.

Francesca obviously knew I'd reached the end of my patience with her. She dropped her eyes and studied her jeweled hands lying in her lap.

"Well? Out with it!" I crossed my arms and fumed at her.

"She writes with a heavy hand," Francesca said as if her statement made everything crystal clear. "She's angry."

"That makes two of us," I said and stomped out the front door.

On the front porch, I flopped into my rocker and closed my eyes. I didn't want to believe Dee could be an angry, aggressive liar. Or a drug dealer. Or an arsonist. I found it hard to believe she was any of those things.

Smiley scooted his rocker closer to mine. He didn't speak or ask any questions. His presence was enough. He opened a tattered Zane Gray paperback and soon moved his lips as he read. He had recently discovered his love for westerns and had carted a sack full from a garage sale. Did my heart good that he was expanding his horizons.

After taking a deep breath and blowing it out, I smoothed out the wrinkled poem, folded the papers, and slipped them inside my purse. Zelda Dee Sizemore was indeed a mystery, but it could be one that might never be solved.

Pearl snipped on a boxwood nearby with her large scissors, her choice lately instead of yard clippers. She hummed "Send the Light" as she worked. I lifted my knitting from my Walmart bag and tried to settle into a rhythm, but jumbled thoughts continued to taunt me. If they would behave and line up like little school children, with no monkeying around allowed, maybe I could focus on one of them at a time.

Irene had been added to my list of troublemakers, which included Stone Phillips and the halfway house neighbor, Lucy McDonald. Perhaps I had overlooked someone. Maybe Nellie? I had scant clues to consider concerning a fire that remained *under investigation* according to the sheriff. I'd picked up an old lighter the afternoon Jack and I found Dee's shoes. No ordinary plastic Zippo, but more like one belonging to someone's collection. A person wearing a hooded jacket had slipped behind some bushes next to the halfway house. Once the fire started, this person disappeared on a bicycle. I had more questions to ask the homeless man, the only witness. But could I count on him as a reliable source? Maybe he was guilty and trying to avoid suspicion. But where would he get the bike?

I looked up as Smiley called my name. "Got an idea of somebody who could run this place. I'm surprised you hadn't thought of her before now, but with all that's been happenin' around here you haven't exactly had much time to think a'tall."

As I considered his words, my hands and my knitting fell onto my lap. He had my attention. But before he could share anything more, Francesca, holding Her Majesty, wheeled herself onto the porch. She didn't share where she had found her wayward pet. "Willy's son is objecting!" she announced in a loud voice. "Some ridiculous notion about losing his inheritance. He thinks because I'm practically penniless, I'm latching onto his daddy for his money. He's forbidding our marriage. Who does he think he is? We don't have to answer to our children."

William lumbered onto the porch and sank into a nearby rocker. He leaned forward with his head in his hands. "Never thought my son would think more about money than his own dad's happiness. I've spent a good portion of my savings on a broken-down taxi and no telling how much on repairs. If he only knew . . ." He looked up. "It's *my* money, isn't it?"

I had never seen him come undone before. He had always declared the glass half full. My heart went out to him.

"Called me a crazy old fool for considering marriage at my age," William continued. "Said me buying a car without having a driver's license proved I had lost my mind. Totally."

No one spoke, not even Francesca. After a few moments of silence, William turned and winked toward his fiancé. Then he grinned, looking more like his old self. "You know what we're going to have to do, don't you?"

Francesca nodded and smiled. "I was wondering how long it was going to take you to figure that out. Let's go."

William popped out of his seat and rushed over behind his lady. Her Majesty jumped down and zipped off the porch, probably to attend to some urgent business. But Francesca hardly seemed to notice.

"Well," I said to the two lovebirds. "Fill us in."

William's face beamed as he stuck his old cigar stub into his mouth. "When we finalize our plans, you'll be the first to know, Red." They practically zoomed down the wheelchair ramp.

"Where are they going?" Smiley asked.

"Headed to the taxi to talk about a wedding is my bet. I hope William doesn't drive that rattletrap off again before Mike has a chance to finish working it over—or before he's a licensed driver."

CHAPTER FIFTEEN

Shirley and Smiley, who had helped me solve the murder of my husband's friend, Josiah Goforth, surely could help shine the light on my tangled thoughts concerning Dee and Mr. Lively, as well as the Hope House fire.

Later that afternoon I knocked on Smiley's door. "Your thirty-minute nap has lasted almost two hours," I said, raising my voice in case he was groggy from sleep. "Meet me in the kitchen for a cup of Earl Gray. I need your listening ears." I knocked again, louder.

After a moment came a muffled reply. "Coming, Sis. See you there."

When I entered the kitchen, a smell nearly knocked me flat. It was worse than the stink of kimchi, my son-in-law's favorite Korean dish from The Stone Bowl, Sweetbriar's newest restaurant. Sometimes Henry and I grabbed a bite of lunch there, although Betty Jo always had an excuse not to join us. I held my nose.

"Law, who would've thought leftover slaw and a few rotten onions would do such as that?" Shirley said as she waved her apron in the air. "That's what I get for cleanin' all that mess outta the fridge." We raised the windows, except for one over the sink that was stuck.

Smiley popped into the kitchen long enough to make a quick exit through the back door. "I'll be on the patio," he said with a wave of his hand.

No need to fuss at Shirley, but I made a mental note to list the foods that should be tossed in the garbage instead of down the disposal.

Mr. Lively appeared.

"Call the Rooter-Man Plumbing Company," I said.

He left immediately with a scrunched-up nose.

When a young plumber finally arrived, I asked his name.

"Some folks call me Leaky Louis," he said with a straight face. Then his shoulders shook with laughter. Not a good sign.

An hour later, Shirley's kitchen had a brand new disposal, and our comedian plumber presented me with an outrageous bill, asking for full payment before he left. Since I hadn't had the time to replenish our petty cash, I wrote him a check.

Shirley fumigated her kingdom with an aerosol room freshener called Honeysuckle. Then she lit five vanilla-scented candles rooted in jars of sand.

This crisis, though minor in the grander scheme of things, had popped up out of nowhere like those pesky no-see-ems that can make life miserable in the South. The emergency destroyed my best intentions and consumed my time instead of allowing me to focus on Zelda Dee Sizemore or Mr. Lively—both a puzzlement in their own baffling ways.

Shirley slipped two meat loaves into the oven and filled a cooking pot with water. Supper would include mac and cheese, cornbread, fresh green beans, sliced tomatoes, and spring onions. Set my mouth to watering as I pushed open the back door to join Smiley on the patio. Only he wasn't there.

After scanning the backyard, I spied him and Pearl at the gazebo that, seemingly overnight, had become overrun with confederate jasmine. She had clippers in hand and Smiley directed her trimming, which was a good thing since she didn't know when to stop once she got going.

I stepped over a pile of clippings. "Looking mighty fine out here, Pearl. Since all the rain we've had, this place has turned into a jungle." She looked up long enough to smile. Painting and gardening were her passions. "Sure wish I could pay you for all the work you do in this yard," I added.

She stopped snipping and met my eyes. "The Lord will provide," she said as she turned back to her task. Smiley was overcome with a sudden coughing fit. Was Pearl referring to her money appearing out of nowhere? Did she expect it to happen again?

Smiley cleared his throat and coughed a couple more times. I thumped his back. "Are you all right?" I asked.

He nodded. "Dang allergies."

"Meet me on the front porch when you've finished helping Pearl." I turned toward the house, then climbed the porch steps. As I dropped into the swing, thoughts of Pearl continued to swirl through my mind.

If anything upset her routine, she would become highly agitated, pull on my sleeve, and ask, "Is there anything I need to know?" She had done that since the moment we were reunited after all those years since high school. Yet the money she had found, and then spent, hadn't seemed to upset her in the least. This whole situation was totally out of character for her.

The scent of Old Spice brought me back to the present. I looked up to Smiley standing in front of me. "You've been wanting to tell me something. Right?"

He sat down beside me and settled himself. "Sometimes it's hard to see an answer when it's been there all along, don'tcha know." He shifted in his seat and grinned like he had a secret he couldn't wait to share.

"Come on," I said, motioning with my hands. "Are you going to make me beg?"

Smiley sat up straight as his smile widened. "Juanita," he said without further ado. "She would be perfect for Mr. Lively's job."

I'd been so consumed with Dee and all her problems, I'd forgotten Smiley had a suggestion for a new administrator. My mind shifted to his line of thinking. "Juanita. Hmmm . . ." I had never considered asking her. "But she's so young and—"

"Responsible. Didn't she care for Ida Mae as long as she lived here, even better than her own daughter?"

"Yes, but that doesn't mean she could manage a whole retirement home."

"Maybe not, but you have to admit she has a heart for old people."

"We're not *old*." For sure I had a trick knee and aches that sometimes kept me awake past midnight, but didn't most folks deal with such ailments or even worse ones?

"We're certainly not getting any younger," Smiley said.

Humph. Seems he was determined to keep the topic fermenting.

"And neither is that grouchy Mr. Lively," he continued, "who ought to retire. Why not hire someone full of vim and vinegar?"

I grinned in spite of myself. "I think that's vim and *vigor*, which actually means about the same thing."

"Whatever you call it, she's got it. When I stopped in the

drugstore a few days ago, she was practically running the place, except for the pharmacy. When I paid her for my corn pads, I asked how she was doing. You know, just making polite conversation."

"Well, what did she say? How is she doing?"

"Didn't say exactly, but when she handed me my change her eyes were full of tears. She tried to smile but didn't quite make it. I asked her if things were tough. She nodded, and it was all she could manage before rushing off to the lunch counter to take care of customers."

"I thought Mr. Watson probably paid her a decent salary, but she hasn't managed her full rent payments for several months now. I know she does the best she can, but my little yellow house hasn't been such a good investment. Juanita tells me she's keeping a record of what she owes me and will pay me in full one day. I believe her. She's a hard worker, honest, and a good mother to Frankie."

"I think you've just hired her."

"What about my rental property?"

"It's a good, solid house that would rent quickly to some working folks who could afford a reasonable payment. I would bet Juanita's only paid minimum wage, and she has childcare to boot."

I jumped up, hugged him, and planted a big kiss on his cheek. "I'm going to talk to Henry. If we make her an offer, it needs to be the right one. Do you think she and Frankie would be happy living here?"

"Are you kidding? I think everyone would be overjoyed. Once Dee leaves, and that little Pepper, things will be too quiet and dull. A young woman and her toddler would add life to this old house. And to our old bones."

He was talking about us being old again, but I let it go this time. If he didn't soon ask me to marry him, it looked as though I was going to have to do the asking.

Before we got any *older*.

Smiley removed his baseball cap and looked up. As always, my heart did flips. "Sorry, Sis. I've been doing all the talking instead of listening. I can tell something's really bugging you."

And so I shared my concerns about seeing Irene duck into the sheriff's office. He said not a word, just grunted or shook his head. "What do you think I should do?" I asked. "For whatever reason, she's latched on to making Dee's life miserable. What could Irene possibly know that we don't?"

"If she's up to no good, who would know? Apparently not the sheriff."

"Blind George." I popped out of the swing and planted another kiss on Smiley's cheek before heading to the pool hall. I didn't ask him to go along because not only had he complained about his corns, he was anxious to work on his latest painting.

On my way, I stopped in front of Rodeo Rags. The window display drew my eyes to a pair of women's cowboy boots. Even though I tried not to covet, my heart ached for those fancy shoes, red scrolled leather with silver toes. The tag read: *Laredo Silver Starburst, $175.00.* I tore myself away and continued on down the sidewalk. "Time to search the thrift stores again, Charlie." I could see him smile and give me a thumbs-up.

As I focused on Irene stirring up trouble for Dee, for whatever reason—not to mention the possibility of hiring Juanita as our administrator—my feet clicked along with a burst of energy. I didn't notice Mr. Lively until he swung his red convertible over to the curb beside me. I stopped and leaned on a big umbrella that Smiley had insisted I bring, even though there wasn't a cloud in the sky. At least it served me well as a cane.

"Where's the fire?" he asked, then laughed like it was the best joke ever.

"When is your departure date?" I asked, pointing my umbrella his way.

He shifted in his seat and pushed his sunglasses to the top of his head. "Situation has changed. Perhaps you could extend my time a few weeks? Job offer fell through."

I wasn't surprised. Perhaps he never had one to begin with. "According to our agreement, you have one more week. Besides, you accused Pearl without any evidence. She didn't steal the money, and neither of us knows who did. You failed on your promise, so you're on your own."

"You're one hard-hearted—not to mention hard-headed—woman."

"I'm not running a charity, and we both need to move ahead with our lives." How could he have the nerve to ask to stay longer? His lack of a job was not my problem.

He revved his engine, backed up, and sped away with tires

screeching. The smell of burning rubber lingered.

This confounded man always tried to throw a wrench into my plans. Months ago he wanted to sell our home to the prison system for a halfway house, but I put a stop to that. Now he was trying to blame Pearl for the missing money. I would not allow him to live at the Manor one hour longer than his scheduled departure, one week from today. With my shoulders thrust back, I got myself cracking toward the pool hall—until the horrendous sound of crushed metal and shattered glass rang in my ears.

I spun around. My brain made no sense out of what my eyes were seeing, but I ran toward the red convertible. Its rear end stuck out of the plate-glass window of the Kut'N Loose Salon.

CHAPTER SIXTEEN

A crowd rushed toward the scene, including the sheriff and his deputy, the meter maid, a postman, a man with two big dogs, and people along the street or inside stores who must've heard the crash and came running.

The Manor's soon-to-be-ex administrator sat in his car stiff as a mannequin. He stared into space as a trickle of blood ran from his forehead and dripped onto his shirt. Sheriff Caywood bent over him and kept calling his name, but the man didn't move. It seemed like a long time passed before EMS workers jumped from their vehicle and rushed to him. The car door was jammed, but since Mr. Lively had been driving with the top down, they climbed inside, fastened a neck and back brace around him, and lifted him out. A faint groan indicated he was alive. In no time, EMS had him secured on a gurney. They loadd him inside the ambulance and sped off toward Pardee Hospital.

Two other EMS workers entered the beauty shop that had been ripped open to the world. Inside, a woman, her head covered with aluminum strips, sobbed hysterically. Another woman with dripping wet hair hugged her while the beautician, Loretta, hugged them both. After everyone was examined, it was determined that no one inside the shop had been physically injured. A miracle of miracles. Seconds before the accident, the aluminum-headed lady had left her chair and was making her way to a shampoo bowl in the back of the shop before the convertible barreled through the front window and crushed her seat flat.

The people who witnessed the whole thing—as well as the ones who heard it happen—gathered on the sidewalk. Mike drove a wrecker from his garage and managed to untangle the crinkled red convertible from the damaged building. The front end was crushed, and Mike said it could be a total loss. Henry came with plywood in his pickup truck to cover the hole in the store. Blind George came with brooms and his cleaning lady to sweep the mess of bricks, insulation, and glass into a pile.

I crunched over glass pieces to reach George. He stopped his sweeping and looked up. "If Irene is up to no good concerning Dee, would you know about it?"

"Does a train wreck if it jumps the tracks?" He stepped aside and went back to sweeping.

"Well? Are you going to share your vast knowledge?" I had to dodge his broom, but I wasn't leaving.

He stopped sweeping and leaned on the broom. "Heard that woman talking to one of my customers last night. After a couple of beers she forgot about whispering. She's set on pressuring the sheriff to charge Dee with arson even when the fire chief hasn't declared arson to be the cause. Even if the charges don't stick—which they won't 'cause there's no evidence—the townspeople will paint Dee and all the women as a threat to our fine community. The mayor will send 'em packin', and he'll be applauded for takin' action."

George was right. "But what's in it for Irene?"

"Beats me. All I can figure is she set out to strike fear into Dee's heart, and she's done a good job of it. If you ask me, Dee —and probably the other women as well—know a trainload of incriminating evidence against Irene, and she thinks this way she can keep 'em from talkin'."

"Upon my word . . . she's one rotten schemer. And the mayor's not any better."

"You got it, Granny. But there's something in Dee's favor. Since the fire hasn't been declared as the work of an arsonist, how can she be charged with something that might've never happened?"

How indeed? "Maybe if Irene stirs up enough gossip it will be all that's needed."

As the crowd broke up to go their separate ways, Henry walked over to me. "When I finish here, Mother Hopper, I'll go over to the hospital and check on Mr. Lively. He's probably just shaken up. A right smart, I'd say. And maybe in shock. I'll let you know how he's doing. Maybe it's nothing more serious than embarrassment, plus the loss of his beloved car."

I nodded and thanked him. Then I remembered another errand I had come into town to do. "Actually, I was on my way to see you."

Henry took my arm and led me down the sidewalk to a bench. "Let's sit a minute. You look mighty pale. Tell me why you were coming."

I explained Smiley's suggestion about asking Juanita if she would like to manage our retirement home and then asked him what he thought.

He slapped his knee. "By golly, she might be the perfect solution. When are you planning to ask her?"

"I'm headed to Begley's now, and as soon as she can take a break from her drugstore duties, maybe we can find a private place to talk."

Henry helped me stand, made sure I was steady, then returned to finish boarding up the Kut'N Loose. I continued in the direction I had been going before the accident. Mr. Lively had asked me to extend his time at the Manor because he had no job to go to. Now he had no car. I could not be responsible for a man who not only made poor decisions, but also was a major source of irritation. I had to think of our home, Sweetbriar Manor, and my friends who lived there. I was not hard-hearted, just practical. One week was my limit for that man, then he'd have to move on—even if it were on the Stagecoach Express.

We slid into an empty booth with two vanilla shakes. Juanita listened with wide eyes and her mouth hanging open. When I finished, a tear slid down her cheek. "What if I can't handle the job? I've never done anything like it before."

"You had never worked at a drugstore before either. Besides, you've juggled a dozen different jobs here."

"I don't know . . ."

"You feel an obligation to Mr. Watson. I understand. I also appreciate your loyalty. Stop by the Manor after work. We can talk some more. Then think it over. If you decide you'd like to work for me, give him a two-week notice. That's fair."

We said our good-byes, and I headed home. In front of Blind George's, Henry called. I put my phone on speaker so I could hear him better. Feeling weak-kneed, I leaned against a light post.

"Seems the poor fellow had a slight stroke," Henry said. "His dead-weight foot landed on top of the accelerator. They'll probably keep him overnight before dismissing him. Seems he hasn't been taking his blood pressure medicine lately."

"Oh my." I couldn't think of much else to say. I truly hoped his *sugar* was a kind person who would take him in.

"Are you still there?" Henry asked. "Mother Hopper?"

"Yes. Sorry. I'm here."

"What did Juanita think about your offer?"

"Grateful, but not sure she can handle it. Promised to let me know in a few days after we talk some more. I didn't think to tell her that she and Frankie can live upstairs, and some of us can help her out at times with her toddler."

"Not sure you or any of us could keep up with that little fellow. According to Betty Jo he goes full speed ahead from the minute he wakes up. She's kept him a few times, you know, and afterward she's totally exhausted."

"I wasn't talking about all day every day, just every now and then."

"Are you going to go see Mr. Lively? Betty Jo or I could take you."

"We had a heated exchange right before . . . before the accident. I don't think I should. Might upset him again."

"His stroke probably would have happened anyway."

Our conversation ended when raindrops splattered on the bench, the sidewalk, and my head. I popped open the big umbrella, and it kept me as dry as a tobacco field in August while I hurried home.

Thankful for a generous gabled roof on the backdoor stoop, I left the umbrella and my wet shoes there before entering the kitchen. I needed a cup of strong tea with a dash of cream and lots of honey. I put the kettle on. Smiley joined me, and I was thankful for his good listening ears. But I was not prepared for another piece of his advice. I promised to consider contacting Mr. Lively's former employer, a nursing home over in Summerset. Maybe he had been fired and his glowing recommendations fashioned out of thin air. A thief would certainly have no qualms about lying. Besides all that, they might have unexplained missing money.

After Smiley left in search of his western novel he'd misplaced, the front doorbell rang. Voices from the foyer floated into the kitchen where I was fixing a second cup of tea. Shirley pushed through the swinging door into the kitchen, the sheriff following close behind. His wet shoes squeaked across the floor. He stopped at the workbench island, removed his dripping hat, and pulled up a stool. Shirley marched over to the stove and pulled out pots and skillets and baking sheets.

The racket made it impossible to talk, so we watched her and waited. I grabbed some paper towels and handed them over. Whatever reason he had for coming, Shirley didn't like him being in her kitchen, besides making a mess. No one offered him a cup of tea.

After sopping up a puddle on the counter and another on the floor, the sheriff turned to me. "I understand you were a witness to Mr. Lively's accident downtown."

"I didn't see anything until after it happened. When I heard the crash I turned around, and his car was sticking out of the Kut'N Loose."

The sheriff waded up the wet paper towels. "After he came to his senses, he was able to talk. It seems he has a mild concussion, along with a slight stroke, but no side effects, such as paralysis. Doctor's running some tests and keeping him overnight for observation. He's lucky nobody got hurt—or worse—when he plowed through that window."

"He came a hair from running me over," I said. Not exactly true, but it scared me as much as if it had happened. My right eye started twitching like it does when I exaggerate the least bit.

The sheriff frowned as he fished his buckeye out of a shirt pocket. "What did the two of you argue about?"

"Why is that important?" I sipped on my lukewarm tea.

Hershel had no reason to ask about the rift between us. He squirmed on his stool and leaned closer. "He says you caused his blood pressure to shoot up, which brought on the stroke, and, therefore, the accident is your fault, and you're the one responsible for the damages to his car and to the building." He studied his buckeye before dropping it back into his pocket.

"That's a ridiculous mouthful you just spit out." I jumped down and stuck my cup of tea in the microwave. When the beeper sounded, I returned to my perch.

He turned his attention away from eyeing Shirley and back to me. "Actually, this is one time I agree with you, but I had to follow up on his statements before filing my report. He doesn't think he's covered for total car replacement or for the property damages, so he'll probably be underwater. He says you fired him. Is that true?"

"He wouldn't know the truth if it knocked him down and sat on him. Doesn't he have any family who could help?" I blew on my tea, took a sip, then stirred in more honey.

"A granddaughter in California. Student at Berkley, but she may have to drop out due to some health issues. Seems he sent her money when he could. Now he's broke, jobless, and soon to be homeless."

I blinked as the sheriff stared into my eyes. Was this Mr. Lively's *sugar*? Even if she was, he had no excuse to steal for her. "What do you expect me to do about this unfortunate situation? I'm not his keeper, after all. He's the one responsible for how things turned out, not me." It seemed our administrator had a reason for his thievery.

Before the sheriff answered—assuming he was going to— Dee opened the back door wearing a dripping raincoat. As she removed it she nearly stumbled over her dog trying to escape Her Majesty. The two animals raced around the island until Dee snatched up Pepper and held him close. I grabbed a broom and managed to shoo the cat through the kitchen door and into the dining room.

"Happy Halloween!" Shirley yelled. In her frustration she shook a sponge mop in the air. Then she bent to the task of putting her kitchen in order.

The sheriff stood and sidestepped the mop while reaching for his hat. He nodded to Dee. "We need to talk. How about the dining room?"

"Pepper's shaking all over. Get him dry and settled first?"

"Don't take too long."

Dee looked like a child who was about to receive her punishment. "Ten minutes?"

He shrugged as deep wrinkles gathered across his forehead.

Francesca wheeled herself through the swinging kitchen door clutching her cat to her ample bosom. "You've got to do something about that dog. He's made Her Majesty a nervous wreck."

"Out!" Shirley shouted as she swung her arm and pointed toward the dining room. Her face, red and puffed up, reminded me of a traffic cop. All she needed was a whistle.

Francesca wheeled around, for once doing as she was told,

and in the process loosened her grip on the Persian that escaped in a flash of fur. I grabbed the broom.

"You're the one!" Francesca yelled. "You've always hated my cat. From the beginning. I'm calling the Humane Society."

Her Majesty zipped into the dining room before my broom touched her. Francesca looked up at me. Her chin quivered, and her eyes filled with tears.

I reached out to touch her shoulder, but she jerked away as if she had been burned. "Willy and I need to find us another place to live," she said in a trembling voice. "Where a pet is treated with respect. Obviously, that is *not* Sweetbriar Manor."

She wheeled away with her nose in the air. I didn't try to stop or reason with her since anger had turned her deaf. Part of what she said was true. I had no love for cats because the ones on our farm hadn't been pets. They lived in the barn and dined on mice and moles and other creatures they could catch. Besides keeping the snakes away. They were pretty much wild, and Charlie and I kept our distance, as did they. Our pets were two big dogs, strays that showed up at different times and stayed for years. And Miss Margaret, of course.

Once Francesca cooled off, I predicted she and Willy wouldn't move, but we would have to work something out as long as Pepper and Dee were with us. And that could be weeks from now before all the Hope Women had a place to call home. Unless the mayor and Irene made that move impossible. I didn't think I could take much more. I hurried into the foyer and then into the powder room. Too much tea made the stop urgent.

Still drying my hands, I closed the door behind me and turned toward the dining room. Unruly animals, a dishonest administrator who had to be sent on his way, plus the uncertain future of the Hope Women, had set my nerves on edge.

But what about Dee? I had to admit she had stolen my heart—a girl from the hills of Appalachia who had probably been wrongly accused of assisting her arsonist ex-boyfriend. Had my feelings clouded my good judgment? Why would the sheriff come by to ask her more questions? At the very least, he thought Dee was a person of interest. That had to be why. Like Blind George said, arson had never been declared as the cause of the fire, so why wasn't she in the clear?

"What's going on, Sis?" Smiley asked in my good ear.

I jumped in surprise. Where had he come from? I hooked my arm through his. "Am I glad to see you." I pulled him along. "Dee could be in trouble." No more time for words. I hurried us through the empty dining room and into the kitchen, expecting to witness an interrogation, but Shirley was alone.

After lifting a ham out of the oven, she set it on the stovetop and turned to us. "They've gone into the sitting room. Sheriff said what he had to say was between him and Dee. Ain't that against the law? Don't she need a witness? Or maybe a lawyer? What if he's harassing her? Don't she have rights?"

"Yes indeed." I ran out of the kitchen and down the hallway, ignoring my gimpy knee.

Dee and the sheriff, with their heads bent toward each other, stood beside our large fish tank that gurgled and hummed. As soon as they spotted me they stopped talking. The sheriff shot daggers my way while Dee looked like a scared little girl facing judgment day. Before I could think what might be happening, my heart melted. Again.

"Looks like we're finished here," Hershel said as he placed his hat on his head just so. "For now," he added.

Dee dropped onto a nearby sofa. She chewed on a thumbnail and kept her eyes on the floor.

Seems he wasn't finished after all. "If you decide you need a lawyer, one can be provided. Be assured, I'm going to get to the bottom of this. I'll be back, so don't you even think about going anywhere. Understand?"

She nodded then hugged her arms to herself.

Hershel walked into the foyer and toward the front door. When he realized I had tagged along, he stopped. "Miss Agnes, as I've told you many times before, you've got to let me do my job. I didn't want to focus on that young woman, but I can't ignore a tip, even if I don't like where it came from. If you have any evidence about this case, anything at all, I expect you to share it with me. You don't want to be charged with obstruction, do you?"

"Certainly not. If I come up with something, you'll be the first to know."

"Somehow I doubt that, but we are on the same side you know."

"Agreed," I said. We shook hands to make it official.

He stopped near the front porch steps and turned toward

me. "By the way, I would suggest you keep your distance from Mayor Phillips' office. Seems you've been making a nuisance of yourself."

"How could that be when he just returned from a small-town convention—which he didn't attend."

"What nonsense are you talking about?"

"Check it out for yourself. I'm sure you have ways to find out."

"I'll be back tomorrow," he said. Would he ignore what I'd suggested? "Something about the fire at the Hope House doesn't ring true. And I aim to find out what it is."

"You mean interrogate Dee underneath a blazing spotlight in a dark room?"

He squinted at me. "You watch too many detective shows. If I push her too hard she's gonna lawyer-up, and we might never find out what really happened or why." He turned to go but stopped and faced me once again. "You realize I have probable cause for searching your place since an ex-convict's living here now. Which I plan to do. A warrant is forthcoming. Should have it tomorrow."

"For the whole Manor?" I felt like shaking some sense into that man. What on earth did he mean?

"Exactly." He took out a handkerchief and wiped his neck. "Drugs could be stashed anywhere. Even in your room without you knowing it. Or in that crazy Nellie's room."

The nerve. I raised my cane toward him and glared. "Good evening, *Sheriff.* I hope you sleep well."

"Yep. Nothing better than a good rain."

I watched him run, hunched over, into a blowing down-pour.

Chapter Seventeen

Like my throbbing arthritic toe—as well as the sheriff's prediction—the rain continued throughout the night. But instead of gentle and soothing, a regular deluge pounded the roof. The sound was louder than static blaring from my radio. Sleep visited in bits and pieces until I gave in to the constant noise.

Awakened by a sudden quiet and bright sunlight that promised an end to the storm, I slipped on my robe and headed for the front porch. The whole world glistened as rainwater dripped from the eaves, the gutters, and the surrounding magnolias and oaks. Confederate jasmine perfumed the air. I closed my eyes to drink it in.

Then, quicker than a hungry dog could fetch a bone, dark clouds snuffed out the sun like a shade pulled across the sky. Sheriff Caywood climbed the steps with a long envelope in his hand. "We'll deal with this later," he said as he slipped the envelope inside his vest and handed me a folded piece of paper I hadn't noticed. I opened it and scanned its contents. A search warrant. Suddenly, the air turned too heavy to breathe. I grabbed the porch railing to steady myself.

He spent a good thirty minutes in Nellie and Dee's room while I paced outside in the hallway. When he finally emerged, he looked at me and shook his head. "Nothing."

"Well, I hope you're satisfied." I crossed my arms and gave him my best dirty look. But was I satisfied? Did he look inside Nellie's cemetery vases? Did he spot any boxes of matches or candles? He tucked his hat underneath his arm and headed toward the main house with long strides. I caught up to him in the foyer. "A cup of hot coffee before you leave?"

"Nope. No time. Have to search every room. The information about Dee didn't pan out, but got a tip about the next room on my list." He opened the door leading to the other wing.

"And whose might that be?"

"Yours. And you can't come in until I'm finished."

"This is . . . this is beyond ridiculous," I sputtered. "You're wasting your time." When we stopped outside my door, the starch flew clear out of me. He turned the doorknob, and I shook my finger at him. "Don't you dare turn my room upside down and leave it that way. Put everything back the way you found it. Am I clear?"

He gave me a sideways grin, saluted, and disappeared inside. I was madder than all get out. After all we had been through together, the man didn't trust me. Not only had I exposed the former administrator of Sweetbriar Manor for her crimes, I had once solved a murder without any help from him. It looked like we would always be at odds with one another.

I could see Charlie shaking his head after a twister splintered our barn into a pile of giant toothpicks. "We need help," he had said. "This is too much for us to handle on our own."

"That was an entirely different situation," I said to him while I continued pacing.

Hershel opened my door and stepped into the hallway. He held up a small, plastic zip-lock bag containing white powder. "Where's Zelda Dee?" he asked. "Have to talk with her, as well as all of those women."

"Those women? You've lumped them all together as suspected druggies? The very nerve!" I thumped my cane on the floor to make my point. "I suppose you're including me along with them?"

He held up both hands. "Settle down, Miss Agnes. I know you don't use or deal in drugs, but who would have access to your room? If this is what I think it is, someone probably thought they had stashed it in a safe place. Do you happen to know where Dee might be right now?"

"I suppose she's in the sitting room. She called a meeting of the Hope women, so they all should have arrived by now."

"Back to my question," he said as he planted himself squarely in front of me with his arms crossed. "Who has access to your room?"

"Well . . . uh . . . no one. If I remember to lock my door."

"If? So anyone could have planted it."

"Fiddlesticks. I suppose so."

"Who wants you out of the way?"

"Who told you to search my room?"

He wouldn't say, but I would bet my last dime it was Irene. We moved on into the sitting room where he questioned all the Hope women. Then he continued his search and found no other drugs in the whole place. Before he left, we stood talking in the foyer when he dropped a bombshell. "I would bet my buckeye that the drugs underneath your mattress were planted. Can't prove who did it yet, but I will."

I breathed a sigh of relief.

"However, I have a restraining order to serve before I leave." He pulled the long envelope out of his vest and handed it to me. I had totally forgotten he had tucked it inside his jacket earlier.

Without reading it, I tapped it against his chest. "This is ridiculous and impossible," I said, spitting out my words. "How could I give the mayor a hard time when he hasn't even been here? Was it his secretary? Maybe she fooled me with her sugar-sweet politeness." My heartbeat thumped in my ears as I tried to swallow the lump in my throat.

"It's not from the mayor or Miss Louise, though neither are happy with your line of questioning. Lucy McDonald says you've been harassing her, and she wants you to stay clear of her place."

"That old woman who lives next door to the halfway house?"

"The same."

"But—"

"Stay away from her," he demanded. "And that's how it's gonna be." He walked away, then stopped and came back. "By the way. I checked on the mayor's whereabouts. Like you said, he wasn't at the convention." Then he tipped his hat and was gone.

I watched him dash through the rain, jump into his patrol car, and drive away. Now what? Lucy McDonald had slapped me with a restraining order. Heavens to Betsy. Only a few days ago she had invited me in for coffee. Someone must've convinced her to file a complaint against me.

When the sheriff returned, would he charge someone with drug possession? He and I both believed someone had framed me. I knew of only one person who would do anything to get me out of her way.

I returned to my room, sat in my crooked rocker, and stewed

about the turn of events—until I glanced up at Charlie smiling from his Ford tractor, my favorite picture of him that always sat on my chest of drawers. What would he advise? I'd often heard him say, "Music can clear the cobwebs out of your mind and help you think clearly."

The Bluegrass station Goin' Round the Mountain should do the trick. My room had grown dark, so I clicked on the lamp and then my Philco. Abigail Washburn's voice and banjo filled my room until she was interrupted by our weatherman, Ralph. He announced we'd best prepare for a torrential rainstorm headed our way. He was always over-the-top dramatic with his predictions. "Ready your johnboats and gas up your motors," he added. "Be wise. Like Noah."

By the time the song "Take Me to Harlan" finished, I had studied the restraining order against me. One thing was clear. Our good sheriff had been influenced by a sleazy woman, a former prison guard who was worse than any of the ex-cons now in Sweetbriar. A basically good man could sometimes be totally dense.

My room darkened even more, and I moved to my window to peer at the sky. The clouds looked as dark as a smudge of charcoal, and the air had turned into a greenish twilight. Rain splashed onto the already soaked front lawn and beat onto the water-filled street beyond. I left my room and headed down the hallway that led to the main house. It seemed all the residents were coming out of their rooms to gather there as well.

The grandfather clock in the foyer struck eleven. Wind swept great sheets of water against the tall dining room windows.

"Reminds me of the time I was stuck in the middle of a car-wash, don'tcha know," Smiley said as he came alongside me. I reached for his hand and held it.

Lightning flashed around us, followed by a boom that rattled the windowpanes. "That was close," I said as we moved into the center of the dining room.

Shirley gathered flashlights out of the kitchen pantry and passed them out in case we lost our power.

Jack burst through the front door clutching a drenched Mr. Lively close to his side. The door banged against the wall before anyone could grab it. We pushed it shut against the wind as rainwater streamed from Jack's cowboy hat and Mr. Lively's raincoat.

"Had to detour to get here from the hospital," Jack said. "You would think they could've kept him one more day. Some of the low-lying streets are already flooding. Good thing I had the produce truck or we wouldn't've made it."

I ran to the laundry room and returned with an armful of clean towels. Mr. Lively sank onto a bench, leaned back against the wall, and shut his eyes. "Take your coat off," I said. "You'll catch your death." He opened his eyes and glared at me, but obeyed. I hung his coat on a hook and handed him a towel.

Jack removed his boots and sopped up puddles of water before grabbing a fresh towel to dry his long hair as best he could. "A giant pine tree's down across Main. And the streets are lookin' like creeks rushin' through town. I ain't leaving 'til this is over."

"Something hot is what you both need," Shirley said as she linked her arm through Jack's. "Chicken tortilla soup's on the stove."

I enlisted Lollipop, and we helped Mr. Lively to his feet. But he pushed us away. "I'm perfectly fine. Now that I've recovered from Jack driving through water like a madman."

We all turned away and left our administrator alone in the foyer. He looked like a soggy, irate blowfish.

The rain never slacked off. After lunch we spent the afternoon looking out windows, pacing the floor, and wondering when the storm would end.

Francesca spent her time looking at her tarot cards. That night around the supper table she maneuvered her wheelchair closer to William. Her face was as pale as wallpaper paste as she wrung her hands together. "Something terrible is going to happen," she said as she glanced around. "I feel it in my bones, and I've seen it in my cards. You've been forewarned."

After her pronouncement of doom, the lights flickered, and nearly everyone stood with flashlights in hand. Fortunately, the electric held fast. A collective sigh rose above us.

"I'm headed to bed, Sis," Smiley said after it seemed things had settled down somewhat. "Let's walk down the hallway together. I'm not locking my door in case you should need me before this night is over. Francesca's given me the willies."

Worry lines had settled across his forehead. He slipped his

arm around my shoulder, pulling me close. He felt shaky and cold as I leaned into him.

We made it as far as the foyer. Mr. Lively stood at the head of the stairs waving his arms. "Get some pots. Pans. Anything. Roof's leaking like a sieve."

William, Jack, Shirley, and I moved as fast as we could. Soon, the half dozen or so leaks sounded like a percussion street band in Mr. Lively's living quarters.

"I'll never get any sleep with this racket," he said.

"Put your newfangled *Alisha* next to your ear. And you'd best set an alarm to empty the water before it overflows," Shirley said.

"It's *Alexia*." He huffed. "This old place needs a new roof, among other things."

"Humph," I grumbled to Charlie. "A new administrator is what we need."

We left Mr. Lively sitting in his recliner with his flashlight beside him and *Dancing with The Stars* blaring on his television set.

Startled awake in the early morning darkness, thunder boomed like cannons and shook my bed. Rain lashed against the panes as lightning seemed to dance around my room. How long was this storm going to last? Someone opened my bedroom door.

"Momma? I'm scared," Pearl whispered as she scurried to my bedside in another bright flash. Wearing a granny gown and clutching a stuffed turtle to her chest, her long white hair floated around her like cobwebs. I threw the covers back and patted the bed.

"Come sleep with me. I'm scared too."

"You are?" She crawled in and settled her trembling, lanky frame as close to me as she could. When I scooted away to have some breathing room, she moved closer until I ended up on the edge.

Maybe she would relax some if I could take her mind off the storm. I sat up in bed before I fell off of it. "Tell me everything about the art show you and Smiley are planning. Isn't it on a Saturday in late May? Have you chosen a place? Can people buy some of your pieces? You've had an abundance of new canvases and paints recently delivered from Amazon."

Like flipping a switch in her brain, the subject of the up-coming art show did the trick. She sat up and faced me. "You will come, won't you? Mr. Lively says we're foolish to proceed when nobody will be there."

I reached over and took her hand. "Don't listen to him. You're an accomplished artist plus a good teacher. Who would've thought Smiley had one creative bone in his body? You're the one who brought that to light."

Her bony shoulders drooped. "But what if no one comes?"

"Your friends at the Manor will, and I'll bet the Hope Women will too. I'll ask Dee to read some of her poetry. That should add a spark to the show. What do you think?"

"Oh my," Pearl whispered as she gazed into space. "That would be lovely."

The rain continued to pour. I thought of Ralph, the weatherman, and his predictions. Sweetbriar Manor didn't own a johnboat—or any other kind of a boat for that matter.

"I'm going back home now," Pearl said. "To paint."

"But you have weeks before the show."

"I need to paint. Now." In an instant she was on the move and headed to her room next door.

It was only four o'clock, but I was wide-awake. Maybe Smiley was awake too. I slipped out of bed, grabbed my chenille robe, and went to find out.

In the hallway I ran into Dee as she stumbled through the back door with a towel-wrapped Pepper in her arms. "Ain't that the fieriest storm ever?" She clutched the whimpering poodle closer to her chest. "Not fit for man or beast?" Her hair dripped rainwater down her long blue strands.

"Wait here." I ran into my bathroom and quickly returned with a towel. I handed it to her. "Looks like you need this worse than Pepper."

I held the little dog while she dried off, patting her hair and face. A drop of water glistened on her eyebrow ring. Then she removed her raincoat and let it fall onto the rug while she dried her legs and kicked off her soaked wedge-heeled sandals. After surviving a fire and now a flood, the shoes looked as if they might fall apart. But it was her coat that drew my eyes back to it. Hadn't the homeless man said the person he saw the night of the fire wore a coat with a hood? And the person's frame was small. Like Dee's.

She picked up her coat before she took Pepper from me. "You wouldn't do your business outside, so it's puddle pads for you. Let's go before you make a mess." She took off running down the hall.

I picked up my towel and headed to the laundry room, located in the big house near the kitchen. Since Dee had joined us, we now rotated laundry duty. She had pitched a pure hissy fit when she saw her name on the list, but after I told her she had to pull her weight or leave the Manor, she settled down.

Except for Nellie and Smiley, Dee didn't mix with the other residents at Sweetbriar Manor. She had made friends with Blind George, the only person in town who would hire her. He said the townspeople, including me, were prejudiced against the women who had served time, and he felt they deserved a chance.

The sharp lightning had subsided, but the rain continued to hammer the roof with no sign of slacking off. I hurried toward Smiley's room.

I tapped on his door, and he opened it, barefoot and clad in red-striped pajamas. "Did ya ever see such a storm? Used to sit on our front porch swing with my daddy and watch 'em, but you wouldn't catch me out in this one."

"How about some hot tea?" I asked.

"Give me a minute to dress. The Manor's full of women these days."

"Only one more than usual, but I know what you mean. Maybe I was too hasty to open our home to Dee. Everything and everyone seems unsettled. Makes me grumpy and out of sorts. I'll rest easier when all the Hope Women have moved to their own place."

"You don't think Dee is guilty do ya?"

"No proof that arson was ever committed, but the cause of the fire hasn't been officially announced. The sheriff thinks she might be into drugs, and maybe she was cooking meth in the basement. But apparently there's not enough evidence to arrest her."

"We can talk over our tea. Suits us, don'tcha know."

I leaned over and kissed him. Squarely on his lips. Took him by surprise, don'tcha know. I scooted off toward the kitchen to wait for him there.

The dining room was over half filled with others who apparently couldn't sleep. William sipped on a mug of coffee and nodded a greeting. Francesca stuck her nose in the air and avoided any eye contact with me. This would not do. We were supposed to be friends. I marched over and planted myself in front of her.

"We would miss you and William if you left us," I said as I retied my robe sash.

Francesca huffed. "But not Her Majesty."

"Perhaps Miss Margaret will add the right ingredient," I said as calmly as possible.

"Pepper is the problem, not to mention an ex-con living with crazy Nellie. Now I keep Willy's door locked. Things have changed around here, and I don't like it."

"One day we'll look back at this time and wish we could relive it."

"I doubt that."

"Just remember the chaos we're living through right now is temporary. Dee and Pepper will be gone in less than two weeks, and our lives will settle down." I hoped this was true, as well as Mr. Lively's exit. Even with all of his irritating ways, I wished him no ill.

"Two weeks? Not soon enough to suit me." Francesca turned and wheeled herself toward William.

Mr. Lively appeared by my side. "Looks like you've gotten yourself into a predicament. Animals running wild, a female criminal taking up residence, and now we're drug infested. I heard what the sheriff found." He picked lint off his red suspenders before stooping to my eye level. "What do you intend to do about it? You should've never allowed pets here in the first place. It all started with that silly pig of yours. Plus, you should've never allowed Dee to move in. She's nothing but bad news and probably stashed her drugs in your room. You've got to set some boundaries or the whole world will take advantage." His bug eyes reflected my frazzled red curls before he rose to his full height.

"Exactly," I said, thinking he was the one who needed boundaries. "First off, for your information, Miss Margaret is the most sensible, refined animal I know." I thrust back my shoulders and lifted my chin. "Maybe if she visited more often, the other two animals would calm down. And as far as Dee is concerned? I had my doubts at first, but then I followed my heart, which included my Charlie's advice."

"That kind of reasoning is the most ridiculous thing I've heard yet. Why not invite the whole zoo and include every homeless jailbird while you're at it?"

"Why not indeed? Thank you for your suggestion."

His bulging eyes grew bigger as his shaggy eyebrows twitched. Mr. Lively had unknowingly planted a seed. Miss Margaret's presence would help, but maybe a large, older dog would help even more. Like the ones we had on the farm. Such a dog wouldn't be intimidated by Her Majesty. But how could I find one? Hmmm . . . maybe the local animal shelter had the perfect one. As far as Dee and Pepper, I would miss them both when they left us. I might also miss Mr. Lively. Sure I would. Like a throbbing sinus headache.

Shirley swooshed through the kitchen door and into the dining room, releasing the aroma of bacon frying and biscuits browning in the oven. She carried her small battery-powered radio, placed it on a nearby table, fiddled with the dial and turned up the volume. Our local weatherman expounded in his usual dramatic fashion. In the past, we had given him little attention, but this morning our chatter ceased as we focused on his voice.

"The Sugarcane River, to the north of Sweetbriar, not to mention the Dixon River to our west, are approaching flood stage rapidly. Folks, I'm predicting the flood of the century. Heavy rains in the upstate have turned innocent creeks and streams into roaring torrents, and it's headed our way. By this time tomorrow, many of our low-lying neighborhoods in Sweetbriar, especially the one we call The Bottom, will have water rushing into every crevice it can find. Unless you live on high ground, you must leave. By four o'clock this afternoon. The mayor has issued a mandatory evacuation for anyone living in The Bottom, or near it, as well as those who live downtown, or near it. Leave now."

"Meet back here in ten minutes," I announced. Everyone scurried to their rooms to pack a few belongings or valuables in case the situation worsened and we also had to evacuate. Better to be prepared now rather than sorry later.

Since Sweetbriar Manor rested on a higher elevation than the rest of town, people started showing up at our door. Using his work truck, Jack carried Juanita and her toddler, as well as three other people who lived in The Bottom to the safety of our home. Mr. Case refused to leave his produce business, but he sent baskets of strawberries, blueberries, bananas, broccoli, potatoes, and onions. His wife sent her blackberry cake with caramel icing, a blue ribbon winner every year at the county fair.

Next came the sheriff, his deputy, and a scruffy man in handcuffs—who was promptly attached to a dining room chair. In the middle of all the confusion, Betty Jo called my cell. "Water's nearly up to the bridge coming into town," she said. "We're staying put."

"Absolutely. Your neighborhood never floods."

"Be careful who you take in for shelter. Some people will take advantage. I hope you realize the danger."

"The sheriff's here," I said. "And the deputy. We should be safe." The phone buzzed a most irritating sound.

"You're breaking up," Betty Jo yelled. "What did you say about the sheriff? Did he say you're not safe? What did he—"

The phone died as the front doorbell chimed and kept on chiming. I hurried through the foyer and threw open the door. A small group of dripping people pushed their way inside, including Irene who caught my eye and said, "I know I'm not wanted here, but I had no choice." The rose tattoo on her neck quivered.

For once in my life I was speechless. We stared at each other for a long moment. Not wanted? That was an understatement.

CHAPTER EIGHTEEN

Months ago, I had been the one to expose Irene's scheme to blackmail former convicts to steal for her boyfriend's business, the Last Chance Pawnshop that had eventually become the Hope House. She certainly had reason enough to hate me, even though her part in their plans hadn't been proven. Irene walked away free, but her boyfriend, Boss, had also committed a more serious crime. He killed a homeless man, Josiah Goforth, for his valuable bagpipes. That's what I was able to prove. Another powerful reason to hate me. And here she was standing in my home.

"Of all the nerve," Francesca said as she flounced in her chair. "Don't you know how to move on when things don't go your way? You have no business here. Nothing legitimate, that is."

I couldn't have said it better myself. "I don't suppose you had anything to do with the sheriff serving me with a restraining order or drugs showing up in my room," I said.

"Ridiculous," Irene said. "Our sheriff's a smart man without any help from me."

"Sheriff Caywood's a good man, but sometimes he can be as blind and as deaf as a piece of lighter knot," I said.

"You'll soon find out I'm right when he makes an arres . . ." Irene closed her mouth, turned away, and removed her wet raincoat.

"What's your scheme this time?" I asked as I followed her over to the coatrack. "You have something brewing or you wouldn't be hanging around town. I guess you're glad the House of Hope burned, aren't you?"

"No need for you to know what makes me happy," the woman said with a smirk as she hung her raincoat on the row of crowded hooks. She lifted her chin and slipped into the shadowy dining room.

"What's happening, Sis?" Smiley asked as he shuffled up beside me.

I dug in my purse and latched on to my funeral home fan to cool my face. Why had Irene appeared back in Sweetbriar? Did she have anything to do with the fire? Or nothing? She seemed to be on the inside track with the sheriff. I felt sure she planted the drugs in my room and instigated the restraining order. But how could I prove it?

More people appeared at our door including Blind George lugging two large coolers. "Enough hot dogs, buns, chili, and slaw for the whole town," he said with a grin. His cleaning lady followed carrying a large kettle. The lid danced as she walked, releasing the aroma of boiled peanuts. William rushed over and relieved her of her heavy load.

I was looking forward to lunch but hoped we didn't end up sheltering the entire town. With Shirley's directives, the women took charge of the kitchen and dining room. Dee worked alongside Blind George, and they made an efficient team.

Irene had vanished, so I opened every unlocked bedroom door and stuck my head inside. I had to keep an eye on that woman or find someone who could. I was stunned when she stepped into the hallway closing a door behind her. Nellie and Dee's room. "What do you think you're doing?" I demanded as I rushed forward and blocked her way.

"Looking for Dee. Have you seen her? The sheriff thinks she's a flight risk."

Before I could answer, Irene scooted away toward the main house, her oversized body quivering in her haste. A lame excuse. Dee was in the kitchen helping George. She wasn't trying to hide or run away, and I was certain our sheriff was aware.

I caught up to Irene as she stood near the front door talking to Hershel. When she spotted me, she turned and scooted away. But not before I heard her mention Dee's name. *Lord, help us,* I prayed. *Only you know what is going on.*

I walked over to the sheriff. He pulled a poncho over his uniform and secured a plastic cover over his hat before he glanced my way. "Deputy's in charge of our prisoner. I've got to make sure everyone evacuates the low areas. Sometimes old folks are stubborn and won't leave. Governor's sending in the National Guard, but they ain't here yet."

I nodded. No time for questions.

He tipped his hat and left in the blowing rain as our lights flickered and then went out. I reached for my flashlight and headed toward the pantry and Shirley's stash of candles and matches.

In the dining room, the emergency signal blared from the small radio before Ralph made another announcement. "Listen up, folks. Water is threatening to breach the Turner Dam by five o'clock this afternoon. If the dam doesn't hold, Main Street will be flooded in less than fifteen minutes. Leave now while you can. Get to the Interstate where all lanes will move north. Go at least as far as Pinewood where shelters will be waiting for you. Mayor Phillips will speak in two minutes. In the meantime, get out of Dodge."

Shirley and I placed a candle, rooted in quart jars of sand, on each table with William and Smiley's help. When all the candles were lit, the dining room glowed.

I turned to Smiley. "Since Sweetbriar Manor sits on a knoll above town, we should stay put. Right?" I kept my voice low and my lips close to his ear.

He shrugged. "Only the Lord knows, Sis."

"Yes indeed." I gazed into those dark brown eyes. "Only I wish He would share his knowledge of what we should do."

William ran inside saying his beloved taxi wouldn't start and would be ruined by the floodwaters.

"Call Mike," I suggested. "Maybe he can get it over to his garage and put it on a lift."

When Mike didn't answer his phone, William ignored Francesca's protests and sprinted toward his car parked along the street. He disappeared into sheets of rain blowing sideways.

I called the mayor's office and asked to speak to him. Louise said he was too busy saving important papers, plus their computers, from the impending flood to talk and had left her in command.

"Call the Stagecoach Express. Now," I said. "Anyone stranded in Sweetbriar has to have a way out of here."

"They're on their way momentarily," she said and hung up. She had taken charge, but I hoped she knew what she was talking about.

Jack had convinced the First Baptist pastor to hand him the keys to the church van, which he then used to pick up the rest of the Hope Women and some people I had never seen before. He deposited the motley bunch and left to return the van. A crowd formed in front of the tall dining room windows. We watched the rain sweep across the front lawn. Within the last hour, the number of people inside the Manor had mushroomed. I refused to dwell on our precarious situation, yet my insides trembled and wouldn't stop. I reached for Smiley and pulled him closer. He slipped his arm around me.

"Take a deep breath, Sis. The Lord's got this."

Nearly everyone had arrived carrying a suitcase or a shopping bag or two stuffed with pictures and papers, or some trinkets suddenly considered valuable, all grabbed in haste. Everyone was drenched to the bone. The wet bodies—including dripping hair, clothes, umbrellas, and shoes—sent the humidity to a smothering level. The lot of us stank worse than a soggy dog.

Pearl entered the dining room with two of her paintings tucked under her arms plus a paper grocery bag full of art supplies. She looked like a refugee boarding a tiny boat to cross rough seas for an unknown land. I made my way over to her and convinced her to rest her possessions on the floor.

"Where are we going? Is there something I need to know?" she asked in a whispery voice. Her body shook as if she stood in the middle of a blizzard, and her bracelets jingled like tiny tambourines.

"We'll be dry and safe right where we are." I tried to reassure her as I slipped my arm around her waist. She felt as stiff as a pair of starched jeans. Shirley appeared with a blanket. We wrapped it around Pearl's bony frame, then Shirley led her to the kitchen for a cup of hot tea while I found a place for her valuables in the foyer.

Returning to the dining room, I caught a glimpse of an old school bus outside on the street below as it limped its way past the Manor and disappeared toward town in the driving rain. I prayed for whomever was evacuating Sweetbriar on that thing.

Shirley reminded everyone to deposit their bundles against a wall near the front door where we could easily grab them in case we had to leave in a hurry. No one knew for sure if we could stay put or not. I remembered the picture of Charlie sitting in my room. How could I have forgotten him? I hurried down the hallway. When I opened my door, Irene stood there thumbing through my granny's Bible.

"Get out!" I yelled as I swung my purse her way.

She dropped the Bible and fled. Perhaps she had been looking for another place to stash some drugs.

I rescued my Bible from the floor and Charlie from my chest of drawers, then grabbed my purse and dashed back out of my room. I hoped the sheriff would show up soon. He had some explaining to do about that awful woman.

After William rescued his beloved taxi by helping Mike raise it on a lift, he returned with a big grin on his face, even though he looked like he had been fished out of the river.

Francesca rolled toward him. "Didn't I tell you a disaster was coming? All of Sweetbriar will be swept into the flood-waters and swallowed up. Everything will disappear. Even your taxi." She glanced at her fiancée as he rushed past us.

"Dry clothes," he said as he headed to his room.

"Sorry, dear," she added, raising her voice to his departure. "I know you love that rattletrap, but it's true." She flounced around and peered out the window. "Mark my words." She pulled a bunched fleece robe toward her chest as Her Majesty peered out and meowed a pitiful cry.

Pearl came to me again and tugged on my sleeve. "What's happening?" she asked. "Tell me."

"We're in a safe place. You have my word." I tried to smile, but failed miserably. My anxiety rose like a tsunami washing me out to sea. The mayor and his secretary appeared next, bringing along restraining-order Lucy and her obstinate nephew, who had been rescued from the rising waters. Terry huffed his way to the dining room and flopped into a chair where he fished a pocketknife out of his jeans. He proceeded to open and shut the knife in jerking motions. The sheriff's pris-oner, sitting across from the boy, leaned closer. The deputy walked over to Terry with his hand out. The knife was given over, but not willingly.

"You got anything else in them pockets?" Deputy Larry asked.

Terry shrugged.

"Let's see it. All of it."

Another knife was tossed onto the table, then a crumbled five-dollar bill, some change, and two cigarette lighters. I moved closer to get a better look. The lighters looked similar to the one I'd found at the scene of the fire. Old, maybe vintage, with flip tops.

Larry asked Shirley for a plastic bag, then dropped the knives and lighters into it.

"You got no right to take my knives," Terry said. "And those lighters belong to my Aunt Lucy. She's gonna be madder'n heck when she finds out."

"Behave yourself, and you might get them back when you return home," the deputy said as he turned to Mr. Lively and asked him to lock the bag in his office, which he did.

I squeezed Smiley's arm and prayed for the good Lord to watch over us. I needed the sheriff to return. Soon. Had Terry started the Hope House fire with one of those lighters? But why would he? And didn't he ride an old bicycle that rattled and shook and had loose spokes? Plus, Terry and his bike fit the homeless man's description of what he had seen and heard. Oh my. We needed mercy in abundance.

The mayor's squeaky shoes announced his presence that bristled with irritation. He leaned his scrunched-up face over to mine. "Why did you let those women come here? You're not responsible for them," he said out of the corner of his mouth. He nodded toward the foyer where four Hope women huddled together.

"You've never wanted them in Sweetbriar, have you?" I asked as I rubbed a crick in my neck.

"Nothing but trouble since they came, even before your protest parade. Tourists have second thoughts about visiting our town that used to be a favorite vacation spot. Do you realize the economic repercussions? Next thing we know, the newspapers will be full of a supposed arsonist on the loose, even if there isn't one." He shook his head. "You didn't want them here either, but you've managed to take one of them into your home and rescue all of them from a flood, besides finding them a permanent place to live. Whose side are you on anyway?"

His squinty eyes bore holes into me as I straightened myself to my full height. He must've learned of the Ancient Oak Apartments. I was certain he would try to block that possibility.

Smiley came closer and leaned to my good ear. "No use arguing with him, Sis. He has a heart of stone to match his name, don'tcha know."

"I heard that," the mayor said with a scowl. "I'm looking after the welfare of our town. Which is something Agnes Hopper has no concept of doing. Sweetbriar will become a haven for criminals, and the good citizens will all move away. Far away."

"Didn't I warn you from the beginning?" Francesca said as Stone Phillips huffed away from us in a total snit.

"Happy Halloween!" I shouted, throwing my hands into the air. Shirley's favorite frustrated expression suited exactly how I felt at the moment.

I headed to the kitchen to see if I could help Shirley put our next meal together, for it seemed as if half of Sweetbriar had descended on us to feed and shelter them. For once I was thankful Deputy Larry was performing his duties like a professional by keeping watch over Terry, even though Lucy loudly protested.

Shirley, George, and three of the Hope women had things under control in the kitchen. George had brought his hot dogs cooked, inside their buns, and wrapped in aluminum foil. He lifted several dozen from one of the large coolers, the foil still warm to the touch. Large bowls of slaw and chips sat on the kitchen island as well as a fruit salad made from Mr. Case's produce. "Maybe this food will hold us for a while," I whispered to Charlie.

I breathed a sigh of relief as a line of quiet and subdued people entered the kitchen to fill their plates. William offered a prayer of thanksgiving. While he prayed, I heard and felt a rush of air. I looked up. The back door stood open. Nellie, and Dee with Pepper in her arms, had slipped out into the torrential rain. What could they be thinking? I ran to the door and hollered, but the storm swallowed my voice. Nellie squealed as she darted through water pouring over a gutter. Pepper twisted out of Dee's arms and disappeared into the overgrown lot next door. The women chased after the poodle as I pushed the door shut against the swirling wetness.

"Well," Francesca said. "We got rid of those troublemakers. Right, Her Majesty?"

William grabbed his raincoat. "I'll go get 'em. Save my seat, sweetie."

Before Francesca could protest, he hurried outside, stabbing his arms into his coat sleeves as he ran. In the next instant, Irene followed him. "I know how to handle women like those two," she muttered.

What did she mean by *handle*?

"Hey, pretty lady," the prisoner yelled from the dining room. "Bring me some food. I'm starving out here." He probably meant Shirley, but she was busy. Since I couldn't do anything to help catch a runaway dog or the two women chasing him or the two chasing them, I fixed him a plate. I had totally forgotten about this man chained to a dining room chair. Lucy and her nephew were bent over their plates at the far end of the table.

"Reckon you'll do," the prisoner said, diving into his food.

"Didn't your mother teach you any manners?"

He looked at me with a full mouth and a blank expression.

"The magic words?" I asked, thinking it might jog a long-forgotten time when he was a boy.

He swallowed and gulped his water before ducking his head to his plate once again.

"If you could remember those words, I might be inclined to bring you some dessert before it's all gone."

He looked up. "I'm sorry. Thank you. And please. That good enough?"

Terry snickered, but I ignored him.

"It's a start. Jam cake with caramel icing coming up shortly."

He grinned so wide I could see he was nearly toothless.

"Make that two pieces," Larry called out from across the room. He leaned on the doorframe picking his teeth.

"Seems you're able-bodied enough," I said. He'd rushed to the front of the lunch line earlier pushing others out of his way.

I returned from the kitchen with one piece of cake and set it before the prisoner. I was preoccupied with worries about the ones running around in the storm of the century. "Our situation can't get much worse," I grumbled to Charlie.

No sooner had I groused than a deafening thud hit the front porch. The house shook violently. The windows clattered, followed by splintered wood and shattered glass. An enormous tree had ripped through the front of our house. The antique door, or what was left of it, lay in the foyer underneath an oak that both Henry and Mr. Lively had warned me about. Had in fact urged me to have it removed.

Those of us in the dining room seemed to be rooted to the floor as we stared at the quivering tree and the pile of rubble surrounding it. The hole in our house revealed the tree had smashed through a section of porch roof before it hit the door and kept coming.

People in the kitchen rushed out to see what had happened. No one seemed to notice the grandfather clock teetering back and forth until Jack flew past us, jumped over the tree, and grabbed the old gentleman. Jack's stiff leg hadn't stopped him from springing into action. He steadied the clock and stopped the weights from clanging about.

One disaster averted, but a loud debate arose over what should be done about the missing front door—not to mention the tree. A heavy mist from the rain swirled into the foyer. If only we had a large tarp to nail over the gaping hole. Suddenly, I knew something that should work. I turned to Mr. Lively. He surprised me by agreeing we had no other choice. He raced upstairs.

Jack appeared, dripping wet and holding a chain saw from the tool shed. After pulling its cord again and again, it roared to life and spewed smoke, which cleared out most everyone in a hurry. I quickly closed the dining room doors. As soon as the surgery was completed, Blind George, Jack, and the deputy dragged the enormous logs outside to the porch.

I grabbed two good-sized raincoats from the wall hooks and gave orders to the mayor and to Lucy's nephew, Terry. With a nod of approval from the deputy, they headed for the potting shed out back and returned with push brooms, a leaf rake, and a shovel, then started cleaning up the mess. They groused over my directives, but they bent to the task.

Shirley brought me her toolbox as Mr. Lively thumped down the steps with his brand new sealskin covering, still in its original package. Before his accident, he had planned to use it to protect his convertible in the old garage behind the house. He and George unfolded it and held it up over the door opening. I scrounged around in the toolbox and uncovered a box of nails. When Shirley found a hammer and a stepladder, the men got to work.

Mr. Lively said he couldn't watch any longer. He shook his head and mumbled, "Expensive, and now it's ruined before I got to use it." He left to take a *nerve pill.* After his accident, Mike had towed the convertible to his shop and vowed to fix what should have been totaled. If the car could ever be driven again it would have to have a new cover, which I was certain had been the best of the best.

Why had a selfish, irritating man like Mr. Lively stepped up to protect our home when he couldn't wait to leave it for greener pastures?

Smiley nudged me. "Sis? Looks like everything's under control here. Come out to the kitchen. You need to eat a bite of lunch."

My stomach agreed. I had forgotten about food. I felt the comfort of his hand against the small of my back as we walked through the dining room. I stopped to share my thoughts with him about Mr. Lively.

Smiley looked at me for a long moment. "All his bluster is a cover-up so he can keep his distance. I would bet he's holding on to a secret that's eating at him, and for some reason he can't share it."

I considered what my best friend had just said as I stepped closer. "Have I ever told you how much I appreciate your insight?" Even if I didn't always agree with it. "The information he refuses to share is the identity of his *sugar*, who is obviously why he took money from petty cash."

We moved into the kitchen. Smiley lifted his baseball cap and scratched his head. "You got me there, Sis. What happened to his claim someone else stole the money and he'd find out who done it?"

"Oh, he found out all right. He accused someone who doesn't have a dishonest bone in her body. All because of money she found stuffed in her easel tray."

Smiley stumbled over his own feet, which he was prone to do, and I reached out to keep him upright. "Ahhh, Sis, you mean he pointed the finger at Pearl?" He studied his sandals before raising his head.

"You look mighty pale." I searched his face. "Are you all right?"

"Fit as a fiddle." He gave a half smile, and his voice sounded a bit shaky. One thing was certain. Whenever this man gazed into my eyes with his big brown ones, like at this moment, he stole my breath without another word passing between us.

I gave him a quick hug. Mr. Lively might always remain a puzzlement. He had denied stealing from petty cash and had accused Pearl. Impossible. But who could have taken it? Maybe I would never know.

I climbed onto a stool at the kitchen island while Smiley filled my plate. The sound and aroma of coffee perking on the gas stovetop brought back memories of early mornings with Charlie on our farm. Eggs and bacon, biscuits and gravy, and two cups of strong coffee after milking our three sweet and gentle Jerseys. Seemed like a lifetime ago. I would forever miss my Charlie, but he wouldn't want me to curl up and stop living. I gazed at the good man who cared enough to make sure I would eat something. Would he ever pop the question? Had he even thought about it lately? Seemed like I was going to have to take charge and do it myself. But I didn't know what I would do if he turned me down.

William stumbled through the back door and slammed it shut. He peeled off his raincoat as he shook his head. "No sign of the women or the dog. Like they disappeared. Vanished."

CHAPTER NINETEEN

Francesca wheeled into the kitchen. William poured himself a cup of freshly perked coffee while Smiley and I devoured our hot dog lunch. Francesca lifted a pink fleece bundle from her lap, unrolled Her Majesty to the floor, and tossed her robe to William. "Put this on," she ordered. "You'll catch your death." The cat zipped out of the kitchen. William did as she said and tied the sash across his ample chest. I slipped my phone out and took his picture while swallowing a giggle.

"Did you realize our front yard looks like a war zone?" William asked. "A real mess. Uprooted oaks, snapped pines, and tangled limbs scattered all over the place." He swept out a pink robed arm for emphasis.

"Yep. Took out our front door too, like it was nothing," Smiley said.

"Never liked that door in the first place," Francesca said. "Remember when "Dixie" blared forth whenever it was opened? I'll have to say, Agnes, that's one thing you did right when you disconnected that most annoying tune." She lifted her chin and circled her long stranded pearls in the air.

"Humph," I grumbled to Charlie. "She just dished out a backhanded compliment."

Her voice rose in excitement as she turned to William and embellished the scene of a tree smashing into our house. "You've got to see it," she added as she led William away to show him the damage.

"Nothing like a disaster to make that woman happy," I said to Smiley.

He shook his head. "You got that right, Sis."

He gathered our paper plates, tidied up the island, and poured us some coffee before returning to his stool. We sipped a bit in silence.

Silence? We looked at each other before rushing to the

window over the sink. The rain had stopped. Totally. Water dripped from the house eaves and the back porch bannister. It streamed across the patio, but nothing poured from the sky or pounded our roof. Was the storm of the century over or had it paused only to start up again? Low, dark clouds didn't look encouraging.

Moments later, the back door fell open. Dee stumbled inside as the deputy popped into the kitchen from the dining room.

"Thought you'd escape didja?" Deputy Larry said with a sneer. "Can't fool me. Sit and don't move." He touched his stun gun as if to make sure it was still there.

Dee sank onto a barstool and sobbed into her hands. Shirley appeared with a scowl for Larry and a large bath towel. She wrapped it around Dee's shoulders before disappearing inside the kitchen pantry with a flashlight. "I know I've got a bag of potatoes in here somewhere," she said.

"What happened?" I asked as I poured Dee a cup of coffee.

"Pepper's run off. Nellie too. Couldn't find 'em nowhere."

"Irene's like a hound dog after a coon," Larry said. "She'll bring Nellie back for certain, but my boss said to keep an eye on you, missy, and that's what I'm aiming to do. Might as well forget about that yippy dog of yours. You'll never see that thing again."

Dee clinched her fists and jumped up, but the deputy blocked her and pushed her back down. Her face looked like a thundercloud. "You don't scare me none."

"Law's on my side, and you got to have some respect."

"Tell me what happened," I said as I gave Larry a fierce glare and then turned my back on him. "Why did you and Nellie leave the house?"

"Nellie said the old garage out back had a dirt floor that would probably still be dry since the driveway leading to it goes uphill. Pepper hadn't done his business proper since this rain started. Not acting like his self at all. Most likely constipated. That's when Nellie said we could make a run for the garage. But Pepper slipped away from us and disappeared. We could hear him barking, close at first then far off somewhere."

"Where was Irene?"

"Irene? I never seen her. Hard to see with rain in your face. Maybe she's caught up to Nellie by now. But Pepper? You reckon he'll find his way back?"

I nodded. "I think you can count on it." Would Nellie and Irene return? Or had they been swept away in the rising floodwaters?

Sure enough, the sky darkened, and the rain turned into another downpour. The wind swirled and howled. A loud, heavy thud hit the ground. The house shook. Dishes rattled in the cabinets. Surely, another oak or the top of a tall pine had fallen.

"Our whole house is bound to be hit. We're doomed," Francesca said as she rolled out of the kitchen.

"You're not helping the situation one bit," William said, following behind her.

I had never heard him speak to his sweetie like that before.

Someone sobbed nearby. I turned and wrapped my arms around Pearl.

"I'm scared," she said.

I pulled her closer and gently rubbed her back. "I know you are. But we're going to be all right."

Shirley saved the day when she poked her head out of the pantry. "Pearl, help me find some jars of canned tomatoes. Bring your flashlight."

Larry led Dee into the dining room. I fixed her a fresh cup of coffee and followed them. He sat her at the same table with the man handcuffed to his chair. The room was full of people milling about or clustered in tight groups. Somehow, Terry had managed to slip out of sight.

The mayor continued to grumble and complain. I had taken just about enough. I stood up. "Let's sing a song," I said in a loud voice. "But before we do, let's pray for Irene, Nellie, and Pepper to find their way back. The good Lord knows where they are even though we don't. Pray harder than you've ever prayed before. Let's hold hands and bow our heads."

In our silence, the rain pounded harder than ever, yet I felt the Lord's presence among us.

William stood and cleared his throat. "Good afternoon, Lord. As you know, we're in somewhat of a mess down here. We need your help. Show Nellie and Irene how to find us, and that little pup too. Lead them to safety just like you took old Moses across the Red Sea. Amen."

Shouts of "Amen!" and "Hallelujah!" flew around us. I didn't know William had the soul of a preacher in him until now. Maybe he didn't know it either.

"Thank you," I said as I looked up into the face of this barrel-chested man still wearing Francesca's pink robe. She beamed from her wheelchair. For once she kept quiet.

I looked around and clapped my hands to get everyone's attention again. "Now, let's sing."

"How about this one?" Smiley said, then began to sing "It Is Well with My Soul."

We lifted our voices loud and clear. Everyone sang, even the prisoner who directed with his one free hand. William's deep voice boomed during the refrain, and I'll have to say we sounded as good as a tent revival meeting.

A strong gust of wind pushed against Mr. Lively's car cover nailed over the door opening. Would it hold? Our singing made a slight pause before we continued, louder than before. It was a sweet time sitting in a torrential rainstorm, the likes of which I hadn't seen since I was a girl on our farm in Kentucky. That spring our pigs, chickens, and tobacco crop all floated down the river, swept away never to be seen again. When the singing ended, I shared my memories with Smiley. "My daddy never got over losing everything, and we ended up having to sell the farm." Tears slid down my cheeks. "I miss him more now than ever. He was a good, hard-working man."

Smiley pulled out a folded handkerchief from his pants pocket and dried my face. Then he put his arm around me and pulled me to his side. His Old Spice had worn thin, but that didn't matter. I nuzzled my face against his soft neck.

"We keep our loved ones in our hearts, don'tcha know. Always with you that way." He squeezed me so tight I couldn't move even if I'd wanted to.

Francesca huffed. "Well, if you ask me—"

"No one did," William said. And that was the end of that.

Smiley straightened himself and looked into my face. "We're going to be okay. I guarantee it. As sure as you and I have been friends since the first day we met. Am I right?"

"Exactly."

Irene sloshed into the dining room from the kitchen. Alone. She looked as if she'd been pulled from a raging river and dragged up a muddy bank. She smelled like a swamp. Her clothes were pasted to her large frame, and her scalp shone through her plastered hair.

"Couldn't . . . couldn't find . . ." She bent over with her hands on her knees to catch her breath. We waited. The rain sounded like a pounding waterfall. Bad news was surely coming.

Irene held on to the back of a chair and pushed herself upright. "Nellie's gone. Heard a scream down by Main Street that's now a churning river. Full of branches and all sorts of yard trash. Spotted a work boot, a lawn chair, and two cats bobbing along. Not a sign of Nellie or that pup that started all this."

"No!" Dee yelled out. She jumped up and shook a fist at Irene. "She's out there somewhere and so is Pepper. We can't stop looking. We can't."

Before anyone moved or spoke, the back door banged against the kitchen wall. We moved toward the noise as Nellie staggered into the kitchen. An over-sized lump wiggled underneath the raincoat pulled up to her chest. I tried to take Pepper, but a low growl made me pull back.

Nellie reached inside her coat, and Pepper squirmed free. Dee dropped to her knees, cradled her pet, and wept as another dog fell to the floor. He was a shorthaired caramel-and-white animal with a long snout and pointed ears. Pepper immediately twisted away from Dee, and the two dogs frisked around each other like they were long-lost cousins. Everyone gathered closer with grins and chuckles until the two animals finally settled down and curled up against Dee, who hadn't moved from the floor.

"Looks like Pepper's got a Heinz 57 pal," Jack said. "They're the best kind."

Shirley brought more towels, and I helped Nellie out of the dripping raincoat. "Tell us what happened," I said. William brought a chair over, and she dropped into it.

Nellie took a ragged breath. "Pepper ran toward the street. When I caught up to him he was standing on the curb barking his head off at a dog caught in a tangle of limbs and trash. He was partway howling and part yelping. What was I supposed to do? The water didn't look too deep, so I waded out thinking I could most likely get him loose. Well sir, soon as I set foot in the water, Pepper jumps in too. I couldn't do anything about that, so I kept going. The current was swifter than I'd counted on, and I fell more than once."

She definitely had everyone's attention.

"Then I felt something lift me and push me toward the trapped dog. Can't explain it and might never. Once I got him free, he jumped into my arms and he ain't left me yet."

"How did Pepper get back to you?" I asked.

"That dog's stronger than he looks, but he was carried down the street a ways. It was a while before we met up again."

Dee moved over to sit in a chair beside Nellie as the excited animals whimpered and nuzzled their snouts together like they were old friends. "Did you have trouble getting back to the Manor carrying two dogs?"

"Some, but I heard voices and headed that way."

My head popped up. "You did? What did they say?"

"They was singing. Something about a river."

"She heard what? Singing? That's impossible," Francesca said. "In this storm? Ridiculous."

"God can work in mysterious ways," Shirley said.

"Amen to that," I said. More *amens* followed.

So now we had a mutt Nellie had named River on board. We were becoming like Noah's ark in the great flood.

Water washed across our yard like a rising tide licking a beach. The two dogs and one cat finally settled down and slept, but all the people were awake and alert.

I was busy praying, and I was sure others were as well.

CHAPTER TWENTY

Our motley group stranded inside the Manor grew tired of peering out the dining room windows, so most of us ambled into the sitting room, even though it felt more like a funeral parlor. With no electric and few windows, the room felt smothersome and was filled with shadows. People gathered in little bunches, speaking in tired whispers. When would the rain ever stop for good? And what would we find outside when it did?

A woman's shrill voice interrupted my thoughts. "Should-'ve let those criminals fend for themselves. They're tough as flint. They would've been all right. Instead, here they are sticking around us good citizens like fleas. That's what happens when the law coddles 'em. Wouldn't happen back in my day. Why . . ."

Lucy McDonald. Here we were, stuck with the old woman who had lived next door to the halfway house. Why in the world did she accuse me of harassing her, then file a restraining order? She had no grounds for such an accusation and had even seemed friendly the morning after the fire when we stood together on her front porch. Asked me to stay for a cup of coffee for heaven's sake. My gut feeling told me she was hiding something, but I hadn't a clue what it could be. She kept spouting her views about our Hope women to a group growing in number. I turned away before she called the sheriff over to complain about my too-close presence. He had recently returned after he and the National Guard checked the town for any stragglers who had refused to evacuate. He looked frazzled, standing hatless and barefooted as he nursed a cup of steaming coffee.

I gazed around the room and took an inventory of my friends. Lollipop, who never worried about anything in his world, unwrapped a sucker and flopped into an overstuffed chair. He hummed to himself as he concentrated on his candy.

Nellie loved on a smelly dog she had named River. Francesca sat in her wheelchair and stroked Her Majesty. William stood behind her, minus the pink robe, and chewed his cigar stub. Shirley refreshed her cherry-red lipstick before heading to the kitchen with Jack and Blind George. "Gonna pull stuff out of the freezer before it ruins and start cookin' supper," she said throwing her hand in the air. Even though our ovens were electric, the big stovetop ran on gas, so everyone would enjoy a hot meal. But how long would our food supply last?

I eased down onto a cushy sofa and scanned the room again. Where was Irene? Then I spotted her near the piano talking into the sheriff's ear. When would that man wise up? "Charlie," I whispered, "I don't have enough zip left inside me to deal with all of this. Will anything ever be normal again?"

I could see my sweet husband's face after golf-ball sized hail had destroyed our crops. Rows of corn, beans, tomatoes, and okra pounded into mush while we watched from the front porch. Yet he didn't give in to despair. He wouldn't give up. He . . .

My eyes grew as heavy as a velvet curtain pulled across a stage. I could feel myself giving in to the urge to sleep.

The next thing I knew, someone ruffled my hair. I looked up into Smiley's face leaning over mine. "Take your time," he said. "Thought you might like to know the rain's stopped. Maybe for good this time. The sun's even trying its best to shine."

His announcement cleared my foggy brain. He took my arm and helped me stand.

"While you snoozed, we've all pledged to stick together. That's what family's for, don'tcha know."

"Yes indeed," Francesca said. "If you have any valuables, keep them close or they'll disappear. Mark my words."

I shot her a look. "We can always depend on you to remind us of the worst possible situation. You delight in being miserable and taking us along with you. Well, sir, I refuse to go. Aren't you *ever* thankful? For *anything*?"

Oh my. I could feel everyone's eyes on me. Why had I let ugly thoughts spew out of my mouth? I sounded like a hateful old woman, and I didn't like it.

Francesca's face turned a fiery red, and she squeezed her cat until it cried.

"I'm so sorry," I said as I moved closer to her. "I have no excuse for that outburst. Please forgive me."

"I'll consider it," she said with an upturned nose.

That meant she would. In time.

The sheriff talked on his phone with Sweetbriar's fire department. I stuck close by him. Everyone was anxious to return home, but it was uncertain what they would find once they got there. The rain had stopped as suddenly as cutting off a faucet. But water continued to flow from the upstate, and the rivers would keep rising. They wouldn't even reach flood stage for twelve more hours. How long would the Manor have to serve thirty or so people as a shelter? Did we have enough food in the deep freeze? Not to mention a place for heads to rest on pillows or a sheet or blanket to cover them. I felt overwhelmed without any *help* from Francesca.

"We need some good news," I whispered to Charlie. Whether from my reassuring husband or the good Lord, the answer rang clear. So far, the dam above our town of Sweetbriar had held.

Sheriff Caywood placed a call to the National Guard. "Here's what I know," he said into the phone. "An enormous oak uprooted and smashed into the front of Sweetbriar Manor. Yep. That's the old folks home. No, nobody's injured here. Blind George's got a john boat and we're fixin' . . . no, that's his name, and he ain't blind. We're leaving now. Going door to door to check one more time. We'll need more boats and maybe tomorrow or the next day plenty of shovels. I know you know your job. We know ours too."

The sheriff spoke to William while handing him the key to the prisoner's handcuffs. "In case his bladder can't wait 'til we're back. He's a shifty sort and will steal if he's got half a chance, but he ain't dangerous." Then he turned to me. "Keep an eye on Dee. Don't let her out of your sight. I'll be depending on you."

"You still think she's a flight risk? Where on earth would she go even if she was?"

Shirley handed the sheriff a pair of dry socks. Where she had acquired them I had no idea. He slipped them on his feet. As soon as he finished putting on his shoes and tying his shoelaces, he stood and jammed on his hat. He looked at me and frowned. "Irene also bears watching," he added in a near whisper. "I'll explain everything later." He rushed out of the sitting room taking Blind George and Deputy Larry with him. The back door slammed.

Jack set the radio on the piano and tuned in to our weatherman, Ralph.

"Listen up, folks. If you live in or near Sweetbriar, Sandy Ridge, Townsend, Absolute, or Pinewood, and you are in a safe place, don't rush out thinking just because the rain has stopped you can get to your home. You'll run into a disaster of catastrophic proportions. Stay where you are. A series of microbursts has left trees and power lines in a tangled mess. Plus, the river hasn't reached its flood stage, so three feet of putrid water in our homes and businesses could rise even more. Stay put. Stay safe. Looks like the dam should hold this time, but engineers are assessing the damage. We've had the storm of the century. I hope we never live to see another one. Tune in for an updated report at six o'clock."

Shirley relayed some information she had learned from the deputy talking on his cell phone earlier. But our day, that now seemed more like a week, had turned frantic after his conversation and she had forgotten to tell me what she'd heard. It seems the inspectors had found a pile of burnt oily rags that had traces of lemon furniture polish near the back of the Hope House. Was this how the fire started? I had smelled the same lemon scent in Nellie's room, but she never cleaned. Maybe I should inform the sheriff. Then my mind switched gears, and I considered Terry. The only evidence linking him or anyone else to the crime was circumstantial. Even if some evidence pointed to Dee, I believed she was not guilty. But I couldn't be objective when I had seen the compassionate side of a scrappy, tough young woman and had taken her into my heart. I could not. I prayed the sheriff was wrong about her.

I marched up to the mayor, who had turned to a tall, skinny woman wearing horn-rimmed glasses and a Red Cross uniform. "We have to put those women where somebody can keep an eye on them," he said. "They can't be mixed in with the good citizens of Sweetbriar or trouble is sure to occur."

"But don't we already live in the same town? Why can't we be good examples for these ladies to emulate?" The Red Cross lady's face scrunched into a frown.

"Not if our good mayor can figure out a way to get rid of

the ladies," I said, giving him my best glare. "Am I right?"

Mayor Phillips ducked away from us mumbling under his breath. I caught up to him in the dining room where he stood alone gazing out at the dazzling sunshine. "How was the convention?" I asked as I stood beside his tall frame.

"What are you talking about?" He never turned from the window and seemed calm and collected.

"I truly don't care where you were, but you can't just up and leave with no way to get in touch with you. I didn't have an emergency, but what if someone had? Good thing you returned before this storm set in."

He turned and looked at me. "Louise knew where I was."

"Well, your loyal secretary kept that knowledge to herself."

Mayor Phillips folded his arms across his chest and scowled down at me. "If you must know, I was in Charleston learning about ghosts and haints, tales and legends."

"Whatever for?"

"A way to lure tourists back to Sweetbriar. Do you realize we have a rich history we can draw from? I've been doing some research and discovered we were once a haven for witches. Actually, that was never proven, but maybe we could embellish such tales to make our town more exciting."

"Merciful heavens. Sounds like spicy entertainment. You've got my full support."

"I do?"

"Certainly. If you'll speak up for the Hope women to stay in Sweetbriar. As a matter of fact, they would make perfect docents around town. Tourists would love it."

"You don't say. Hmmm. I'll give some thought to the idea. That's all I can promise."

We shook hands. I felt like doing a jig as I left him, but I contained myself. The future of the Hope women in Sweetbriar had possibilities.

The sun slipped behind low clouds rolling across the sky, and with no electricity, the hallways darkened. Any person moving about couldn't be identified unless he or she walked close enough to touch.

Since the sheriff said I should keep an eye on Dee, I hurried to the kitchen where I'd last seen her. Shirley was stirring something in a big pot. She glanced my way. "Gone to get some dry clothes. Her and Nellie both."

"What on earth smells so heavenly?" I asked before leaving the kitchen.

"Vegetable soup," Shirley said as she added another jar of tomatoes. Five empty quart jars sat on the counter. Her last summer's canning of soup-mix, tomatoes, okra and corn, put to good use.

"Plus fried cornbread," Jack added with a grin as he flipped cakes in two skillets.

"Oh my," I said, already looking forward to supper.

"Don't forget we have dessert," Shirley called to me as I entered the dining room. I turned around and stepped back into the kitchen.

"Found three pans of that frozen fruit salad in the very bottom of the deep freezer, and it will melt if our electric don't return soon," Shirley said.

"You mean the salad with cherries and pineapple and sweetened condensed milk? The one Betty Jo calls *old people's salad*?"

"That's the one. And we found a big ol' turkey we never used at Christmas. Jack's gonna roast that sucker on the grill tomorrow morning. We're gonna eat high on the hog 'round here."

I ran over and hugged them both before heading to Nellie's room. Her door was slightly ajar, so I pushed it open. Dee was curled on the bed with Pepper tucked beside her. Nellie stood at her window. "Something you need to know," she said as I walked over to her. Down by her feet, River laid his snout onto his paws and closed his eyes.

Nellie stroked one of three cemetery vases sitting on her generous windowsill, but didn't speak. The sun escaped from behind a dark cloud, and the outside wetness shone like glitter had fallen from the sky. We watched in silence for a moment before I spoke.

"Well, what did you want to tell me?"

Nellie touched each vase before taking a deep breath. "Aunt Mildred is very nearly gone forever."

"You mean part way but not totally?"

Nellie nodded as a tear slipped down her face. I reached in my purse and handed her my last clean hanky. River stood and moved closer before leaning against her. She reached down and stroked his head. I waited for her to continue.

Nellie blew her nose. "I should've never listened to my counselor. 'You must put your Aunt Mildred to rest,' she said. 'Let her go. It will bring you peace.'"

"Did it?"

She shook her head and sniffed. Dee rose from the bed, leashed both dogs, and left us. Even though I had been instructed to keep an eye on Dee, I had confidence she wouldn't go far and would return soon.

"Tell me what happened," I said. Nellie sank onto the edge of the bed as I pulled a chair over to listen and to rest my knee.

"I took her to the cemetery one day to scatter her ashes. I set the coffee can down underneath an oak tree and went off looking for the best place, one she would like."

"Then what happened?"

"I got turned around. Lost. I was lost, not Aunt Mildred. When it edged toward dark, the groundskeeper said I had to leave. But I came back the next morning, and that's when I found her. Then I thought if I could let her go a little bit at a time maybe that would be easier."

"So, you started collecting the cemetery vases."

She nodded. "These three are the only ones left of Aunt Mildred."

"But why didn't you tell us? You let us keep searching for her in the coffee can."

"I don't know. Seemed easier to do it that way. If I had told you, would you have believed me?"

"Probably not. So what are you going to do now?"

"I want to keep what I have left of her."

I reached for her hands and held them. "What if Jack made you a nice wooden box to keep her ashes in? Then you could return the vases before you're charged with stealing."

She looked at me with wide eyes. "Jack would do that?"

"Certainly. And Pearl could paint the box, decorate it if you like."

Dee and the two dogs returned.

When Nellie stood, she reached inside her skirt pocket before she stretched out her fist. I held my hand underneath hers as she dropped a cigarette lighter. It was an old, silver one with a flip top. She had never voluntarily handed me any of her stolen items.

"Where did you get this?"

"Found it on the sidewalk when I was leaving the Hope House the night of the fire. Thought about keeping it. Is it important?"

"Maybe. Did you take anything else that night?"

Nellie looked up with her eyebrows crunched together. "You won't go to the sheriff? He doesn't like me you know."

Yes, that was surely true since he had threatened her with jail time unless she changed her habit of sticky fingers. She hadn't, but imprisonment was not the answer.

I shook my head. She reached in another pocket and revealed a handful of poker chips. "Did you go there often to play cards?" I asked.

"Pretty often."

"You can keep those, but if you remember anything else about that night will you come to me?"

She nodded . . . or I think she did.

Nellie spoke to her dog. He stood and shook his whole body before gazing up at her. She leaned down and nuzzled her face against his neck. Could River have been a service dog in his former life? There was no collar, but he could have one of those information chips underneath his skin somewhere. Since the dog had become a part of Nellie's life, a totally different attitude had surfaced. Hopefully, no one would claim him.

After Dee and Nellie assured me they would come to eat as soon as they settled their pets, I headed toward the dining room for soup and cornbread. Smiley, who could sometimes read my thoughts, sidled up beside me. Over supper I'd tell him all about Aunt Mildred, but for now I shared my thoughts about Nellie and her dog.

"Everybody needs somebody to love 'em no matter what," he said. "Unconditionally. First, along came Dee with that big chip on her shoulder. Have you noticed it's hardly ever there anymore? Maybe livin' here with us, plus workin' for Blind George, has done the trick. And now Nellie's rescued a dog that's rescuing her. God works in mysterious ways, don'tcha know."

"Yes indeed." I threw my arms around his neck. I hugged him so hard the air huffed out of him.

He bent over and pulled up his dress socks.

For certain they would slip down again. I made a mental note to buy him some new ones since he insisted on wearing them with his sandals.

"We need to talk," I said. "I've got a bushel of things I've kept inside, and I need your undivided attention. We're wasting time, and we're not getting any younger, you know. Let's find a private spot after we eat."

"Absolutely, Sis. I couldn't agree more. I can see the issues with Mr. Lively are wearing you down, not to mention a house full of cantankerous townsfolk."

"You're partly right and totally wrong all at the same time. Mr. Lively remains a puzzlement, that's for certain, but some things on my mind are personal, between you and me." Smiley didn't react to what I'd just shared, but kept walking. Did he hear me trying to open my heart or was he ignoring me?

He walked faster, and I had to do a little two-step to catch up. I would change the subject. For now. But when the opportunity presented itself for us to be alone, he would have to make a decision about our relationship. One way or the other. I reached out and tugged on his sleeve. He stopped and turned to me.

"You can help me figure out how to approach Lucy, restraining order or not," I said to his puzzled face. "I've figured out why she's trying to keep her distance from me."

"You have?"

"She's protecting someone."

"Hmmm. Not much to go on."

"No, but I have something Nellie gave me that should help."

"Now you've stirred my curiosity, Sis."

"Good. Let's eat first. Then we can talk. How about your room?"

He nodded. Barely. He suddenly seemed afraid of being alone with me.

CHAPTER TWENTY-ONE

After talking over my plans with Smiley, who seemed like his old self again, I found Hershel and asked him to meet me on the back porch that served as a beauty parlor. A few things had become clear, and I needed to share them in as private a place as possible.

He fished out his trusty buckeye, leaned against a door jam, and thumbed his lucky charm. I needed more than luck. While I rummaged in my purse for my funeral home fan as a stalling tactic, I prayed for the right words to come at the right time. "Don't let me blow this, Lord," I whispered into my purse cavity.

He had brought Dee along with him. She collapsed into a nearby styling chair like all the starch was gone from her. She couldn't give up. Not now.

"Found it," I said as I lifted a peppermint and my fan out of my purse. I walked over and handed the candy to her.

"Remember your granny and the color of her blue eyes," I said, fanning my face to beat sixty. "Your eyes as well as your backbone come from her."

Well, sir, that did the trick. She lifted her chin and sat straight as a Mennonite in church, hands clasped in her lap. Smiley joined us, for which I was thankful. He pulled a straight-back chair close to Dee and laid his hand over hers. Now I was ready.

I turned to the sheriff. "Dee had nothing to do with starting a fire at the Hope House."

Hershel pushed off from the door jam, returned his buckeye to his shirt pocket, and gave it a pat. "Exactly. She's innocent."

"She is? I mean . . ." Smiley jumped up and helped me sit in his chair. My head was spinning. "But you—"

"Only way I could see to protect her. Let people think—"

"You said you thought she was guilty and a flight risk. When all along you were protecting her from—"

"Irene," we both answered together.

"Yep," he said with a wide grin. His eyes flew over to Dee where they softened as they lingered there. She gazed at him as if seeing him for the first time, and they both blushed before looking away. "Oh my goodness, Charlie," I whispered. "Those two are becoming an item."

I stood and walked over to the sheriff. "We know who *didn't* start the fire, but do you know who *did*?"

"Have my suspicions, but only circumstantial evidence. And that dog won't hunt."

"Ask your deputy to bring Terry here."

"So, you suspect the same. But on what charge? He's not likely to volunteer."

"How about endangerment to others with an open knife? Didn't Larry take it away from him?"

"Something like that might work." He rushed away and soon returned with a sulky boy and his Aunt Lucy.

"What is the meaning of this?" Lucy said in a snit. "We demand an apology, and I want our possessions returned immediately, especially my lighters—they belonged to my father I'll have you know." She glanced around the room. "What are all these people doing here?"

Prompted by Lucy's angry words, Smiley led Dee from our back porch gathering, and they disappeared into the kitchen. I guessed he would always avoid confrontations, but that was okay with me. He had plenty of other fine qualities.

Lucy glared at me. "Well?"

"I'm staying put. We have something to discuss with you and your nephew."

Hershel nodded to Lucy and then glanced at her nephew. "Have a seat."

They did. Terry slouched in his chair and picked at his fingernails.

"Let's talk about the night of the fire," Hershel said.

Terry jerked his head up. "You ain't got nothing on me."

"But we do," I said. "We have a witness who puts you at the scene."

The sheriff's mouth dropped open, but then he recovered enough to speak. "Go ahead, Miss Agnes."

"You were seen creeping around the Hope House just after midnight and slipping behind some bushes before the fire broke out. Then you jumped on your rusty old bike and high-tailed it out of there."

The sound of a dripping faucet filled the silence.

"Terry?" Lucy whispered in a shaky voice.

Tears began to flow from a twisted face as if Terry were in severe pain. Then as sobs shook his small frame, he told us what happened that night.

"I . . . I found a bunch of old lighters in a drawer beside my bed and . . . well, I wanted to see if they still worked. After I stuffed 'em in my pockets, I snuck out the front door and picked up my bike out of the yard. I'd only gone a few blocks when I seen the mayor riding his bike down the street. I turned back before he seen me and then decided to find some place closer to Aunt Lucy's. It was dark behind the Hope House, so I ducked behind some bushes. I'd brought some oily rags, fig-uring that would help. The fire took off like a flash and raced through the pine straw. I haven't slept since that night. It was an accident, but a lady died in that fire. I didn't mean for any-one to die. I swear. Will I get the electric chair? Will I?"

"I had no idea," Lucy said with a gasp as she stood. Then she rushed over to her nephew, stood behind him, and placed her hands protectively on his shoulders. "He's just a boy," she said in a pleading voice.

"Yes," I said, "but he has to take responsibility for his ac-tions."

Lucy nodded, then bowed her head.

Terry's body was suddenly racked with sobs. "I'm . . . I'm so sorry. I never meant to burn the house down, and I surely never meant to kill nobody. You gotta believe me."

"I believe you, son," the sheriff said. "We'll deal with some of your bad decisions later, but for now be assured that you didn't burn the house down or kill anyone."

Everyone stared at him with wide eyes. He certainly had our attention.

"The explosion," I said, breaking the silence.

"Yep. Like Jack figured and shared his insight with me, someone was cooking meth in the basement. That someone was Mary Wilson, the one supposedly in charge of running the place. She had plenty of drugs in her system, so it's possible she got careless and miscalculated something that set off an explosion. The fire you started, Terry, never reached the building. It was purely a coincidence the explosion occurred not long after you rode away.

Lucy and her nephew froze for a moment with mouths hanging open. Then they shouted, danced, laughed, and cried until the sheriff held up both hands. They stopped and turned to face him. They were now somber and as meek as two lambs waiting for judgment.

"For the next six weeks, Terry, you will report to me at eight o'clock every morning, except Sunday when you will attend church."

"Yes, sir," Terry said, giving a sharp salute.

"Your duties will include assisting the Hope women, who will assign you chores each day. Could be cleaning bathrooms, washing windows, pulling weeds, or running errands. Whatever they decide. But in the near future you will begin each day shoveling out muck from homes in the Bottom, tearing out sheetrock, and loading trucks headed for the dump. Jack has agreed to oversee your efforts. And they better be stellar. Whenever Jack's ready to dismiss you for the day, you'll be working for the Hope women. Understood?"

"Yes, sir," Terry said with a sharp nod.

"What about Irene? Where is she?" My stomach twisted into a tight knot. After all the trouble she had caused, had she slipped away scot-free? Again?

"Handcuffed in the dining room with our other prisoner. Figured if I gave her enough rope she'd hang herself. And she did."

I ran over and hugged our good sheriff. Relief flooded my very soul. "How did she manage to do herself in?"

"Well, it was all due to her cell phone getting sketchy service here in Sweetbriar. More than once she talked to someone—I'll find out who eventually—and shared her troubles about her cohort in crime, Mary Wilson. Seems they were in some drug business together. Mary owed Irene money, and she had come to collect. Of course the fire changed all that. There was no money to be found, and Irene was afraid her drug dealings with Mary would be discovered."

"That's why she set out to put the blame for the fire on Dee, thinking her drug business with Mary would go undetected," I said as the truth rose to the top like cream in a milk bucket.

"You got it," Hershel said. "Now I've got to write up my report. Think I could get a cup of coffee?"

"In a skinny minute." I turned to leave the back porch.

"Wait," Lucy said as I reached the kitchen doorway.

"I . . . *we're* sorry to have caused so much trouble. I'd like to help any of the Hope women, especially Dee, in any way I can. Will you let them know?"

"Certainly," I said. "Your offer will mean everything to them."

Terry stepped forward clearing his throat. "Include me in what Aunt Lucy said. I'd like to do something. If I have any time left after my chores," he added.

Everyone chuckled at that last remark. I shook his hand and left to make a fresh pot of coffee.

Two days later, a patched-up school bus crept through The Bottom of Sweetbriar. Most of the Manor's residents were hanging out the windows. We came prepared with shovels, push brooms, cleaning supplies, sandwiches, and bottled water. We would set up lunch at Mr. Case's Produce located at the end of the street and up a slight rise.

No one spoke as we surveyed the devastation. The floodwaters had left a measuring line three feet high on the buildings, and thick mud coated the streets and sidewalks. The air's rotten stench was worse than a bayou's. More evidence of the storm was piled high alongside the curb. A tangle of tree limbs, shingles, drywall, and insulation, as well as undetermined trash, had been dumped onto a plaid sofa, a blue armchair, and two mattresses, fragments of people's lives. Where one mound ended another began and stretched as far as the eye could see.

Terry worked among a host of volunteers bent to their tasks. He threw shovelfuls of stinking mud into the back of a dump truck. Shirtless, filthy, and sweaty, he had tied a bandana over his mouth and nose and never looked up as our bus drove past him. He was becoming a man.

When I spotted my yellow house, the rental I'd bought as an investment, my heart broke. Wind had peeled off the roof, and pieces of the tin were stuck against a **chain**-link fence in the side yard. I had insurance, but I didn't know if it would it be enough to rebuild. For certain, Juanita and Frankie couldn't live there now and maybe never. Thankfully, she and her two-year-old, curly-headed toddler had moved into the Manor, the young mother acting as our new administrator.

The streets were filled with activity—people working to bring some order back into their lives. A row of splintered telephone poles lay underneath new ones. Dozens of power company men, strapped to poles or standing in buckets lifted high in the air, worked intently to restore power to The Bottom, for this part of Sweetbriar had been hit the hardest, and the poor would suffer the most. From a large white tent in front of Case's Produce, volunteers handed out food and bottled water to a line of people. A man on a bulldozer pushed through the mud, clearing a path to Main Street. An assembly line of men shoveled filth out of a thrift shop, onto the sidewalk, and into the back of a pickup.

"We'll face it together, Sis," Smiley whispered in my good ear. "Together with the good Lord's help, don'tcha know."

The breath I'd been holding swooshed out of me. "Indeed," I said as I looked into his amazing eyes. "That we will."

After a long, hard day of labor we returned to our home. The oak that had fallen and crashed through a portion of our porch roof and smashed the antique door had been cut into sections and drug into the yard. Deep scars in the porch floor remained, and a shredded roof hung overhead.

The front of the house was a patchwork of plywood and tarps. The swing hung by one chain, while a single rocker remained. The hanging ferns had vanished. Yet a pot of red geraniums sat untouched on a side porch railing.

"Happy Halloween," Shirley whispered as everyone gathered in a silent clump at the bottom of the porch steps. "We got us a mess."

A gloom settled over us like a dark cloak. The foyer showed some water damage with buckled floorboards plus leaves and dirt that had blown underneath Mr. Lively's tarp. Yet our home had somehow willed itself to survive.

The storm left its mark on the big house, but the two attached wings of rooms had only a few missing shingles and some drooping gutters, plus a broken window or two. A true miracle. Every resident agreed, even Francesca, that we would make room for as many homeless townspeople as we could.

I sat on the porch steps and tugged off my farm boots, the ones I'd worn when tromping through muddy rows of beans or corn or when mucking out the barn. Those memories brought a comfort.

Inside my room—now wearing clean clothes and my slippers—Charlie smiled from his Ford 8N, his photo resting on my chest of drawers. All was quiet. The residents, including the Hope Women, had picked up brooms and mops and cleaning rags and left the old Victorian lady to help others less fortunate.

Late that afternoon our power came back on. Shirley found a sack of unspoiled onions in the pantry, and we chopped up a half dozen or more and threw the pieces into a large Dutch oven. Then she browned three packages of stew beef that needed to be used before they ruined. After she added seasonings and had everything to her liking, she put the lid on the pot and slid it into the oven, then started peeling potatoes and carrots. A soothing aroma filled the kitchen, and my anxious thoughts about Sweetbriar Manor's future lifted into the air and evaporated. We had a lot of work ahead of us, but we were going to be okay. I thanked the Lord as I swept the kitchen. Someone knocked on the back door.

"Could you get that?" Shirley asked.

When I threw open the door, Mr. Lively stood there wearing his usual rumpled clothes and his Confederate suspenders.

I grabbed his hand and pulled him inside. "You didn't have to knock."

"I know I should've . . . I know . . ." he sputtered.

"Before you say another word, I want to thank you for saving our home from further damage by sharing your new tarp. How much did that set you back? Maybe two hundred at least?" I leaned on my broom and studied his hangdog face. He wouldn't look me in the eye.

"I . . . I came to tell you before I left, but it seems you know already."

"Yep. Why didn't you ask me for a loan? I wouldn't have even charged you interest."

"I intended to put the money back before you noticed, and then my sugar, my granddaughter, was desperate for some financial help. So there you have it. I'm guilty as charged." He finally raised his head. With sad eyes and slumped shoulders he resembled a defeated man awaiting his sentencing.

"Yes, you are guilty of stealing, but the worst part was trying to blame the crime on someone else."

"That was inexcusable."

"I agree. Would you like to know who left the money in Pearl's easel tray?"

"I would."

"Smiley wanted to do something for Pearl. She is an excellent art teacher and refused payment for her lessons. He decided to leave her some money without letting anyone know. His plan worked."

"You don't say. What are you going to do? About me? Soon as I get settled I can send you an agreed amount each month until it's paid back. And with interest if you like. I beg you not to press charges."

"I've been thinking this over, and here's what I've concluded. Your willingness to give up your new tarp saved our home from further damage. I think the money you took, which was a bad thing, was used for a good purpose. Sometimes the Lord works things out like that."

Mr. Lively straightened himself to his full height and thumbed his suspenders. He smiled slightly with a glimmer of hope in his eyes. "What exactly are you saying?"

"No charges will be filed against you, but you will send me twenty dollars a month until the full amount is paid. If you don't, I'll contact your new employer to garnish your wages. This sounds harsh, but you can't justify stealing for any reason. Do you agree?"

He agreed and we shook hands. Then we walked over to the kitchen island where Shirley always kept a note pad and a pen. I requested his new address as well as that of his granddaughter's. He questioned me with ruffled eyebrows, but jotted down hers as well. I didn't tell him I planned to send her the money as soon as he paid the full amount.

"Got a job with an accounting firm, and you'll see I included that address as well. Seems I enjoy working with figures more than I do people. Took me a while to come to that conclusion, but I had a lot of time to think while emptying all those pots and pans sitting underneath a leaking roof. You've got to get a new one by the way. Work it into the budget and cut corners elsewhere if need be."

"Sounds like good advice."

His eyes widened in surprise. We shook hands once more as we said our good-byes with no hard feelings. I wished him well, and I meant it. He opened the back door, then stopped and looked back.

"Thank you." With a quick wave he turned and was gone.

CHAPTER TWENTY-TWO

The Manor's residents, which now included Juanita and her toddler, plus the Hope Women who would stay with us another week or so, scooted chairs around the dining room tables. Eight people from The Bottom, including Mr. Case, squeezed folding chairs among us. Seats and elbows bumped in the process, but everyone smiled or even joked about the tight fit—even Francesca, though by default.

She picked up her knife and pointed to me. "Mark my word. If you keep on trying to feed the whole world, we'll . . . we'll have to . . ." She flounced in her chair while her cheeks turned rosy red. "We'll have to eat in shifts."

Smiles broke out all around the dining room, plus chuckles from those of us who knew Francesca best. My often grumpy and demanding friend had shown her softer side.

Shirley, Jack, and William served steaming bowls of beef stew that smelled heavenly. No one complained that peanut butter and crackers had taken the place of our usual hot cornbread or that we drank bottled water instead of milk. Our supplies would be replenished in due time. After Smiley thanked the Lord for our home, for keeping us safe, and for the food set before us, even Francesca joined in the *amens*.

After our late supper, everyone pitched in to clear the tables while Dee and Nellie cleaned up the kitchen.

"Lord have mercy," Shirley said on our way to the sitting room. "Whatever has gotten into these people, I hope it lasts. We're behavin' better than most families."

"Indeed," I said. "Sometimes a crisis brings out the best in folks."

Francesca rolled herself up to the piano. Instead of her usual Bach or Beethoven, she began playing "It Is Well with My Soul." William directed as we lifted our voices.

Out of nowhere it seemed, Hershel suddenly stood among

us. The singing slacked off until it finally quit all together. Francesca pulled the cover over the piano keys with a bang and glared at the object of our interruption.

He leaned down to my good ear. "I've got some information you ought to hear about, Miss Agnes."

"The kitchen should be empty by now," I said. "Let's go there."

And so we did. Meanwhile, William and Francesca fussed over the next hymn choice. Things were getting back to normal, like most families.

Once we reached the kitchen, the sheriff got right to the point. "Irene's been transferred to the state prison. Our Sweetbriar jail didn't have adequate security for the likes of her. Thought you might rest easier knowing she's no longer in town."

"Is that why you really stopped by? To tell me about Irene?"

He stared at me with a puzzled look that quickly cleared. Then a slow blush crept up from his neck. He knew what I meant.

"Before you leave, Hershel, we need to clear the air about something."

"Okay." He blew out a long, slow breath as he pulled up a stool. "Let's hear it."

"What do you intend to do about Dee?"

"What do you mean?"

"She was falsely accused and interrogated. Even if you were using a smokescreen to keep her under your watchful eye, she could file a lawsuit against you and your office, as well as your deputy if she were so inclined."

He removed his hat and stared into space. "I'll take that cup of tea now."

I put the kettle on to boil. "Green or black?"

"What?" He shifted in his seat and looked at me with a blank expression.

"Your tea."

"Oh. Black. And the stronger the better." He drummed his fingers on the counter. "I'm sure you have a suggestion. About Dee?"

The teakettle whistled, and I poured the water over the tea bag in his cup. "Sugar or honey?"

"Neither. Got any lemon?"

"Fresh out." I set his cup in front of him and climbed onto

my stool beside him. "What do you think your daddy or grand-daddy would do?"

He blew on his tea and set it back down. "Don't rightly know."

"You should. They were honorable men. Both of them."

"And I'm not?"

"Yes, but sometimes you get sidetracked."

"You think I should apologize to Dee. Might be best to let sleeping dogs lie."

"But hard feelings can fester and burst like an ugly boil."

He fidgeted on the stool. "Is Dee angry enough to be a threat one day?"

"I don't know, but she ought to be."

He swallowed a big gulp of tea and picked up his hat. "Where do you reckon she is right now? Didn't spot her in the gathering just now."

"So you noticed her absence did you? Must be outside walking Pepper. If you're so inclined, I'm sure you could find her."

He moved toward the back door, but turned and walked back. "You folks need anything, you let me know."

"We'll be just fine," I said. "You do the same. If you need anything, that is."

"Yep. Will do." He saluted and winked, or I think he did, before he pulled the back door shut behind him.

By the time I returned to the sitting room, cots from the Red Cross had been erected to take care of the five men from The Bottom who would live with us until they could return home. The three women would sleep on the enclosed back porch after we made more room by pushing the beauty-shop chairs to one side.

Everyone had retired—except for Francesca and William who sat on the piano bench he had pulled close to her wheel-chair. They had their heads together in a deep discussion.

"Well, that settles it," William said as he slapped his knee. "I'm sure Agnes will help us get it all together."

I plopped down beside William, suddenly feeling every one of my seventy-something years. "Exactly what have the two of you been cooking up?"

Francesca's grin was uncharacteristic for her. Maybe William was finally sanding down those rough edges. "We've been planning to marry since the night Willy presented me with my rose ring. We've just moved the date up a bit, and the wedding will be right here at the Manor."

"Exactly when is this wedding?"

"This coming Saturday."

"In three days? But the front door will remain boarded up and the wood floor in the foyer buckled, not to mention that chopped-up oak tree spread across the lawn. Our home and yard is a total mess and won't improve greatly for several months."

"All the more reason to go ahead. By the time the weather cools in October, the Manor and the town will be back to normal, and we can take a trip in our taxi without feeling guilty about leaving. We want to marry now, roll up our sleeves, and go to work.

"Whatcha think, Red?" William asked. "Will ya help us get the ball rolling?"

"But what about flowers? The wind has stripped nearly everything bare."

Francesca scanned the sitting room. "Aha. Just as I thought. That arrangement sitting on the mantle will work just fine."

She pointed to a sad bunch of silk daisies I had been meaning to toss. "Nellie's cemetery roses would serve as a better bouquet."

Francesca wound her pearls into a knot. "Humph. Some people are never satisfied. We think those daisies will do just fine."

William loudly cleared his throat.

Francesca glanced over at him, then released her pearls. "I'm sorry, whatever you think would be best."

Did she just say *I'm sorry?* I pushed myself up from the bench. "We'll discuss this in the morning. I'm bushed. Time to turn in."

As I trudged down the hallway to my room, Smiley stood near my door with his hands clasped behind his back. He looked up and grinned, or he tried to before it disappeared and a deep frown wrinkled his forehead. "What took ya so long, Sis? Sheriff must've been long-winded. He's usually a man of few words. Any earth-shattering news? I want to hear all about it."

I studied this man who had stolen my heart. He looked like a young boy on a high dive too nervous to jump. "Are you all right? You look a mite pale. Do you need to sit down?"

He swallowed hard, sucked in a deep breath, and presented me with three drooping red roses. "All I could find in the yard. But they smell good. Maybe you could save the petals.

Isn't that what ladies do?"

"Well, I—"

"Can't let 'em go to waste. Whatcha think?"

"I'm not sure. Exactly what are you saying?"

"I'm saying life is mighty short, and we ought to get crack-in'. Tie the knot while we've still got some fire in the old furnace."

My heart pounded in my ears. "What about your promise to your Lucinda?"

"She would approve. Of us. I think. If our getting married makes her mad, she'll have to get over it. What about your Charlie?"

I nodded, unable to speak. Charlie would want the very best for me, and that meant getting hitched to this dear man who had just stammered out a discombobulated proposal.

Every ounce of weariness left my bones as we floated to the kitchen for two cups of Earl Gray—with lots of honey.

While we waited for our tea to cool a bit, Smiley laid a crumpled up handkerchief between our cups. He gently smoothed the material out flat to reveal a diamond ring, a single small solitaire.

We looked into each other's eyes. My heart thumped in my ears, and I was speechless.

"This was my granny's. I know she'd be proud if you would wear it. Would ya, Sis?"

I threw my arms around his neck and pulled him close. "What took you so long?" I kissed his ear, then made my way to his sweet lips.

The morning air was already hot and humid, but a breeze stirred the confederate jasmine, causing its sweet scent to drift over us.

Nellie presented bouquets—her cemetery roses sprayed bright pink—to me and then to Francesca. She had snipped a boutonniere for the grooms, which they proudly stuck into the buttonhole of their jacket.

Francesca and I wore thrift shop dresses saved from the floodwaters by the astute shop owner. Hers was a pink lace affair that complimented her Lady Rose ring. I had chosen a white blouse and a lightweight denim skirt. Suited my new red boots with the silver toes. A wedding present from the Manor's residents.

The Salvation Army captain and the two grooms waited in front of the tall dining room windows on Sweetbriar Manor's side porch since the front porch still had a dangling roof overhead. Nellie pushed Francesca's wheelchair up the handicap ramp. I followed behind them as "The Morning Has Broken" from Josiah's bagpipes shook the air and sent shivers from my toes clear up to my red curls.

Though impossible to hear them over the music blasting forth, the crowd clapped and cheered as we passed by, which included Henry and Betty Jo. My son-in-law winked and gave a thumbs-up. A movement by his feet caught my eye. Miss Margaret. She squirmed and twitched her tail, a sure sign she was ready to spring forth, but Henry swooped her into his arms just in time and whispered in her ear. Betty Jo turned to look my way. She actually beamed as she dabbed at her eyes. My family.

I hoped the crowded porch wouldn't collapse, for it seemed the whole town had turned out. The mayor and his secretary, Terry and his Aunt Lucy, the sheriff and . . . Dee stood close to him, and they gazed into each other's eyes like they were the only two people on the porch. Mercy. His apology must've been a good one. I had guessed the two of them would become an item. It did my heart good.

William walked toward us to get his sweetie, and Smiley came for me. The music stopped. The captain cleared his throat. A hush fell over the gathering as a wren's birdsong filled the spring morning.

When Francesca and I handed our bouquets to Nellie, a smile spread over her face. Even though she only had part of her Aunt Mildred in a small wooden box decorated by Pearl, Nellie seemed more content than I'd ever seen her. God is full of surprises.

Smiley, my cherished friend and soon-to-be husband, reached for my hand. My heart was so full I feared it might burst.

"Dearly beloved, we are gathered here today . . ."

THE END